G000109003

FESTIVAL IN TIME

Tracey Scott-Townsend

Wild Pressed Books

First Edition.

This book is a work of fiction.

The publisher has no control over, and is not responsible for, any third party websites or their contents.

FESTIVAL IN TIME © 2022 by Tracey Scott-Townsend.
Contact the author via twitter: @authortrace

Cover Design by Tracey Scott-Townsend

ISBN: 978-1-9163774-4-8
Published by Wild Pressed Books
http://www.wildpressedbooks.com
All Rights Reserved.

No part of this publication may be reproduced or transmitted in any form by any means electronic, mechanical, photocopying, recording or otherwise, without the prior permission of the copyright owner.

Previous novels by Tracey Scott-Townsend

The Last Time We Saw Marion (Inspired Quill 2014)
Of His Bones (Inspired Quill 2017)
The Eliza Doll (Wild Pressed Books 2016)
Another Rebecca (Wild Pressed Books 2018)
Sea Babies (Wild Pressed Books 2019)
The Vagabond Mother (Wild Pressed Books 2020)

For further information about all the titles go to the publisher's website or the following social media platforms:

Twitter - @authortrace
Instagram - @authortrace
Facebook - Tracey Scott-Townsend Writer
Website - www.vagabondmother.com

For my Communities,
LFC: the 'village' in which I raised my children;
HHfR, the refugee and volunteer community in
Hull; and my fellow poets, artists, readers, writers
and gardeners. We have more in common, etc.

FESTIVAL IN TIME

1

Annette, 1972

The weather forecast was for rain and more rain, after a long sunny spell. Mum had actually banned me from going to the festival, but wild horses wouldn't keep me away. Sure, I'd have to miss the Friday night bands but I'd still get to see Genesis. They were my favourite group of all time.

Looking back, I should've gone on my own. If I had, our whole lives would have turned out different.

If you'd ever met my little sister Janie, you might have understood why me taking her along could turn out to be a *really* bad idea. But whatever. I decided to give her the benefit of the doubt. My best friend Mary had chickened out when her mum threatened to cut off all her hair if she defied her.

So Janie was the only option I had left.

I was indulging in a fantasy about meeting Peter Gabriel backstage when Janie appeared at the top of the stairs, toilet flush muffled by the carefully closed door behind her (*well done, Janie*). I watched as she neatly sidestepped the same

1

creaks I had on the stairs – looking suspiciously as if she'd also done this before.

I helped her into her backpack. I'd put the flask and sandwiches in there the night before along with my extra jumper. She looked at me sideways and pulled in a shivering breath.

'All right,' she said. 'I'm doing this. I'm going to a music festival.' She looked at me properly then and nodded, fringe falling back into her eyes. Normally she didn't go out of the house at weekends unless it was to the library.

I wondered if she'd still be playing with her dolls on Monday. The only band she'd ever heard of at the festival was a brand new one called Roxy Music. It would be their first festival performance, but her best friend was a second cousin of one of the band members and it was one of the ways I'd managed to persuade Janie to come as we'd whispered in the dark the night before. I'd said she could get a souvenir of some sort for Sally.

We stepped out into the dawn light and I locked the door behind me. A thrill of anticipation made my fingers tingle; was I doing the right thing bringing Janie with me? The corners of her mouth twitched. She glanced up at our parents' bedroom window and wriggled her shoulders into a more comfortable position under the backpack's weight.

'Come on, then,' she whispered.

Ha. She wasn't going to let me down.

Maybe we could finally start to have some fun together.

———

Sunrise spread over the flat Lincolnshire fields and raindrops reflected pinks and yellows on the bus windows. The strong smell of fertiliser seeped through the frames and off some of our fellow passengers, their clothes steaming from the bus's heater. A pall of cigarette smoke hung in the air. I didn't know how anyone could smoke at that time of morning. The bus was crowded with farm labourers, factory workers and a bunch of hippies, I guessed they were festival-goers like me and Janie. Saying things like yeah man and far out. My stomach turned over again with excitement. *This was the real me!*

The farm workers stared at the hippies and us, wrinkling their noses as though *we* were the ones with the funny smell. We passed a field of miserable-looking cows lying half-under some trees, and after that it was potatoes as far as the eye could see. Only the year before I'd taken this same bus route for my summer job, potato-picking in one of those very fields. I wouldn't be doing that again, now I had a Saturday job at Woolworths.

The bus stopped at a set of traffic lights before a bridge over the River Witham. I nudged Janie, pulling the hairbrush out of my backpack. Janie mumbled in her sleep, something about elephants at the circus – a recurring dream of hers. I pinched her to wake her up properly and she yelped, rubbing the top of her arm. It couldn't have hurt *that* much through her parka!

'Did you have to do that?' she snapped.

'We're nearly there and you look like you've just got out of bed. Which I suppose you have, in a way.' She'd practically sleepwalked through the deserted streets of Lincoln on the way to the bus. 'Come on, we need to make you look presentable. Plait your hair, it'll be easier. I'm going to do your eyes for you.'

A woman wearing a white hairnet looked me up and down while I checked through my makeup bag for the eyeliner. I stared hard at her and she blew out a cloud of smoke, turning her head away before I did. *Ha.* Janie had dried dribble at the side of her mouth, but fortunately I'd packed a damp flannel like our mum always did. I passed her it when she'd finished plaiting her hair and she wiped the whole of her face, passing it back to me afterwards. I zipped it back into the washbag and set about underlining her left eye just as the bus jerked forward.

'Ouch! You poked me in the eye.' She smeared the eyeliner further by rubbing it, silly.

'For God's sake, I'll have to start again now. Here, wipe it off with the flannel.'

Patiently I unzipped the washbag again and let her have a look at herself in my compact mirror. Her eye watered. The bus crawled over the bridge and stopped at a bus stop.

'Quick, let me do it now.'

The crowd of sugar beet workers filed off the bus at the entrance to the factory, like Utopians being sucked into the Troglodytes' cave in *The Time Machine*. That was never going to be me, working in a place like that. I'd rather run away and join the circus.

By the time the bus set off again Janie looked at least five years older. I'd given her a coat of peach-coloured lipstick as well as kohl rims to her eyes. She didn't look like my little sister anymore.

2

Janie, now

Time seemed to dissolve in the garden. Janie leaned her arms on the gate and felt her mind loosening as her eyes roved the beloved paths, their stones salvaged from the riverbank. The beds were scribbled with the green of this year's vegetables, pushing their way upwards from the earth. Everything coming alive at this time of year. The purple sprouting broccoli she'd planted last June was still sending out healthy side shoots. The sugarsnap peas would be ready to eat in a week or so.

Too late for Janie.

She'd built the garden wall herself, with reclaimed bricks. She'd taken a night class in Oban, *Rudimentary Bricklaying.*

Driving home in the dark on the twisty mountain roads with the radio on and the windows open to the crisp night air, she'd felt like herself again after losing herself to maternity. Like she had when she first left home and realised she didn't have to be delicate Janie anymore, traumatised by an event in her youth. Sometimes, on her night-time drives she'd see a shooting star arc across the sky. Once, there had been colours flickering in the air, reflecting off the car's bonnet. She pulled into a viewing area that looked out over the bay, got out and leaned on the roof, chin in hands. The Northern Lights danced and spat over the sea beyond Oban – coils and banners of green and pink and red – nature's fireworks.

By the time she got back into the car she was cold and emotionally wrung out. The kind of feeling she usually got listening to music or after the increasingly rare sex she had with Paul, a sense of connection.

Arriving home that night she saw the light on in Paul's studio – the shepherd's hut she'd renovated herself, with a view to Bed and Breakfast accommodation, but Paul had begged to have it as his workspace. Creeping up the steps, she lifted the latch on the door. Inside, the baby monitor crackled on a shelf and there was Paul with his back to her – rocking on his feet, a paintbrush in his hand. On the easel in front of him was a nude depiction of Janie. She never thought of the woman on the canvas as herself. Once she'd been converted into brushstrokes and paint she belonged to the artist. He could make her what he wanted her to be. His ownership of the image gave her a mystery she didn't feel in real life, where she was tired and overworked. It was the garden that made *her* sparkle with life. Or her youngest child suckling from her breast before he went to sleep. The things she had grown.

But on this night she was buzzing with the Aurora Borealis and she wanted to hold onto that feeling. She felt as vibrant as on the night they'd met, when she'd been modelling for a life drawing class and he'd been there for the first time, an unexpected, youthful presence amongst the old-age-pensioners that made up most of the class. There had been an electrical atmosphere in the room and she'd known as soon as she met his eyes – something she never normally did with class participants – that they would end up together.

Taking the steps stealthily, she approached Paul from

behind in the shepherd's hut. When she touched him he jolted, then groaned as she slid her arms around his waist. His belt loosened, jeans slipping down his thighs, he'd started without her. With one hand she'd grasped his hip while with her other she traced his arm down to his wrist where she felt his bones under the pad of her thumb, traced the veins standing proud on the back of his hand. His shirt was undone. He had his hand inside the star-patterned boxers she'd bought him for Christmas.

Neither of them said a word. She settled her fingers firmly over his and moved with him, pressing her body to his. He held the paintbrush out to one side, as if painting an image of her in the air around them – frantic brushstrokes whipping dust motes into contours. With her other hand she stroked his stomach and thighs and moved her fingers around his balls, squeezing as hard as she dared. She rocked with him, holding him upright. He exploded into her hand.

Now Paul had gone. He'd emptied the shepherd's hut of his equipment and installed it in his brand-new studio in Glasgow. Their children had grown up. Their home had been sold; it was time to abandon her garden.

3

Justin Citizen, now

Half a mile away in the sea, all around the perimeter of Justin's tiny island, he could see hundreds and hundreds of boats. Fishing boats, rowboats, rubber dinghies – lots and lots of dinghies. And there were orange-life-jacketed men, women and children hanging on to the edges and some of the people were slipping under the waves. Somehow he could see them close up. He sobbed as another child went under. Dinghies sank in horrific slow motion, and he saw empty orange life jackets bobbing on the sea's foam, collecting on the shore until Justin – helplessly perched on a hill in the middle of the island – could barely see over the top of the rapidly-growing orange mountain.

Further out, Justin caught glimpses of the grey bulk of warships, and a few fancy yachts. Even the funnel of a submarine. He fought to regain control of his lungs and called out to people in the smaller boats closer by. Well-kept sailing boats piloted by men and women in navy-and-white, and boats into which fishermen hauled their catches. Slowly these people began to listen to him. One by one their boats moved closer to the shore and the sailors started helping the people in the water to safety. Justin raised his voice. He spoke about the changes that needed to happen so that nobody would fall into the water.

The mobile phone on his bedside table beeped loudly.

Taking a shuddering breath, Justin fumbled for his specs and picked up his phone.

> Seen the polls this morning? Up to 35%, Uncle Jus.
> You'll get there! Keep going as you are, love you xxx

It was only 7am. His niece, Ivy, would be up with her baby, he supposed. Little Olivia, a late first baby for her mother. Ivy was almost forty-three. Ivy's own mother had been only seventeen when she was born. *That* had been a shock for his whole family.

His niece had been the inspiration behind his recent campaign proposal (indeed, had helped write it) to pay mothers or fathers a proper allowance if they wished to care for their own babies at home rather than be forced back into the *workplace*, as Ivy called it. Nursing parents of newborns would be able to claim a breastfeeding credit. After all, under this proposal, the population's overall health stood a chance of improvement – Ivy had researched all the statistics – there would be less work-related stress and happier families.

Ivy worked from home, having given up her job at the paper, and now earned money as a freelance journalist. She and Justin would sometimes Skype late at night, he after a tiring day's campaigning and she finalising a piece for the next weekend's supplement. Ivy often let her uncle know of any stories – quite often *about* him – that he'd find useful. If Olivia woke up, Ivy would hold the baby up to the screen for him to see.

To his deep regret, he'd not had children with either of his two ex-wives, though both now had families with their second husbands.

He responded to Ivy's text with a thumbs-up emoticon (he chose yellow this time) and added a smiling face with heart-shaped eyes. Replacing his phone on the bedside table he swung his legs out of bed and stood gingerly. Although the heel pain all but crippled him in the mornings, his feet were usually (thankfully) better by the time he presented himself in public – it didn't do to show weakness, he was told. Hobbling through to the bathroom, holding the furniture as he went, he came to a stop in front of the sink and examined his reflection in the mirror. Bloodshot, red-rimmed eyes. Sad, downturned mouth. It was the dream eking through. The sadness of the world. He turned the cold tap on full. The sound of rushing water brought to mind the roaring and whistling of the crowd at one of his recent outdoor rallies. Feeling the hint of a smile on his lips, he gave his face a vigorous drenching. Smugness never did anybody any good.

After his shower, dressed in a clean, open-necked shirt and khaki trousers, Justin sat at the breakfast table. His cat jumped onto the cushioned chair next to him, purring as it fixed him with an intense gaze. Justin chewed and swallowed, chewed and swallowed. Despite his feline companion he felt lonely. The breakfast table stood next to the large, square kitchen window. The view looked out onto compact back garden: overgrown lawn sprinkled with dandelions, buttercups and daisies and overhung with straggling roses that climbed all over the fence. The few bees that were left in the world loved Justin's garden.

He seemed to hear a resonant, low note and looked away from the window into the dining room, through the arch in the kitchen wall. His guitar hung beyond the archway and it was calling him. He usually allowed himself at least half an hour to play before setting off to work in the mornings. He wouldn't have so long today, but one song would be better than not playing at all.

After lowering himself to a stool beside the wood-burner

nook he lovingly stroked the guitar's chipped, stickered body and picked out the first notes. When he was sad the song that came to him was *Suzanne*. He played it for a while, singing the words under his breath. The cat came to sit in its basket near the stove.

As Justin strummed the final chords of the song, he rose to his feet, glancing through the archway at the kitchen clock. Time to get ready for the day's serious business.

4

Annette, now

I had a weird feeling about Ponytail-Pete that day. I sometimes had, what do you call them? Premonitions, I suppose. The back of my neck would tingle, or I'd get a sick feeling in my stomach. This time it was the sick feeling. Pete and I as good as lived together but I liked to keep my personal space, so I occasionally demanded down-time. Two days before, he'd spent the night at my house and asked me to marry him, again. *Go on, go on,* he'd said, (badly) impersonating Mrs Whassername in *Father Ted.* He made me laugh, but the stubborn old mare in me turned him down as usual. I didn't see the point; we were happy as we were. Him with his black eyes, his nose-ring and the scar on the side of his face, he'd have done anything for me and it was no secret I took advantage of his good nature. But he knew I loved him. *Didn't he?*

That morning I had my hand on the gate. He'd been miffed with me and I thought making up would be fun. But for some reason I couldn't bring myself to go up the track to his house. Every time I tried to open that gate, I hit a force field and the chill in my stomach deepened. I just *knew* something bad had happened – I couldn't face facing it. So instead I went home and texted Dex, another member of our band. *Would you go up and check on Pete?* I asked. Because of my funny feeling.

I felt sorry for putting it on Dex but I was still glad it wasn't me who found Pete's body. It was bad enough having the scene described to me. By the time I saw Pete again, he was lying peacefully in his wicker coffin, as if he'd died in his sleep and not in a heap of crockery on the kitchen floor. A bloody brain aneurism. I hope he *did* know how much I loved him.

A whole two years passed before I could bring myself to have sex with anyone again. My cottage in Leitrim sat in the *back of beyond* and I didn't get out much. I spent my time concentrating on music and working at the community centre in the nearest village. At home my attention went on my dog and horses.

Colm Blair-McGoogan was an Earl, or something similar in the Irish gentry. I never wanted to know. Although of course I could see it plastered all over the house stationery. But as far as I was concerned, he was a down-to-earth and musical bloke – the two qualities I valued most highly. He first spotted me busking with my band on the streets of Carrick-on-Shannon and stopped to chat for a while, mostly with me. Just a bit of banter. He told me later he was attracted by my *indefatigable sass*. Ha! He asked us to play for him at a party. We agreed and Dex took down the details while the posh bloke dropped something as he walked away in his tweed jacket and flat cap. He'd left fifty euros in my open fiddle case; pizza night for us, then.

We turned up for the party in Dex's battered old van. The map had guided us up a winding mountain road, threading through a dense patch of woodland. On the other side of the woods was a small village and beyond that we found our destination. Fionula pressed the buzzer on the gate as we all strained to see out of the windows at the front. The gate swung open and we drove another half a mile down a tree-lined drive which led us to the black tarmac in front of the house – a mansion, in fact. Green Irish lawns swept away from the building at the front and sides, and we found a tall stone wall with two wooden doors in an archway around the back; the posh bloke had mentioned it in his instructions. Fionula hopped out again and pressed another bell. A voice directed us through the archway into a stable yard, where we parked and unloaded our instruments. A grey-haired woman came outside and led us into the house, taking us through the kitchen into a corridor. That's where Colm was standing. He ushered us back into the kitchen, encouraged us to sit at long wooden benches either side of the wide table. While we were eating – Fionula, Dex, Cara, Kenny and me – he asked if we knew a favourite tune of his. Later, when the party was in full swing, he brought out an ancient fiddle and joined us on stage. We were gobsmacked. He said we must sleep in the house after the party instead of bunking down in the van as we'd planned.

Colm Blair-McGoogan. I became fond of him despite our (massive) differences of opinion and lifestyle. He was a decade older than me and a member of the class I used to turn my nose up at – but with his open-heartedness and tolerance of all things different from himself he soon made me see I was the bigger snob. This bloke, who could have had his pick of any beautiful woman he wanted, chose a beak-nosed, hunch-backed loudmouth who wore charity-shop clothing and chain-smoked rollups.

So yeah, I fell in love with him in return. And then he went and died as well. Heart attack.

And this is the thing. Colm left me some money. Quite a lot. What did he think I was going to spend it on? He knew I lived my off-grid lifestyle by choice. I was never after his money. But he left it to me anyway.

I was grooming the horses. Romy was being a nuisance as usual, grabbing the curry comb and wanting me to throw it for her, when Mick-the-postman (as opposed to Mick-the-barman) pulled up in his green van. We exchanged pleasantries, as you do, then he handed me a letter from my older brother, Nicholas. A Wing Commander in the RAF, no less. Lived in Germany: *Ever so busy, don't cha know?* Nicholas's letters always sounded like he needed to tell me off for something. Just for being me, I suppose. I'd accumulated a whole list of misdemeanours, harking right back to when I was sixteen, and probably before *that*, in Nicholas's book. He was visiting our mother, on her request.

Mum, he said, was now on a load of new tablets for various complaints. He was sorry to tell me this but he said Mum wouldn't – she had cancer and she was waiting for a scan. I got one of my funny feelings when I read that, the chill at the back of my neck. Someone would have to keep an eye on her, Nicholas said – had I thought of moving back to Lincoln? He was there at the point of writing the letter and he'd take her for the scan himself but he couldn't stay. Janie, he pointed out, had a family of her own to look after.

It sounded like he was unaware of our sister's recently broken marriage. Janie obviously didn't want to blemish his opinion of her as the perfect wife and mother. Yeah, I knew I sounded bitter. Especially when I read his suggestion that *I* should give up *my* life – not to mention my horses and my chickens and the two goat kids I'd recently adopted, and my job at the community centre and the band – to become a live-in carer for our mother. In short, Nicholas's reasoning was that it was my responsibility because, *forty years* ago, I'd instigated almost a decade of being out-of-touch with Mum, and I needed to make up for it now. Seriously? Nicholas didn't know the half of it.

5

Annette, 1972

The bus deposited us in the village square, beside the war memorial. Janie and I were the last to disembark, shuffling out after the hippies in their maxi-dresses and Afghan coats. Some of the women and one man wore ponchos that looked sewn together from pieces of blanket. You wouldn't catch me dressing like that. I tugged down my denim mini-skirt and gasped when puddle-water splashed the backs of my legs as the bus took off again. At least I wasn't stupid enough to have worn my lovely white boots. The slightly-too-small wellies on my feet would keep them dry if nothing else.

The sky was now thick and grey – all the pretty colours of sunrise melded into the weather. Janie had chucked away her bravado, though she now looked at least sixteen – my age – amazing what a difference eyeliner and lipstick had made. But she clutched my sleeve and hopped from foot to foot. Bloody hell, I felt responsible for her. I would've been better coming on my own. I toyed for a sec with the idea of packing her off back home on the next bus, but I didn't want to use up precious money on the bus fare, and she probably wouldn't go on her own. I planned for us to get a lift back to Lincoln after the festival – there'd be loads of people going that way. I'd already hitchhiked loads of times with Mary, ha. Our parents would kill us if they found out.

'C'mon. Buck up, Janie.' I stood with my rucksack at my feet and her clinging miserably to my arm. She was trying to adjust the heel of her sock inside her boot. The fine rain darkened her hair and splash-marked her parka. I fumbled in the pocket of my furry jacket and jammed my maroon beret onto my head. From a crumpled paper bag I extracted a coiled liquorice lace, Janie's favourite sweet. She let go of my arm and sucked the end of it into her mouth. Her eyes wandered off to the left, the direction the hippies had walked in. She looked like Twiggy, or another of those starlets with the kohl eyes and that wistful expression. I'd never thought of her as pretty before. *Hmm.* She was supposed to be my sidekick.

'Let's follow them, then,' I jerked my head towards the hippies. 'That must be the way to the festival.'

The end of the liquorice lace disappeared into her mouth and she perked up, even managed a grin and looked like my little sister again. We shrugged our backpacks on and clunked off down the road out of the village, my toes already pinched in the stupid wellies. How I missed my cork wedge sandals, or better still my white boots – what kind of a look was Wellington boots? But my job potato picking out this way last summer had showed me how muddy these fields could get. We trudged on.

Rain glistened on the grey road. Soon we had to step onto the wet grass verge so two tractors could pass us safely. Janie moaned that the backpack was cutting into her shoulders.

Okay, I felt a bit guilty about weighing it down with my heavy jumper. Only a bit, though. She was fitter than me and didn't have my back problem, it was only fair she should help me out. I pulled my beret down over one ear and tucked my chin into my neck. My back *was* aching, actually. But I didn't whinge about stuff like that. We stepped onto the road again and plodded on.

A line of cars and vans that'd been held up by the tractors crawled past us. I noticed a group of bobbies walking ahead. They turned around and stopped as the vehicles approached. One put up his hand to halt the traffic. Janie hurried to catch up with me. Her mouth hung open and she panted, grabbing my arm again.

'Why are the police here? What do you think's happening?'

I shrugged her off. 'I don't know, do I?'

'Oh look, the bobbies are getting in that van. The chap's opened the back for them – look.'

'haha.' I said. 'The hippies in that van are going to be wetting their pants.'

'How d'you know there are hippies in the van?'

'You saw the driver, didn't you? Anyway, most of the people at the festival are going to be hippies. Don't you know anything?'

She paused to consider. 'Not as much as you, obviously.'

'Less of the lip, you.' I gave her backpack a clout. Stumbling and regaining her balance, she turned and glared at me with tears in her eyes.

'That was just bloody mean!'

'Hey, get you. Swearing! What on earth would Mum say?'

'Just shut up. Leave me alone.'

I was thinking up a suitable response when a yellow-and-orange taxicab pulled up beside us. Two long-haired blokes sat in the front – one of them reminded me of Peter Gabriel – and a girl with frizzy curls, wearing a beaded headband, sat on the back seat. She looked a bit like Janis Joplin. They were all looking at us. I realised my mouth hung open so I snapped it shut, hoping none of them had noticed.

The driver wound down the window, smoke billowing out of the car.

'Want a lift, girls?'

My heart thumped. 'Yeah, sure,' I adjusted my beret again. A raindrop dripped down the back of my neck.

Janie narrowed her eyes. Before she could dig her wellies into the mud at the edge of the road, I grabbed her arm and pulled her forward, saying, 'Thanks,' to the driver.

The girl in the back unwound her legs and opened the door, shuffling along the seat. She patted the red leather. 'Come on, then. You should be able to squeeze in with your bags.' Her voice was like Janice Joplin's as well.

I pushed Janie in front of me and we both piled in with our backpacks. I pulled the taxi door closed behind us. The smell of our damp clothes mingled with the patchouli scent that filled the car. Janie wrinkled her nose, making a small noise, about to protest. I gave her a sharp nudge. She gasped and shot me a furious look, but she did at least close her mouth.

The car started up and I felt like a member of the Royal Family, until it came to a stop again before it had really got going. The girl beside us leaned forward between the front seats.

'What's going on? What's the hold-up?'

'Dunno,' said the bloke next to the driver. 'There's a couple of angry-looking fellers and a woman with some sort of protest sign in the middle of the road. "Stop the Festival" it says. Boring locals, I expect.'

'Can't stand anyone else having fun,' muttered the driver. He jerked on the handbrake and waited, his fingers tapping the steering wheel. The car engine rumbled.

The girl with frizzy hair slid out and approached the protesters in the middle of the road. 'Is there some kind of problem?' Beneath her short, tasselled dress maroon velvet bell-bottoms swung around her legs, moving like liquid with her swaying hips. Smiling, she sidled up to the woman holding the banner. I caught the words 'messing up the countryside,' followed by, 'court injunction,' from the man with a big stomach on the right of the group.

The girl held her arm outwards, shepherding the others

without them seeming to notice. She nodded and smiled at them. Whatever she was saying seemed to help – edging the protesters closer to the verge until there was enough space for our driver to move the car forward at a crawling pace. Once we drew level our girl leapt back in the car and slammed the door shut. She knocked Janie's bag sideways, turning to kneel on the back seat and laughing breathlessly. Janie let out one of her gasps at the girl's two-fingered salute out the back window.

The rest of us were laughing as we bumped along the road at only a slightly faster pace than we could have walked. Never mind the speed, Janie and I were arriving at the *Great Western Express Festival* in style.

The remains of Tupholme Abbey (we recognised it because we had once been for a family picnic there) glowed faintly yellow through the morning's thick greyness. The fields around the ruined abbey were packed with tents and humps of polythene as far as my eyes could see. Closer to, I could make out people lying under the polythene mounds. Damp festival-goers picked their way across the muddy ground between the humps in every direction. It reminded me of a battlefield.

We came to a stop at the gates and the blokes in front twisted their heads round to look us up and down.

'Thanks for the company, lasses. We'll drop you off here. Enjoy the festival.'

The girl leaned right over us, her elbow digging into my stomach. I held my breath. She released the door catch to let Janie and me out of the cab and I breathed again.

'Maybe catch ya later, love,' she said in her husky voice. The blokes waved at us and we stumbled out, dragging our bags behind us. The ground rocked under my feet, I'd never admit it but I felt a bit lost standing there watching the big yellow taxi chug away down the track. The main thing was not to let Janie sense it.

'Come on then,' I dragged her by the arm. We showed our

tickets and they let us in through the turnstile. I needn't have worried about Janie looking too young, they hardly glanced at our faces. Once on the other side it all felt a bit of an anti-climax. A drizzly morning. No bands playing yet. We shouldn't have come so early.

Janie shoved her hands in her pockets.

'What now?'

'Let's go and have a look,' I made an effort to sound assertive.

We walked round for a bit. I had to encourage Janie to step over people, the ground was jam-packed with bodies. A girl about my age with matted hair sat on a hay bale strumming a guitar and a young bloke with thick sideburns sat wrapped in polythene on the ground humming along to the chords. One-man tents scattered amongst the polythene tunnels made bright splashes of colour in the grey drizzle. A band I didn't recognise were tuning up on a stage I didn't think was the main one.

A cheer went up just ahead of us. Our fellow passengers on the bus from Lincoln were dancing around a crowd of mirror-image friends at the entrance to a big tent with a sign outside. Peering through the drizzle I read the scribbled words: *crash tent.* Ah. Sleep sounded good to me, after all the excitement. Closer by, some lads had built a shelter out of bales of hay and planks of wood. One lad, aged about fifteen maybe, had his belt unbuckled as if he'd just got dressed or was about to get undressed. He was bare-chested and stood cupping a joint in the palm of his hand, all cocky-like. He blew smoke towards us as we passed him.

'Wanna toke?'

I shook my head. 'Nah, you're all right. Ta.' I could tell he was eyeing up Janie but she had no idea. She was staring at a sign on a smaller tent ahead. I pulled her along, but she twisted her head back.

'What does that mean?'

Blow jobs 10 bob. I burst out laughing. 'That's for me to

21

know and you to find out.' To be honest my only experience of actual sex was with a lad from the Boys' Grammar School when my school combined with his for a Christmas disco. I surprised myself, really, as I hadn't even particularly fancied him. I chose to put my decision down to the Babycham someone smuggled in. The brief, fumbling (and bloody painful) act took place in an empty classroom. For weeks afterwards I was scared I might be pregnant but that was one thing I didn't mention to Janie. Mum would probably kick me out if she knew I'd done *it*. Still, at least I wasn't a virgin anymore and I'd know what to do should the opportunity arise (haha) again with a lad I *did* fancy.

Janie reddened. 'Be like that, then.' I suspected she was relieved not to know. She hadn't wanted to know the details when I told her I got my period for the first time. That was three years ago. I wondered if she'd started hers yet.

My eyes roved over a further mass of kids lying encased in some kind of paper sleeping bags that made them look like maggots.

Further off loomed the stage.

'This is what we came for,' I pointed at the tall metal towers rigged with lights. At the speakers, stacked on top of each other. 'You wait until the music starts. To think we're going to be standing in front of *Genesis*!'

'And Roxy Music,' she breathed.

'Yeah, right.' Whoever they were.

'Sally's going to be so jealous.'

'That's the spirit. It's going to be amazing.' A shiver of excitement made the hairs on my wrists tingle. I brushed raindrops from the sleeves of my fake-fur jacket and shivered again, this time feeling a chill.

'Let's go inside that crash tent and I can put my big jumper on. I need to get it out of your bag. We can have a rest then, if you like. Or eat some breakfast.'

She looked around with a hopeful expression as if she expected to find a café.

'Where can we get some breakfast?'

'I brought a flask of tea and some sandwiches. Well, you did. They're in your bag as well.'

She gave me a look.

'Okay. Let's go in then. I'm hungry.'

6

Janie, then, then, and now

Then

Two-month-old Billy was asleep on her chest, snuggled inside the red jersey wrap she'd carried all her children in. Juliet perched tensely on the chair next to her mother, clutching the hem of Janie's loose shirt in one hand and the toy rabbit she'd had since birth in the other. Juliet had hated the noise and bustle of the auction place: the sharp crack of the hammer and the breath of excitement as each auction neared its climax was a misery for her. Paul, his arm around drowsy two-year-old Allegra, had let out a yell when they won Catmally Station. Allegra almost fell on the floor and Juliet burst into tears. Janie nearly did as well. The property's dilapidated condition suddenly became more real as she pictured what it might actually be like to live there with three young children.

Paul's brothers took a sabbatical from the family firm in Sunderland to come up and stay with them for a month. During their stay they made two rooms habitable for the

24

family and did some groundwork on the rest of the house and outbuildings. Janie hadn't even considered until they moved in how dangerous it was for small children to live on a working railway platform. The proximity of the tracks meant they'd had to secure the front door as well as the fence and gate that led into the garden. Visitors had to ring an old ship's bell to be let in.

The brothers had done such a good job and the living arrangements had been so harmonious it had given Janie the idea to take on working guests, who helped build and plaster and paint. Over the years they usually had at least one or two strangers – often soon to be friends – living in the house with them or in converted outbuildings, until Catmally Railway Station was restored to its former glory.

They joined the *Workaway* scheme, as hosts. They took in four separate young refugee men whose asylum claims were in process. They provided accommodation for overseas students. There were always people staying at Catmally.

Then

Paul invited one of his tutees from Glasgow College of Art to live with them for a while – this was long after Janie's nightly visits to the shepherd's hut had stopped. She and Paul were so busy they had often gone a week without touching each other. Looking at each other, even. Janie, faintly aware of this remiss, kept meaning to do something about it.

The student received free accommodation in exchange for light au pairing duties. By then Juliet was twelve, Allegra ten and Billy eight. Janie worked part-time in the science department at the secondary school in Oban and Vanessa's duties included getting the children's tea three days a week.

Janie arrived home early one afternoon thanks to an electrical fault at the school. She parked in the car park, walked around the side of the house onto the platform, unlocked the back gate and walked into the kitchen to find that Juliet had collected her siblings from school. She stood at the stove, cooking their tea. Vanessa was nowhere to be seen. Sand-coloured hair lightly fastened into unruly plaits, the young woman flew through the kitchen door a short while later. Janie noticed the flush saturating Vanessa's freckled cheeks and pale neck, the shock in her eyes at seeing Janie, standing with her arms folded. Vanessa stood, out-of-breath, fiddling with the ends of her hair. But the way she lifted her chin made Janie's heart feel like lead.

'Where have you been?' her voice sounded like lead, too.

'I got called in to college for an interview. It's for a prestigious award, I couldn't say no. Don't be mad. Juliet can cope fine on her own, look at her. She's a great gal, aren't you, hen?'

Vanessa exchanged a complicit glance with Janie's daughter before dragging off her jacket and throwing it over the back of a chair. She moved to the sink and washed her hands, then peered over Juliet's shoulder at the chilli she was stirring in a pan.

'Mmm, smells good.'

Juliet's feet did that little dance of hers when she felt uncomfortable.

'I'm perfectly aware of my daughter's capabilities,' Janie said through gritted teeth. 'The point is that you are under obligation to fulfil certain duties. We agreed. I don't want Juliet to have to be responsible for the others just yet. You can't simply take off like that without letting me know. It's not fair.'

Really it was her own guilt at leaving her children in the care of an unreliable stranger. She'd never been able to get to know Vanessa properly, there'd been something over-guarded about her from the day Paul brought her into the house. Janie had a flash of presentiment then but she'd quickly swallowed it down. Paul had been getting so touchy whenever he felt criticised.

After so many others of all shapes, sizes and nationalities,

Vanessa was the first guest she didn't feel comfortable having in her home. What *was* it about her?

'Ach. Okay, I'm sorry then.' Vanessa sounded as if she really wasn't. 'I'll try not to do it again. But I think I have a good chance of winning this award. I'm excited.' She plonked herself on a chair at the head of the table and opened a newspaper. Janie could tell she wasn't actually reading. She glanced at her daughter before opening the oven to check the progress of the potatoes Juliet had put in.

'You've done a wonderful job, darling. Have you had time to do any homework?'

'Haven't got any tonight,' Juliet moved to the sink and filled a glass of water which she drank slowly. Meagre light from the window picked out the faint down on the curve of her cheek and lightened an escaped strand of reddish hair. Janie watched her throat contracting as she swallowed the water and felt her own throat tighten. If only she didn't feel so tired. If only she felt a better mother to Juliet, who seemed to have grown up too soon.

The house shook as the Highland Express pulled into the platform and screeched to a halt. A cluster of passengers Janie had passed leaning against the outer wall of their house moved towards the carriage and climbed in. Janie watched a mother struggling to lift a loaded pushchair up the step, eventually helped by the guard. A whistle was blown. Something clicked in Janie's head. She felt her cheeks go hot. The train strained to pull off towards Glasgow, leaving the tracks singing in its wake.

She touched her daughter's shoulder.

'You could go and read for a while, then, hen. The potatoes will need another half-an-hour I should think.'

Juliet glanced from her mother to Vanessa, sensing an atmosphere. She gave her mother a small smile.

'Okay. I'm off to get changed.'

Janie turned back to Vanessa, glad there were no passengers outside to hear through the open window.

'How come you arrived back when you did? The train isn't due in for another ten minutes.'

Vanessa reddened, biting her lip.

'I got a lift. A friend was travelling up to Oban for the weekend. What is this, anyway, an interrogation?' She managed to look innocent and derisory at the same time, not even pretending to have any respect for Janie.

Janie could have slapped her.

'It's just odd, that's all.' She paused, fumbling with a tea towel. 'Please don't put my children in danger again.' She kept her voice steady but her hands trembled as she replaced the tea towel on a rail. She picked up the wooden spoon by the cooker and gave the chilli a stir. She placed a lid on the pan, turned the heat off underneath it and moved towards the doorway to the sitting room, from where she could hear her younger children chattering in front of the TV. A need to be swallowed into the cushions between Allegra and Billy overtook her. They were the only thing that mattered. Her children. She moved through the doorway.

'Hardly in danger. Talk about mollycoddling,' Vanessa's mutter behind her was just loud enough to be heard. Janie counted to ten in her head. The girl had to go.

Now

She finished wiping the shelves in the kitchen cupboards and rinsed the dishcloth before she wrung it out and draped it over the edge of the sink. On the platform across the rails, a young couple waited for the train to Oban. The laddie had bare, tattooed arms and Janie imagined him shivering, with his hands rammed deep into the pockets of his jeans. She bet he had goose-pimples – there was a chill breeze out there on the platforms today. The wee lassie was wearing a too-large leather jacket that probably belonged to the boy. They stood slightly apart but were slowly moving their faces towards each other. Janie watched from her distance, sad that they probably believed the feelings they had now were going to last forever. Eventually the gap between them disappeared and the lad slid his arms inside the girl's jacket, pulling her tightly against him. Janie looked away, her throat swelling.

Her mobile rang, and she picked it up to see her childhood friend's name blinking on the screen. After a traumatic start to their real-life friendship, she and Lara became penpals. They visited each other's homes a couple of times, but eventually fell out of touch. Then when they were in their thirties, Lara friend-requested Janie on Friends Reunited.

Lara had rung to wish Janie *Bon Voyage* and force a promise out of her to visit London before the summer was out.

Lara was divorced, too, and struggled to make ends meet in a tower block in North London. 'Marcus is going to end up in real trouble if he's not careful. I blame his uncle Fergus. Anyway, how's your adorable Billy? I haven't had a good squish of his cheeks for a while.'

Everybody loved Billy. 'He wouldn't thank you for squishing his cheeks anymore,' Janie laughed. 'Anyway they're covered in what he calls bum-fluff.'

'Eueww! If I come across him in the dark I'll bear that in mind.'

Janie was about to end the call when she remembered to ask about her friend's troubled relationship with her father.

'He'd promised he would fly over for Jocelyn's birthday this year,' Lara said. 'She's seven years old already and he's never even met her!' hearing the crack in her voice Janie's throat tightened with empathy. Lara's almost-orphan status coupled with her kick-ass attitude had filled her with admiration as a child. But her friend's long-lost reunion with her father in her thirties, in fact about the time she and Janie reconnected, seemed to have broken her hard-bitch (Lara's words, never Janie's) carapace.

After the call, the house felt quieter than ever. Janie

examined her clean, empty kitchen and blinked back tears. Her lovely kitchen. The walls they had kept yellow since Paul and his brothers first painted them to offset the dimness of the room's outlook – the kitchen faced directly onto the covered platform. Yet this long, narrow room was the one she most thought of as home. The cosy space in which the family and all the guests that had stayed with them over the years had gathered for convivial meals and conversations.

She used to sit in a rocking chair over there by the wood burner to feed Billy, amidst the chaos of building work. Paul would bring her drinks. The girls played on the rug at her feet. Staring at the cold stove she wanted to conjure those little children – that besotted husband – back again. Turn back a few pages and reread the story until it made a bit more sense. *When did everything start to go wrong?*

Tonight she would have dinner in the local hotel with a few of her friends. Her last boxes had been taken to storage at a local farm earlier that afternoon. The car was jammed full of the items she might need over the next few months. Tomorrow she would climb into her car and drive without thinking, all the way to Lincolnshire. There she would meet Annette at their mother's. Annette had promised a surprise for Janie. With her usual sureness she declared she was going to make her sister "deliriously happy". Janie would believe that when she saw it.

7

Annette, now

I caught a bus into the city centre, carrying me fiddle in its case. It drew some interested glances from the pensioners, mums and babies that made up the bulk of the passengers. A toddler stroked the case lovingly.

'Alfie, leave the lady alone,' snapped his mother, pulling him more securely onto her lap. I watched a lake go by outside the window, remembering childhood bicycle rides there with Janie, minnow-fishing with Nicholas when I was even smaller.

The fiddle case got me into conversation with a grey-bearded old man. He told me he once played in a folk group. As we talked about Johnny Cash and Bob Dylan I felt a wave of warmth – an encroaching memory I usually refused to allow in, because it stirred other recollections I'd rather not entertain.

In town another busker played guitar further up the high street, his voice amplified by a portable PA system. Bugger, that was the best spot. I opened my fiddle case near the War Memorial instead. There were still faded poppy wreaths from the previous November around its base.

Two women with white hair who must've been twins stopped in front of me when I started playing *Mairi's Wedding*. Both women wore blue velvet coats with fur collars. They stood unmoving with their arms interlinked before suddenly turning on the spot in sync and walking off without apparently communicating. I bowed to an old man who dropped a handful of coins into the fiddle case at the end of the tune. His knees clicked when he straightened up and we exchanged a sympathetic grin. With *Rose of Tralee* I brought an old lady to tears. She emptied her purse of change and patted me on the shoulder when I'd finished.

'You've made my day, lovey. That was my wedding song.' Her accent was Irish and it made me swallow emptiness in my throat. A child jigged to the next tune, its mother rocking a baby in her arms. Grey-beard from the bus stopped by, tapping his foot. When I started to play *Danny Boy* he sang along in a rich, folksy baritone. We played two more tunes together, before he said he had to get on. Together, we'd drawn quite a crowd. Grey-beard refused my offering of coins.

By the end of the two-hour session I'd made forty quid – not bad for an afternoon's work. I bowed to the scattering of applause and packed up my instrument, my back aching.

Checking the time I calculated Mum would be delivered home from her day-centre in an hour. I found I was tearing at the skin around my fingernails with my teeth, still not quite believing the situation I'd got myself into. When I asked my band mate to look after my place in Ireland for me just while I checked on my mother, I guess I was refusing to accept the reality. I told myself Nicholas must've been wrong about the state of Mum and how much care she'd need. It'd be fine, to be sure. But after a week of observing how frail she'd become I realised I couldn't just drop her and go back. I'd been unwittingly deposited in an alternative version of my life where I lived in a small terraced house with Mum and our two dogs. We'd drive each other bonkers.

In Ireland I would have arrived home from work at the

community centre and by now I'd be carrying an armful of wood inside for my sitting room fire. I'd have taken out water for the horses – the old grey mare and the tangle-coated foal nobody else wanted. I hoped Fionula remembered the exact spot behind the ears I'd shown her where the foal loved to be scratched. The goat kids would be bleating in their pen and Romy would be jumping around my feet, wanting me to throw her ball. Instead she was undoubtedly annoying the hell out of Mum's neighbours barking at squirrels on the trees behind the back fence, because I'd had to leave her outside in a makeshift kennel. It'd been a choice between that or leave her cooped up in the living room with an ancient Jack Russell that had no respect for boundaries.

I needed space. I needed my animals. My stomach cramped, just thinking about how trapped I was.

After leaning on the memorial wall and rolling a fag I wandered up the High Street towards the Stonebow – a medieval archway, one of Lincoln's old gates. The structure incorporated a guildhall with leaded windows. A dim memory of a school trip there when I was about twelve, getting in trouble for running my hands along the surface of the long, shiny table in a wood-panelled room, and again for daring to climb onto a raised dais and sit on the mayor's throne while my classmates laughed at me. I'd lost touch with them all, even Mary who'd been my best friend in the world.

Absent-mindedly I glanced into shop windows as I shuffled along with the fiddle-case, a familiar, dull ache in my upper spine. Under the darkness of the stone arch I shook my head at a pair of women dressed in long, pleated skirts and navy-blue jackets, proffering leaflets that promised *Salvation!* 'I'll save meself, thank you.'

Where could I get a cup of tea around there? The department store café was already closing according to the sign in the window. *And my mother thought I was in the back of beyond in Ireland.* There some bars on the upward slope of the High Street, maybe I'd have a pint before

33

returning to my duties as a clueless carer. Thank god Janie was arriving to help bear the load the next day. She was bound to be better at that kind of thing than me, what with her being a mother and all. Again my stomach clenched at the thought of the cramped conditions we'd be living in together.

I turned my head to check my reflection in an estate agent's window before going into the bar next door.

For sale by auction, a poster with a torn corner caught my attention. The main photograph showed a stone house and a series of outbuildings with fields surrounding them. A smaller picture displayed a disused railway line, running alongside a rough track outside the house's garden. A huge garden, more like a smallholding really.

A decommissioned railway station! Just like the one Janie'd had to move out of.

My hand tightened on the handle of my fiddle case as I saw the property's location: in the very village where *it* took place. The event that changed my life forever. This must be Fate, trying to tell me something. I chewed on my fingernails while I contemplated my situation. I had the Earl's money – I never thought I'd find a use for it – sitting like a lead weight in my bank account. What if. . . what if I rushed into a decision so incongruous it might turn out to be genius?

A decision that might solve all our problems, at least the accommodation-based ones.

Checking out the reserve price I looked for the date of the auction – 7 o'clock this evening! To be held at the auction house on the corner of St Andrew's Street. Good job there was a spare key to Mum's house in the hanging basket by the front door. I'd text her and let her know I was going to be late and she would just have to manage on her own for a while.

They had a good selection of craft beers in the bar I went into, one I remembered as being a nightclub that Mary and I once managed to sneak into, two years underage.

A pint it is, then.

8

Justin, now

His head still buzzed from the volume of applause at his Hebden Bridge rally the day before. During the night it had resounded through his dreams. And he'd dreamt he was singing to the people who filled the centre of town and the streets leading out of it. They'd been perched on rooftops and walls and one or two spectators had even been sitting on the tops of lampposts – both in reality and in the dream. But he'd only sung in the dream – Bob Dylan. The audience, the whole town had joined in and the applause afterwards was beyond rapturous.

The times certainly were *a' changing*. He sometimes wondered, if he'd stuck to folk singing, could he have achieved more than he had as a politician? Bob Dylan had been awarded the Nobel Prize for Literature after all – his lyrics recognised for their influence. Could that have been Justin? Perhaps he should begin each rally with a song.

He had his guitar with him in his tour bus cubicle and it had proved useful last night, which come to think of it, was probably the reason he'd been singing in the dream.

'You can't sleep on the bus,' his advisors had told him. 'It's not professional. Let us book you into hotels.'

'I'm more comfortable on the bus,' he said, and he really was. Preferred being responsible for himself. 'Anyway, hotels would be a waste of donated money. We need to spend it for the good of the many, not on me.'

His chief advisor straightened his tie, top lip slightly curled. 'Well, I'm sorry, but I'm not sleeping on the tour bus. I need a private room.'

'That's fine. You work hard and of course you need a good night's sleep. Whatever you feel works best for you. But I'm happier sleeping in the bus, honestly.'

'Humph. Well, thanks. I'll see you in the morning, then.'

The advisor looked as though he'd swallowed something bitter as he turned and walked through the hotel doors. It was no good, they couldn't seem to get along however hard Justin felt he'd tried. These days they seemed to have totally opposite views despite being in the same party. Justin decided to forget it all for a night and go for a quick one at the pub down the road from where the bus was parked. Inside, customers slapped him on the back and insisted on buying him drinks. The place thronged with excitement and noise. A folk band was playing on the stage in the corner and Justin's knee began jiggling. He was about to get up when someone placed another pint of beer on the table in front of him. He put up a conciliatory hand and gave them a smile.

'Thanks, that's much appreciated. But hey, could you look after that for me for a minute? Here, take my seat, won't you? I've got to go and fetch something.'

He fought his way out into the cool air and walked the two short streets back to the bus. All the curtains were drawn. The driver was falling asleep in front of a DVD at the dining table in the back. Justin exchanged a few words with him about the loneliness of a political tour bus driver, before reaching into his cubicle for his guitar.

'Listen,' he placed his hand on the driver's shoulder on his way out. 'Don't wait up for me, hey? I know it's been a long day for you, too. I'll see you in the morning.' The driver gave him a grateful smile and nodded.

'Cool, thanks Boss. You know the code to get back in, don't you?'

'I do,' said Justin. 'You have a good night's sleep – I won't be back too late.'

He was reminded of the days when he had the easy (for the most part) companionship of a wife at home after a long day's politicking. His second wife had left him five years ago and he'd been alone since, apart from the cat (who was currently being looked after by his first wife). He felt like a priest – married to his job. Political bus drivers weren't the only ones who got lonely.

———————

The band were taking a break at the bar when he returned, their backs to the room. Justin tapped one of them lightly on the shoulder. He swung around and stared glassily for a moment, then his eyes widened and he spluttered on his beer.

'Justin Christian, as I live and breathe.' Justin had to take a deep breath himself. It felt odd to hear his original name. He felt a little pain at the spot where his clavicles met.

'Where've you been hiding, mate? Haven't see you since the early seventies!'

Justin almost choked with laughter. Clearly, his old friend never watched television or kept abreast of politics. Perhaps the drugs had riddled his brain.

'Oh, here and there,' he said lightly. 'Got into a different line of work after the band split up. But look, I've got my guitar on me now. Fancy doing a few of the old numbers together?'

'Sure, man. That'd be cool. We're on again in about five minutes, I'll let the others know. See you on stage!'

The laugh continued to rumble in Justin's throat. It was great that he looked so ordinary – like a myriad of other men

37

his age from all walks of life. He was often described as a man of the people. He propped his guitar in a safe place and squeezed onto the end of a bench at the table where he'd been sitting before. He reached across the table and picked up the beer he'd been bought earlier.

'Hey, that belongs to...' someone said, and then they noticed who was holding the glass. 'Ah, you're back. I need you to settle a point of conflict between me and my friend, here. You see, I was thinking the economy could be better served by...' he went on and on until Justin's brain flapped in his head. He tried hard to pay attention. But at the same time he was aware that, for the first time in years, the thought of being on a stage made him nervous. In the middle of all the noise and intensity there was a screech from the microphone. Justin had to stop the man's spiel by politely raising a hand.

'I do apologise,' he said. 'But I'm afraid I have to get up again now.' The man placed his hand over-firmly on Justin's arm and fixed him with a determined expression as his mouth fell open. Justin looked directly back into the man's eyes. That was his way, to never waver his blue-eyed gaze. People didn't appreciate shiftiness. 'I do apologise,' he said again. 'I'll be back to resume our conversation as soon as I'm able.'

He patted the man's arm with his free hand. This seemed to satisfy him and he unhooked his claw-like grasp. The lead singer tapped the microphone with the tip of his finger and the noise in the crowded pub settled down a little. Justin grabbed his beer for a last, desperate gulp.

'Excuse me, excuse me.' He reached behind two men with large bellies to extract his guitar from the corner where he'd propped it. One fellow jolted as if he'd had an electric shock when Justin's shirted arm brushed against his thick, tattooed one.

'Thank you,' Justin heard himself say, feeling hot from the beer. The man had a serpent tattoo on the back of his bald head. 'Eh up,' said his friend, noticing Justin. The friend had wispy, pale-brown hair spraying from the top of his beetroot scalp. 'Aren't you...?' he nudged the other one. 'Look 'ere, Fred – it is. It's that soft lad as thinks we should give up our nuclear arsenal. Stupid git. Putting our country in danger. I'd recognise 'is wimpy face anywhere. It's 'im, isn't it?'

'Why man, you're right. It bloody is. What're you doing 'ere, then?' Beefy tattoo man took a few steps to the right, partially blocking Justin's exit. Justin thought he might sick up his hastily-gulped beer. He decided to practise the steady-eyed gaze that had worked on the local at the other table, hoping his eyes were emitting their usual, honest beam.

'Aye, well. 'E's not worth bothering about, is 'e?' said tattoo man, glint receding from his eyes. ''E's never going to win, is 'e? We'll be all right with that new iron lady the other side have got for us. She knows how to make our country strong again, she does.'

Sweat trickled down the back of his neck. He should have stayed in the bus. He needed his strength for tomorrow. *Burnley*. The microphone fed back into the audience again and people put their hands over their ears.

'We have a special guest joining us for the next few songs,' the singer, not Justin's band mate of old, on the stage announced. 'Where is he, now? Ah, there he is, working his magic with Fred and Bert over there – the magic we've all witnessed today in our town centre – yes, seriously, I'm not having you on. Here he comes! Please welcome to the stage, the one and only... Mr Justin, err, Citizen.' Justin edged his way forward, elbowing people out of the way as delicately as possible, feeling hotter by the minute. He stopped mid-step, realising that he was possibly committing professional suicide. Was it too late to disappear back into the crowd? *Yes*.

'Come on now, Mr Citizen, let's have you up on the stage. You've got your guitar with you I see. Always come prepared, eh? Now why didn't you treat us to a bit of that this afternoon? Silence the naysayers with a song...' He continued his patter while Justin struggled towards the stage, thankfully leaving the intimidating Fred and Bert far behind in the melee. On the opposite side of the stage he could see his old mate from the 1970s making a shocked gesture – out-turned palms and theatrically rounded eyes. Mouthing what was probably something like: *'You're Justin Citizen – THE Justin Citizen? OMG mate. So that's what you've been doing all these years!'*

A round of applause accompanied him onto the stage. The band played the opening chords to *Like a Rolling Stone* and Justin soon forgot everything else. His singing went down a storm and before the end of the night he had the whole pub joining in.

Including Fred and Bert.

The next morning he emerged from his sleeping cubicle red-eyed and tired. Hung over if he was honest, and he was. To a fault, his advisors had told him – but he didn't see how being honest could be a fault. The driver looked a lot fresher than him.

'Did you sleep well, Andy?' Justin fumbled to get his glasses on straight as he poured himself a cup of coffee from the machine bubbling away in the tiny kitchenette.

'I did, thanks to you, Mr C. Letting me off duty like you did. I'm not sure you can say the same about yourself though. Looking a bit the worse for wear if I may say?'

'Oh dear, was I snoring again? My ex-wife complained a lot about that.'

'It was more the singing, Mr C. You were singing throughout most of the night – in your sleep, I imagine. Proper rowdy, it sounded.'

Justin started laughing and couldn't stop. Soon Andy joined in. Then Justin had a coughing fit – only just managing not to spill coffee everywhere.

'Oh dear,' he finally managed to speak again. 'I do apologise for that. I knew I was singing in my dream – got the whole town singing along. But I hadn't realised I was singing in real life.' He caught a glimpse of his reflection in the strip of mirror below the light fixture and saw that his eyes, though slightly bloodshot, had a merry appearance, reflecting his positive mood. This was turning out to be a good campaign.

He took another mouthful of scalding coffee and placed the cup down.

'I'd best get in the shower and put a clean shirt on. I've got a meeting in the hotel dining room in half-an-hour and then it's back on the road again. Burnley today, isn't it?'

'That's right, Mr C.' Andy was running a comb through his thick, black hair. 'Only an hour or so's drive through the villages. A friendly lot in Burnley, they are.'

But Justin's attention had been distracted from the conversation by his phone, which he'd left on charge when he came in last night. It now bleeped as he switched it on, and several messages came up on the screen. The first few were from his niece. Later messages had arrived from his press secretary, his deputy-leader and even one from his second ex-wife, with whom he was still good friends.

He felt the colour drain from his face as he clicked on the links they'd pasted into their messages. Every one of them a news headline. He scrolled quickly through the articles underneath.

'Are you all right, sir?' Andy moved back over to the table. He hardly ever called Justin sir. 'Here, you look like you need to sit down. Have another coffee.'

Andy pushed him onto a seat and topped up his cup. The black liquid steamed and blurred Justin's vision.

'Try a piece of toast, as well, Mr C. You're probably hungry after using all that energy singing in your sleep.'

For once Justin was unable to summon a smile. He couldn't even look at Andy. His hands shook as he continued to scroll down the news on his phone screen.

'They've got it all wrong.' He lowered his face into his free hand, muttering to himself. 'Well of course they have. It's their business to distort the truth, isn't it?'

Andy coughed hard in his throat. 'Now you're getting me concerned, sir. You don't look well.'

He sat opposite Justin, who lifted his face from his hand and stared out of the window. Outside, the usual morning rush had already started. But there was something else. People had begun to gather on the pavement next to the bus. This wasn't unusual, often it was young people – his most passionate fans – holding out notebooks and pens, waiting for his autograph. He looked vainly for the *Vote Truth. Vote JC* placards they customarily held up. But today he could see none of the friendliness that had flowed from the town yesterday.

An older man now moved closer to the window, spreading a popular newspaper out on the glass by Justin's face. He jabbed his finger at Justin. The newspaper was one of the several owned by a prominent supporter of the party in government and a close friend of the Prime Minister. Below the thick, black headline on the front page were two photographs. One was a grainy black-and-white image of him as a young man, holding the hands of an even younger girl, a child, with a thick fringe hanging over her eyes. She was pulling away from him. The expression on his face made him look vacant. The other photo was a close up, floridly-coloured likeness of Justin Citizen at one of his recent rallies. The camera had caught him mid-speech and it looked as if his lip was curled in a sneer. Justin was aware of Andy's sharp intake of breath as he, too, must have been reading the headline:

JUSTIN CITIZEN AND THE UNDERAGE FESTIVAL GIRL!

9

Annette, 1972

Janie had made herself comfy again using her backpack as a pillow. The "crash tent" was full of lots more sleeping bodies now; some filthy and covered in mud, others arrived that morning like us. Janie had fallen fast asleep for the second time and looked like a little dormouse (one of her favourite animals – she had lots). I'd dozed briefly and was now wide-awake. So I wrote Janie a note (in lipstick) on the back of a flyer someone had given me and tucked it into the pocket of her parka – half sticking out so she'd see it as soon as she woke up. *Stay here. Back soon.* Then I climbed over everyone and went back outside for a breath of fresh air.

It felt good to be on my own and not have to worry about Janie getting spooked by the slightest thing like when we went out to find a loo earlier; first some drugged-up hippy, then the high, corrugated-metal barrier running around the edge of the site (though I must admit the searchlights on top were a bit excessive). Janie said it was like being in a prison camp, and we *had* seen masses of police at the entrance. Reading books like *Nineteen Eighty-Four* and *Brave New*

World can't have helped her sense of paranoia. Everyone knew music festivals were full of stoned hippies, didn't they? I didn't know what the police thought hippies were going to *do* when they got high – nod their heads a little too hard to the music and cause an earthquake?

This felt like being part of something huge. Something ground-breaking. A massive festival in – wait for it – *Lincolnshire*. Nowhere near as romantic as Woodstock or the Isle of Wight. While I was walking around with Janie I heard a guy in a burger van tell a customer that the Hell's Angels had arrived. The bikers had taken one look at the twelve-foot high fence, he said, and decided that the police could manage fine without them. Off they all roared again. Such excitement! Mary was going to be *gutted* she'd missed it all.

Thank God I didn't let Mum's threats stop me from coming. Every now and then I shivered with fear at what I'd done – dragging Janie along with me. I hoped Mum and Dad weren't going to worry about her too much. They knew she'd be safe with me, didn't they? After all they'd trusted me to accompany her home on the bus from Skegness last year when they both got a lift – in comfort – in Uncle Damien's car. That was the first time I ever busked. Janie and me knelt at the back window on the top deck and sang every song we knew. *Linden Lee* and *Kookaburra Sits in the Old Gum Tree* (in a round) amongst others. We didn't realise we were actually busking until people started throwing money at us on their way off the bus. We bought fish and chips on the way home. After that I busked a few more times with Mary in the town centre, though she wasn't as good a singer as Janie and kept worrying we'd get moved on by a bobby.

Mum and Dad had been paying me a pittance to babysit Janie from the time I was thirteen, but now she was the one who was thirteen – yeah, thirteen, not seven – she was supposedly still their little baby.

Bloody hell, it hit me anew. What if our parents called the police? As I moved through the crowd I calculated the odds of bobbies finding me and Janie amongst thousands of people in waxed-paper sleeping bags and humps of polythene and those that would be jumping around in front of the stage later. After all, we all looked the same, didn't we? Youth. That's what they said on the telly all the time. I hoped Janie's eye makeup hadn't worn off.

A chill breeze dashed raindrops into my eyes. I pulled my jumper down and used its hem to carefully dab the water away, then angled my beret to deflect the rain. There were people everywhere now, walking around and queuing at the vans for late breakfasts. A smoky, edible smell filled the air. A lad wearing a leather jacket and a mullet haircut leaned against a hay bale by one of the food vans, finishing off a hot dog in one hand while holding a joint between the finger and thumb of his other. When he spotted me he beckoned me over and I went, I had nothing else to do. Close up, the pungent smell of dope overrode the food scents. He wiped his food hand on his jeans and dragged a waterproof cover from the pocket of his leather jacket.

'Here yer are, darlin,' he said. "'Ave my poncho. They were givin' 'em out. It'll 'elp keep yer dry.' He helped me pull the thin polythene cape over my head and settled it round my shoulders, his face one big grin. His hair curled around his ears.

'Ah, thanks,' I said. 'That's really kind of you. Look, it fits!'

'Aye an' it suits you better than it does me. Been 'ere all night love?'

'Nah,' I said. 'Just arrived this morning. Anything good on today?'

I don't know why I said that – I knew exactly which bands were playing. I'd been studying the programme for weeks! He dragged his leather sleeve off his wrist so he could look at his watch while I shifted my feet in the mud, trying to get my back more comfortable.

'Yeah, love. There's this new band playing in an hour or so. Roxy Music, they're called. You want to go and 'ave a look at them. Gonna make it big, they are – wait and see.'

'Ooh, I've heard that name,' I said. 'My sister wants to see them – her friend's mad about them.'

'Girl of taste then, she is, your sister. Well, she won't be disappointed. 'Ere well, I've got to get off now love. See a man about a dog if you know what I mean? Want a toke on this before I go?' He proffered the joint at me.

'Oh, go on then, ta.' I drew the smoke into my lungs and tried not to cough. I'd tried a few joints outside the back of the New Penny on rock disco nights, but this one tasted stronger.

'Good stuff, innit?' said the lad. 'You wanna watch out though. There's loads of bobbies 'ere, disguised as hippies. Sneaky bastards.' I handed the joint back hastily and said goodbye. The polythene shimmered around me. My head felt sort of floaty – the ground newly-soft under my wellies.

I wandered into a small marquee. The sign over the entrance said *Folk Tent*. Folk music. The words felt odd as I turned them over in my brain. Folk. F-o-l-k. Bob Dylan, he was folk, I thought. Joan Baez and Woody Guthrie. I'd heard of them and I was sure they were folk. Jethro Tull? Perhaps they were folk-rock – was that the same? I stopped to peer at the list of names and my head swung. I hoped I wasn't going to be sick. I recognised Roy Harper because our English teacher once played us a song called *I Hate the White Man*. We had to write an essay about it. I pushed the flap aside and went in.

The damp mugginess inside smelt like the animal enclosure at the circus. My skin tingled.

After a while I heard someone playing a guitar quietly. I turned to search the gloom. A young bloke sat on a stool in the soft glow of light from the open doorway. He had wavy brown hair and a short, silky-looking beard. He hadn't noticed me. I was drawn forward by the quiet intensity of his chords. Soon he began to pick out notes. His eyes were half-closed but he must have sensed my approach because he looked up suddenly. I moved and the raindrops on my poncho glittered like fairy lights. He offered me a gentle smile, his eyes intensely blue. I pressed a hand to my stomach to stop it turning over again. Like a kid on the story mat at infant school I found myself sinking to the floor and crossed my legs. I almost put my thumb in my mouth – a habit of mine it took Mum years to break, with all sorts of nasty-tasting solutions.

When he started singing it felt like someone was tugging my insides. I folded my arms tightly. Noticed his eyes flicking between his fingers on the neck of the guitar and my face. When they were on me I could feel two burning spots on my cheeks. He sang so quietly to begin with that I could hardly hear his voice and the first few verses were just a lull of low tones that made me want to go to sleep, but at the same time be aware. I noticed he stuttered over his words and had to begin again. Then his voice strengthened and got deeper, and it was only then I started to hear the lyrics properly.

The way we live is like
A huge experiment gone wrong,
I don't want it to be this way.

At the end of my life
I don't want to feel
I never tried to save the day.

Don't want to remember
The peace I never rendered,
All the hearts I never mended.

Oh, what a useless way
That would be to die.
Don't let it be that way.

A feather tickled my skin. I jumped, glanced behind in case someone was playing a trick on me, but the rest of the tent was empty. Shivers ran up the scar on my spine and exploded at the back of my neck. The song made me want to change the world. Take up a banner and protest, like the demonstrations against the Vietnam War. *Don't let it be that way.* I could hardly breathe, the ache in my belly hurt too much.

He ended the song with a few gently picked-out notes, like he didn't want to finish even though the words were over. When he lifted the guitar off his lap and placed it carefully on a stand I took a deep breath. I wanted to applaud but it would have felt clumsy. The song was too gentle to end violently with clapping hands. I believed every word he sang – yeah, me, who Mum was always saying was self-centred. I usually only listened to progressive rock like Genesis and Pink Floyd. Or pop bands. I liked a big sound; songs that expressed big concepts or were plain fun. The naked truth of the singer's feeling was painful.

He sat still on the stool, his palms upturned on his lap. He even had his eyes closed. I looked at him properly, at the long lashes lying on his cheeks. At how his hair looked so silky I wanted to stroke it. He wore a cheesecloth shirt and a patchwork waistcoat. There was a hole in the right knee of his jeans.

'That was all right, that,' I said, wanting to wake up the brash me everybody knew under the layers of sensitivity prickling my skin from the inside. I wiped the back of my hand under my nose. 'Yeah, not bad at all as a matter of fact. You playing in here later?'

He opened his eyes, stood and smiled, picking the guitar up from the stand. *Don't go,* I was thinking. I scrambled to my feet, too.

'I'm playing a small set this afternoon at about four,' he said. 'But my main spot is tomorrow evening. Come in later if you fancy it. Thanks for listening to my practice session.' His voice was gentle, like the way he sang. Was he looking at me the way I was looking at him? My judgement felt scrambled.

'All right, I will then.'

I stood wobbling for a moment, still slightly under the influence of the dope. 'Erm, what's your name again?'

He fixed me with his steady blue gaze. 'Justin Christian.'

His smile was lovely.

Outside the tent it was still raining but I didn't care. I was floating from the song. Still, I needed to make sure Janie was awake so we could make it to the main stage in time for Roxy Music. Not many people would have heard of them, I thought, so they might not have a very big audience. Janie would probably be their most enthusiastic supporter.

10

Janie, now

In the end she decided to spend one night with Juliet at her leafy garden flat in Edinburgh, basically in the opposite direction from Lincolnshire. But hey. She was a free agent now, she could do what she wanted. She received an annoyed reply from Annette in response to her text. The phone rang and rang on the back seat, and at the petrol station when she stopped for fuel she turned it off without looking at the screen.

She hadn't looked back as she drove out of Catmally Station car park. She hadn't spoken to the regular 9am passengers either, while she was locking her front door for the last time, her head down. *She was usually so friendly,* they must have been thinking. She had sometimes brought out a tray of bacon butties and a large pot of tea. That was what it was like around there – everyone was friendly. Except her, on the last day.

She'd walked around the corner of the building with her chin tucked in, patchwork bag weighing heavy with last-minute items she'd picked up on her way out. She'd planned to leave the carriage clock on the mantel in the snug but changed her mind – it had belonged to Paul's grandmother and she thought Juliet might like to keep it. She'd intended the old, chicken-shaped egg bowl to be a gift for the new owner who was keeping on the chickens – but no. She couldn't bear to part with that either, because Paul had bought it from a bring-and-buy sale in the community hall shortly after they'd moved in. (He'd also bartered a painting for their first two chickens on the same day). She needed to keep some happy memories. After all, the children were also associated with Paul and she wasn't getting rid of them. She would keep the chicken bowl for Allegra.

The final item she grabbed at the last minute was a framed photo of a former station master standing outside the then-gleaming station house. She hadn't planned to remove it from on top of the piano (which was staying) because the photo had been found in the property by one of Paul's brothers when they first took possession of the building, and she felt it belonged there still. But Billy loved it. He used to call the faded, moustachioed official in the picture 'Granddad', she had no idea why. The black and white image bore no relation to either of the two grandfathers he'd known. Sometimes it had given her the chills.

Billy had been a baby when they moved to the station, could he have in some way led them to the auction that night? It was true she'd been breastfeeding Billy in the living room of their small, rented house in Glasgow when she idly turned over a page of the local paper and saw the advert for the property. The baby had made some movement against her stomach and she'd looked down at him. He detached himself from her breast and craned his head back slightly as if to better focus on her face. Then he'd smiled. His very first, open-mouthed smile. *Oh, Billy.* And when he'd returned to his feed, his eyelids eventually fluttering in sleep – she'd looked back down at the advert in the paper and was overcome by strong determination.

The "prospective residential" building, set amongst mountains in the heart of Argyllshire, was exactly the kind of location she'd been seeking to live in, and Paul would be able to work from. They'd been saving for a deposit on a home of their own since Juliet was born. Paul had received a large grant for a site-specific painting project involving local communities... were there any rules that said you couldn't move into a site-specific art project once it was completed?

The tears pressing behind her eyes meant she couldn't bring herself to raise her face for a cheery response to the passengers' greetings as she left. She wanted to blot herself out of the picture. The station would be someone else's home now and the passengers would just have to hope the new owner enjoyed their company as much as she had.

She drove out of Catmally on the winding road between the mountains. On the lower slopes, pines bowed in the ever-present breeze. Long grass created a rippling blanket on the fields. A haze of yellow bled into the edges of her vision; the sky's pale blue would deepen to ultramarine later. The sun had already warmed the loaded car. The gears groaned as she changed from fourth down to third. With her back sweating, she wriggled her shoulders against the seat, thinking she ought to have set out before the heavy traffic she'd be bound to meet between Glasgow and Edinburgh. She'd have to find somewhere to park until the traffic had abated – another stress – but she was looking forward to spending an evening with her busy daughter, and finally being allowed to meet the young woman with whom Juliet had started a tentative relationship.

11

Annette, 1972

Roxy Music weren't half bad, in actual fact. The lead singer was a bit of a dish, I couldn't help noticing, even though I was still thinking about the lone singer in the folk tent, *Justin Christian.*

Back to Roxy Music. You should have seen the light in Janie's eyes as she watched her friend's favourite band. I realised again how pretty my annoying little sister was, as if it had only just happened that day. Maybe I saw it because I'd managed to remove her from her natural environment – her bunk bed or the library down the road from our house.

The song finished and Janie jumped up and down, screeching as if she was channelling her friend Sally. She had red spots like roses on her cheeks and the eyeliner made her eyes seem even brighter. I could see a skinny boy a couple of people in front of us turning around to give her the eye. A rush of protectiveness surprised me. I put my hand on her shoulder and kept one eye on the weaselly lad. He made a rude gesture with his fist in his elbow. I gave him the two-finger sign and he leered at me before turning back to the band. Fortunately, Janie hadn't noticed any of this, but it made me realise that soon her innocence would be blown wide open. Her childhood teetered as I watched.

'Take it easy,' I said above the noise of the cheers. 'Don't wanna wear yourself out. There's loads of other bands to watch yet.' She turned to me, spit bubbling on her lower lip.

'This is great,' her eyes were wild. 'I like it here. The band's brilliant! Wait 'til I tell Sally.'

'All right. Well look, they've finished now. Yeah, okay – you can scream a bit longer if you must. Fine.' The rain came down harder. 'Janie, seriously. Stop now – they've gone and they're not coming back onstage, can't you see that?'

'I want to go and get their autographs!'

Her eyes reminded me of when she used to wake up and scream because she couldn't find her teddy. I craned my neck and saw there was no way we'd be able to get to the back of the stage before the band had disappeared completely.

The polythene that served as the stage roof flapped in the wind. I had my beret on but Janie's hair was soaked. Good job she was wearing waterproof eye makeup.

'C'mon.' I dragged her by the arm. 'We need to find somewhere to shelter from the rain for a bit.'

'But I want Roxy Music's autograph.' My patience wore thin. I tugged her parka sleeve.

'Bloody hell. Look at that fence in front of you. Have you got a journalist's pass? No? Surprise, surprise. So how the hell d'you think you're going to manage that? Now come with me and we'll try and dry off a bit before the next band. Otherwise I'll bloody leave you out here in the rain on your own.'

A massive surge of wind sent clumps of soggy straw whipping through the air. A strand caught Janie in the eye and she clapped a hand to her face. She whined as I continued dragging her by the parka sleeve through the straggling crowd. Our feet were sucked by the mud as we tramped towards the "Giants of the Future" tent.

I'd never heard of any of the bands, and the one playing didn't seem much like a giant to me. I'd probably go and make a cup of tea if they were on *Top of the Pops*. Tiredness swamped me. I wished I'd followed Janie's example and taken the chance of a proper sleep earlier. *But if I had I wouldn't have met Justin Christian.* I wouldn't have heard him sing, all alone in that tent. The band on the stage now – Walrus – weren't my cup of tea. My back ached. Genesis weren't playing until tomorrow.

Janie continued to whine about having her eye injured for the second time that morning.

'Well at least it wasn't my fault that time,' I snapped. 'I can't control the bloody wind.'

I missed Mary and tried not to feel too miserable. I would have said I was an optimist but was it ever going to stop bloody raining? I pictured Mum going frantic in the kitchen at home. Reading the note out loud like in the Beatles song I'd discovered Janie crying along to, about a girl leaving home. I'd found Janie sobbing, cradling her cassette player on her bunk bed one Saturday morning, and I took the opportunity to laugh at her even though I secretly agreed it was one of the saddest songs ever.

Damn.

I wish we'd waited and caught the afternoon bus to Bardney. By that time our parents would both have gone to work. They wouldn't have got the note until later and it would be too dark for the bobbies to find us and I'd definitely get to see Genesis tomorrow.

There was nothing for it – we'd have to keep a low profile for the rest of the day.

I moved closer to Janie, cupping my hand around my mouth against the noisy flap of polythene and a couple of hippies shouting at each other nearby. 'Let's go back to the crash marquee and I can redo your makeup.'

She gave me a suspicious glance.

'Why am I supposed to be wearing makeup, anyway?'

Hmm. 'Surely you want to look a bit older than thirteen if you happen to spot any members of Roxy Music walking around?'

Her panda-eyes brightened.

'Oh yeah, of course.' As if she thought any of them would look twice at her. I could see it ticking over in her brain – the story she was going to make up and tell Sally.

In the relative comfort of the crash marquee, fresh, warm-smelling straw bales had been scattered around, and plenty of people lay resting under the canvas. The atmosphere smelt of rain and tobacco and dope. A cloud of smoke hung in the dank air at the top of the tent, you could hear the thunder of rain on canvas, and gusts of wind nearly lifted the marquee off the ground. The amplified sound of the band out on the main stage – Nazareth, I wasn't that bothered anymore about seeing them – drifted in and out of earshot. People handed each other sandwiches and swigs of beer and tokes of their joints. A couple of guitars twanged in opposite corners of the tent. I offered my last sandwich to a pretty girl with a massive afro. Later she handed me the end of a joint that an older boy had passed to her. I guessed he was her brother, since she was a bit on the young side to be here with a boyfriend. But I couldn't see his face properly as he was half turned away, chatting to another guy.

My spirits rose, helped by the dope I suppose. Janie had fallen asleep again already. I kept thinking of when I was going to see Justin Christian for the second time. I wanted to get to the front of the audience and make sure he was able to meet my eyes the way he'd done when it was just the two of us.

When I woke up from a doze, Janie was chatting to the girl with the afro. Peering closer I could see they were comparing little glass animals. Janie always had a pocketful of them, her favourite was the giraffe. Janie looked annoyed to see me awake. She was probably worried I'd say something to embarrass her. I couldn't be bothered. I lay there sleepily, watching her frown deepen; Janie was always secretive over her friends. The other girl wasn't much older than Janie – probably only fourteen – freckles dotted on her nose and cheeks and she had lively amber eyes which caught the light from the open marquee door. She'd confirmed earlier that she was here with her brother and his girlfriend, and two others who I hadn't seen. After a while I stretched and sat up, flexing my back. I could hear that it had stopped raining. Pressing the illumination button on my watch, I checked the time. *Damn.*

'Janie,' I said sharply. 'Get your coat on, we're going out.' If I didn't hurry, I'd miss the beginning of his set. She ignored me and shifted herself to turn her back on me. The other girl gave me a smirk and reached forward to lift the glass elephant from Janie's palm.

'Janie. Come on, we didn't come to this festival so we could sit in a tent all day.' I stopped and readjusted my voice. No sense in riling her. 'Anyway we're going to the folk tent, so you'll be able to keep nice and dry once we're in there.'

'I'm not going,' Janie mumbled, still with her back to me, 'I like it in here.'

The air in the tent became thicker.

'You are coming,' I said. 'I promised Mum I'd look after you so you have to stay with me. Anyway, you must be hungry by now. I'll get us both a hot dog on the way.'

Now Janie half-turned her head to look at me. 'I can't. I'm waiting here with Lara. Her brother and his girlfriend are bringing us something to eat anyway. You go to the *folk* tent by yourself. I'll wait here.'

With her blue eyeshadow and black-rimmed eyes she looked like a different girl. A young woman. I shook my head at her. If we'd been alone in our bedroom I'd have given her a Chinese burn and she knew it. Now I knew how Mum felt, not being able to control us. Janie wrinkled her nose. 'Go on. I'll be fine with Lara. I'm not a baby, you know. I'll meet you back here later.'

Helplessness burned a hole in my chest. But I breathed slowly and shook my fringe to cover my angry eyes. Honestly, what could happen to her here in the safety of the crash tent?

'Fine, then. You'll regret missing half the music later when your friends ask you what bands you've seen.'

'Annette,' Janie sounded incredulous. She raised her pencil-accentuated eyebrows. 'I've seen *Roxy Music*. I'm not interested in the *folk* tent!'

A strand of hay was woven into her hair, whether deliberately or accidental I couldn't tell. Lara sniggered. Janie smirked and then both girls broke into peals of laughter, stuffing their fists in their mouths.

'Just wait here and don't go anywhere without letting me know, okay? I mean it. Stay here. I'll be in the folk tent.'

I could hear them repeating *folk tent* in silly voices as I picked my way carefully over the clusters of bodies and walked towards the imagined promise of the dreary afternoon. Trying to ignore the leaden feeling inside me, Janie would be fine – like she said, she was with Lara and soon they'd be joined by two over-eighteens and I wouldn't have to feel responsible for her for a while. At least I'd be able to watch Justin Christian without Janie moaning in my ear about how bored she was.

The sky hung thick and grey. Mud sucked at my boots like it wanted to pull me under. Water dripped off the corners of polythene and canvas awnings. The further I walked from Janie the less bothered I was by leaving her with that girl. I was going to see Justin again! I wove through crowds of denim jackets and afghan coats. The thud of an amplified bass permeated the general chatter and echoed off a wall of canvas and food vans. Nearer to me someone played a flute in the doorway of a tent.

Out of the corner of my eye I noticed a tanned hippie-type wearing an embroidered velvet top and flared jeans. He was jerking his thumb towards some leather-jacketed guys in a sort of hitchhiking gesture. I couldn't see who he was looking towards. A second-sense caused me to step out the way. Good job because two other men who *looked* like hippies but didn't *act* like them pushed in front of me and grabbed both leather jackets by the arms. Static hitchhiker shoved a police badge in their faces. 'I'm arresting you...' Around me a few other people spat on the ground. Someone muttered, *undercover pigs*.

I moved away quickly, thinking of the joints I'd had a smoke of earlier. A guitar solo wailed across the field from the main stage where the audience seethed behind the mostly-empty press pit. It was a pity you couldn't get closer to the stage, the band must have felt lonely up there – so far from the audience. Wishbone Ash it must have been – not a favourite band of mine and I wasn't bothered about missing them, but you couldn't fault the skill of the guitarists. Mary liked Wishbone Ash. If she was here we would have had to split up or toss a coin. We'd have had a laugh about the drug squad. Mum would have telephoned her mum by now and Mary's mum would be acting all righteous and *can't you control your own children?*

In the doorway of the folk tent I peered into the gloom. *There he was*. Waiting at the edge of the stage. The audience had clustered onto hay bales. I scanned the rows and assessed whether I could fit in at the front. *Sure*. I squeezed into a gap in the middle between a long-haired youth in a green waxed coat and a delicate-looking girl with silvery-blonde hair that clung wetly to the back of her brown velvet jacket. She gave me a far-out smile. I responded by stretching my lips.

A lump grew in my throat as Justin moved into the spotlight. He took his stool, keeping his eyes downcast at first. He fitted his hand around the neck of his guitar and tapped the body of it before looking up. Scanning the audience with those intense blue eyes, he started with the back row and finished by acknowledging everyone at the front. Finally it was my turn. His eyes rested on my face.

'Hello again,' Justin said. Speaking to me alone. His face opened into a smile.

12

Janie, now

Mum and Dad moved house when Janie left for university, not even making a room up for her to sleep in during her first Christmas holiday. At least they hadn't got rid of her books, left stacked in the smaller of the two spare rooms. Just before her first summer holiday from university she met Paul and decided not to go home, and she hadn't lived in Lincoln since.

Janie finished parking the car in a narrow space outside Mum's. She swallowed the lump in her throat and levered herself stiffly onto the pavement. Stretching, her arms and hands tingled as she wiggled her fingers to bring life back into them. Spotting her reflection in the car window she bent to smooth her hair, tangled from rubbing against the head rest.   Still with a fringe and shoulder-length, it was more-or-less the same straw-colour it had been in her childhood. She straightened and stretched again, hands on hips, fingers in the small of her back.

The evening sun felt warm on the top of her head. It shone off the metal hanging basket at the front of the house. Temporarily dazzled, she closed her eyes. The scent of lilac from the laden tree in the small front garden wafted over her. *Deep breaths.*

She heard a door handle rattle. Digging her thumbs into the flesh of her waist, Janie took another breath. There was her sister Annette, who she hadn't seen for several years. Even thinner now, and older than Janie expected – the effect of the windblown lifestyle she'd led, Janie supposed. Nevertheless there was still something about her sister's character, an intoxicating quality Janie had always felt smothered by. Nothing you could put your finger on, just a vibration she emanated. Janie fleetingly imagined her sister full of bees as she hurried down the short path towards her.

Annette had cut her long, grey-blonde hair into a neck-length bob. A wide cotton headband held it off her face, exposing her broad forehead and Romanesque nose. She wore a bright, floral skirt and black leggings and a black tunic hung away from her gaunt chest. The movement of her navy eyes reminded Janie of a blackbird.

Annette strode towards Janie, thin arms conducting the singsong notes of her high, girlish voice.

'Come on then, what are you waiting for? Mum's inside. It's about time you took your share of the responsibility!'

Straight in there. Janie didn't know why, but tears were creeping down her face. *Damn.* It hadn't taken long.

'Are you crying?' Annette interrupted herself to say. 'You are, aren't you? Bloody 'ell, you've only just arrived. You need to get tougher than this, kid. 'Ere, have some tissue. Mop it up before Mum sees you.'

She refused the bundle of tissue – of doubtful cleanliness – Annette had pulled from her skirt pocket, and instead fumbled in her bag for a few neatly-folded squares of her own. She quite liked that Annette hadn't demanded an explanation. Perhaps it was simply that her sister understood life could be quite sad. *I don't really know you,* the thought flitted through her head.

'You've always been fussy, you.' Annette stuffed the

scrunched-up toilet-roll away. 'So, do we do hugs? Come on, I haven't set eyes on you for years.'

The curve of Annette's back felt pronounced, Janie hadn't hugged her sister for longer than she could remember. She pulled away.

Dogs barked from inside the house.

'Oh,' Janie said at the door. 'You've brought your dog as well.'

'Well, listen. Nicholas may have forced me away from me horses and chickens and goats but there was no way on earth I was leaving my Romy behind. Love me, love my dog, as they say. So you better not have any objections. What about your dog, anyway? Did Paul take him?'

'No, he died two years ago,' Janie finished sniffing. 'Riley was eleven, you know, that's not bad for a Labrador.' She blinked the last of the wet from her eyes.

'Oh, I didn't know. Yeah, I suppose he would have been – eleven I mean. Sorry and all that. Life and death, it goes on, doesn't it?'

Annette's eyebrows pulled together and she pursed her lips as if she wanted to say something more. Her navy eyes penetrated Janie.

Janie shifted the basket of cakes she was carrying on her arm, picturing them both lying in bed at night, Annette forcing secrets on her as she had when they were children. For some reason she still felt afraid to listen to Annette's peculiar intimacies. She'd told Janie on the phone that she had a surprise she would love. Janie felt a lurch inside her. She'd have to pretend to have fallen asleep as soon as they got into bed. Then she remembered they were grown-ups now and would be sleeping in separate rooms.

13

Janie, now

Janie, Annette and their mother sat around the old dining table. It still bore the three Woods siblings' illicitly-carved names from the Christmas Nicholas was given his first penknife. Janie kept angling her head so she could see the notches, barely resembling letters, that made up her name. Just visible on the table's outer edge to her left. Nicholas hadn't allowed her to use the knife, though she'd felt she could have done a better job than him. While Nicholas had knelt under the table to make his own mark, Annette had carved her name directly in the table's centre, and received a series of slaps from their mother for her sin. No amount of sanding and revarnishing had restored the table to its original condition. Their parents could have used moving house as an excuse to get rid of it, but here it still stood.

It was late in the evening. Janie had suggested they stop due to their mother's apparent exhaustion, not to mention her own. But Mum had insisted it was important for them to discuss "unavoidable matters". Stuff about insurance policies and worse still, funeral plans. There was a cold spot in Janie's chest. Her brain buzzed and she was sure she wouldn't remember any of it. Everything felt unreal.

Nicholas was notable by his absence.

'He's too terribly busy and important,' Annette said to Janie, half-under her breath.

'He took time off work to give you a lift up here from the ferry,' her mother reminded her. Nothing wrong with her hearing, then.

'He could have stayed until after Janie arrived.' Annette dabbed at a spilt drop of tea with her overlong sleeve. 'He's the oldest, as he likes to remind me.'

'Stop that, Annette, get a cloth. Nicholas is very busy, as you know.'

'Exactly.' Annette's knees creaked when she stood up to take the five steps to the kitchen for a dishcloth. She paused to stretch her back. ' Like I said. Too busy and important to give up a few extra days of his precious leave.'

'He *has* been Skyping me every day.'

Janie had noticed the iPad. Nicholas must have bought it for Mum.

'I've kept him fully informed of my situation.' Mum's voice, like her body, was a faded echo of itself. 'Now that's enough about Nicholas. He'll be here when he's needed.'

They finished the last of Juliet's cakes with their second pot of tea. Janie hadn't been able to resist sneaking a photograph of the plate before they'd taken their first bites. She may have become a child again in this house of her mother's dominion but her own daughter's handiwork reminded her of her true status. Juliet planned to set up a coffee shop with her partner once they had enough money.

'Are you going to post that on Facebook?' Annette asked with faux innocence. Janie's hands tightened on her phone. 'Do you post a picture of everything you eat? I can't be bothered with the internet myself. You can't smell the roses – or the food for that matter.' Janie slid the phone back into her pocket, realising she was grinding her teeth. Annette's constant teasing still had the power to make her feel small.

'It's nothing to do with the food itself. It's about pride in my daughter's achievements. You'd understand if you had any children of your own.'

Annette took in a sharp breath. Noticing the hurt look briefly crossing her face, Janie regretted saying anything.

Later, Mum allowed Janie to use her iPad to order a takeaway on *Just Eat*. Mum insisted on making Janie fetch her handbag so she could press the £25 into her hand after Janie had paid on her card.

It was eleven o'clock by the time Mum permitted the sisters to help her out of her chair. She looked white and drained. Annette's collie paced in a circle while they shuffled across the room, and Mum's Jack Russell lifted her nose and whined. The room felt stifling.

Mum's voice sounded hollow, 'I'm all right, stop fussing.' Together they reached the bottom of the stairs. 'Let go of me.' But she sank to her knees on the third step. 'Fine, you can help me as far as the bathroom and then leave me alone. It's been a long night, that's all.'

After a pointed look at Janie, standing frozen at the bottom of the stairs, Annette saw their mother to the bathroom. She stayed up there a while, waiting outside the door to help her into bed. 'Let Poppy come up when she's ready,' Janie heard Mum saying in a wavering voice. She thought she heard the rattle of a pill bottle, too. Janie collected the pots and takeaway cartons and sorted them out in the kitchen. She was so tired she felt ready to fall asleep on her feet. The dogs bickered with each other by the back door. Janie let them out. A security light came on and flooded Mum's tiny garden, making silhouettes of trees along the back fence. Janie watched the dogs doing their business and returned to the kitchen where she rifled in the cupboards. She found a carrier bag in which to deposit their mess in the wheelie bin by the gate, then followed the dogs inside and locked the back door. *Now, please – let me sleep.* She collected her bag and had her foot on the bottom step when Annette appeared at the top, finger to her lips. She made her way downstairs with exaggerated care. Drama Queen, Mum had called her when they were children.

'There's something else I need to discuss with you before you go to bed,' she mock-whispered. 'Come and sit down again a minute.'

'Not tonight. Please, Annette, it's been such a long day.'

'I just want to tell you about the surprise I mentioned to you on the phone. You'll like it, I promise – and I don't see why Mum won't, too.'

While Janie stood hesitating, Annette rushed over to the bureau and started pulling out sheets of paper. Janie squeezed her eyes tight shut like she used to when Annette tried to get her into some sort of trouble. She opened them and forced her voice to come out calm.

'Not tonight Annette, I mean it. Can't you see what a long day I've had? This morning I was in Edinburgh. I drove for nine hours to get here and I haven't even had a chance to go up to my room yet. I assume I'm sleeping in the small room?'

Annette's face flashed with anger. 'Oh, for God's sake, are you really going to start quibbling over the size of your room? Don't you think I'm tired, too – looking after Mum these past few days? I'm just trying to cheer you up after all that doom and gloom. This is a *good* thing I want to talk about.'

Janie felt dizzy, but she drew herself up and reminded herself they weren't children anymore. 'I wasn't quibbling about the room, nor criticising you, Annette. I promise. But I'm dead on my feet. I can't discuss anything else tonight. There's already been a lot to take in. We'll talk in the morning, okay?' Before giving Annette a chance to respond she grabbed her bag from the banister, and made her way up the stairs as fast as her tired legs would allow her.

14

Justin, now and then

JUSTIN CITIZEN AND THE UNDERAGE FESTIVAL GIRL!

The man's face reared up at the bus window, his lip curled back in a sneer similar to the captured freeze-frame of Justin's mouth on the second newspaper photo. The man's bared teeth were unfeasibly white, as were his knuckles from gripping the newspaper, flattened against the glass. Justin's mind absorbed the inference of the thick, black letters. Stars spiralled in his head and an ache pressed at the back of his neck. He dropped his phone on the table and plunged his face into his hands again, fearing he would black out if he continued looking at those words any longer. The buzzing voices on the pavement outside seemed to be working up into a swarm of bees – high-pitched and insistent. The crowd from the film *Jesus Christ, Superstar* came into his mind, "Crucify him, crucify him."

Justin felt himself dropping down a hole. Spinning as he fell and glimpsing extracts of his past flying by. How was he going to hold his head up and get through the angry mob gathering on the pavement outside the bus for his meeting in half an hour? *Should he even fucking bother?*

It was as if he was standing outside himself, looking down at the pitiful man in the bus seat with his head in his hands. While he fought for breath within the cave of his hands, Andy reached across him and tugged the curtain closed. Justin was no longer on public view. But it didn't stop the crowd voicing their anger. Andy hadn't spoken a word since reading the headline. Justin felt him move away, knocking knees with him under the table as he pushed himself out from behind it. He slammed the door of the compact bathroom.

Surely Andy couldn't have believed what he'd read? But an insinuation was there in black and white. Perhaps nobody truly trusted anybody anymore.

Ivy had warned him about the nastiness of the press, not that he hadn't *technically* been aware of it. And they *had* been dig, dig, digging since he started this campaign. He hadn't believed there was anything that could damage him, an ordinary bloke really.

Where could they have got this story? Not from... *her?* He hadn't seen or heard from her for years but he'd always believed in her integrity.

More than anything, he felt sad. His heart beat harder with a different fear. If the media continued to dig the hole they'd started (in his mind he could see the piles of earth building up on either side – the pit looking suspiciously like a grave) they might start sifting through the grains of soil they'd unearthed. And they might find the one true grit of information that existed in the story. A grit that might destroy his relationship with someone he was very close to.

Then

Performing in the folk tent at the Great Western Express Festival, Justin Christian was at a crossroads in his life at

69

the ripe old age of twenty-two. He'd been playing in one band or another since the age of fourteen. First it was The Christian Brothers – a sort of Beatles and Everley Brothers crossover. The band consisted mainly of himself and his two oldest brothers, Felix and Joshua, joined sometimes by one or another of the other two. But they got asked to play at so many church benefits – with a specific remit of the kinds of tunes they could play – that they quarrelled and split. Funny, since his parents had brought their sons up with no religion. *Christian* was a bit of a bind, to be honest. Anyway, his brothers veered towards progressive rock whereas Justin's first love had always been folk. Woody Guthrie was his idol. He also admired Bob Dylan and had recently taken to writing one or two protest songs of his own. His thoughtful, peace-loving lyrics resonated with the hippies and the commune-dwellers in the London circles he habituated once he had left his parents' country home. Justin made a nice living as a session musician but had also begun to build up a dedicated following of his own.

The Great Western Express Festival was his biggest chance yet to gain a wider audience. People had come from all over the country and further afield, attracted by the amazing line up. The festival was the biggest ever after the Isle of White. But it had taken a gargantuan effort to orchestrate the event. Justin had been invited to play and then told it was cancelled. Then it was on again. Local landowners had taken out an injunction. Local residents complained. But eventually, with the proviso that there would never be another rock festival in Britain if it caused excess noise and litter or congestion of the local roads, the much-awaited event finally went ahead. What a pity about the weather. The abysmal conditions felt appropriate to Justin: the times, he felt, were a' changing for him personally as well as in the world in general.

15

Annette, now

I only visited Catmally Station once. It was lovely, surrounded by mountains. But Janie's kids were noisy and distracting. My dog, not Romy – this was another one, Bear – got hold of one of their guinea-pigs and shook it to death. The guinea-pig's shrieks were blood-curdling. I couldn't forget Janie's daughter's expression when she ran out and saw what had happened. Her eyes stretched wide, her face still for half a second while she computed what she was looking at (blood-soaked fur floating through the air and an eyeless guinea-pig on the ground. My dog with his muzzle apparently painted red). Then her mouth turned into a black hole and an unearthly scream came out. I would never forget Janie's face either – flooded with a similar shock to Allegra's but also a kind of resignation. Like it was the sort of thing she'd expect from me (or my dog). As if I'd always spoiled everything for her. My visit to her family idyll ended early and I had to change my train tickets and my ferry booking. Cost me a bloody fortune.

But it only proved what I'd already suspected. Kids and me – we just didn't mix.

Allegra had never forgiven me, even though she was grown up now. A shame 'coz I got the feeling she and I might have had a lot in common if we could only have got to know each other better. Allegra was off travelling in South East Asia. Brave young girl.

I thought *I* was brave and adventurous when I was young. I went off and explored India. Spent a month or so in an Ashram. Later, back in the UK, I spent some time at Greenham common, and then I bought a horse and a bow-top caravan from the travellers at a camp just out of London. The travellers themselves inhabited gleaming motor caravans but they always had horses to trade and there were usually a couple of those colourful old horse-drawn carts on their sites. The travellers showed me how to hitch the grey gelding to the cart. They took me out on the road and gave me a driving lesson before they'd allow me to take him away by myself. I had a dog then, too. His name was Trident – in honour of my ex-Greenham Common friends. We gave our dogs names such as Bullet and Bunker, Missile and Strike. It was a peaceful way of reclaiming the horrible terms of our protest days. That was years before I ended up living in my cottage on the side of an Irish mountain.

Janie and I were now in the same situation – we'd both given up our mountains for the flat lands of Lincolnshire. And we'd both lost the partners we loved. We were *ekes*, as we used to call it when we were little. Only Janie didn't know it yet.

Possibly she thought she'd be going back to Scotland.

Late that night I was still clutching the roll of paperwork in my hands, the receipt for the deposit on a different railway station than she was used to, this one surrounded by fertilised fields and bang next door to a sugar beet factory. I had a rollercoaster in my stomach at the thought of telling Janie – I realised now that maybe she wouldn't be as excited as I'd hoped. I shouldn't have done it without contacting her first, but what was I supposed to do? The auction had been the *very* evening of the day I saw the advertisement. Like, if I'd never taken the opportunity to go into town that afternoon I wouldn't have known. It must have been Fate – surely Janie'd see that?

Romy groaned in her sleep. Then she got up from the shaggy rug and lurched unerringly towards me, sleep-drunk and groggy-eyed. After one bungled attempt she jumped up and curled herself against me as tightly as she could. Poppy the Jack Russell also lifted her head, sneezing. She pulled herself stiffly to her feet and stretched in the same way as Romy, took a searching look at me before pointing herself towards the stairs and Mum's bedroom, where the door was open for her.

Romy and I nestled together in silence, apart from her breathing. I almost drifted off. After a while loud snores rattled down the stairs. God, *Janie*. No wonder Paul left her.

In the end I decided to show what I'd done, instead of tell. I made Janie drive. She huffed and puffed, muttering to herself as we packed the car with a picnic basket and a tartan blanket, and umbrellas just in case – Mum had about fifteen of them.

'It's *your* special day out,' said Janie. 'I'd rather have a day to relax and catch up with Mum properly before we start gallivanting around the countryside.' We were out of Mum's earshot. 'But if you absolutely insist on it, then why can't you drive? The car's insured for third party.'

She reminded me of a dog, growling. For some reason it made me feel fond of her, she was so familiar. I pressed a hand to my back.

'I'm not allowed to drive.'

'What do you mean, you're not allowed to drive. Who says so?'

I cleared my throat. 'Uhm. Well, the DVLA, actually.'

'What do you mean? You have a driving licence, don't you?

73

You must do, you picked me and Juliet up at the airport in Dublin when we visited you.'

'I have a provisional licence,' I said. 'That's all. It's seen me all right in rural Ireland. All I had to do the time I got stopped was promise the Gardai my full licence was in the post. And I managed to get away without being stopped that one time I drove to Dublin to pick you up. You must have noticed I was nervous, I found it horrific. You drive, it'll be safer.'

Janie's mouth dropped open. She gave me her famous evil eye – it must've been useful when she was a teacher.

'But you drove Poppy to the vet the other day, when Mum was feeling unwell, she told me this morning.'

'Yeah, well – I couldn't say no, could I? That was a one-off. I was lucky.' I stuck my chin out at her. Who needed a pesky dog when they had Janie? 'Nobody found out and Mum was happy the car got a run and Poppy got her check-up. She doesn't need another one for six months – and anyway, you're here now.'

'Yes but I might not be here for. . .' Janie tried again. 'You can't simply go around driving without a proper licence. Imagine the stress it would've caused Mum if you'd been pulled over and arrested. Thank God nobody found out.'

'Nobody found out what?'

Mum's voice sounded far away but when I turned, she was right behind me, struggling to carry Poppy in her arms. Her black eyebrows almost met in the middle as she frowned. 'Nobody found out what?' she repeated.

Janie and I exchanged glances. *Don't tell her.* But she couldn't help herself, 'She hasn't got a driver's licence!'

As soon as she'd said it, she had the grace to look ashamed. 'Sorry,' she mouthed. Anger flared in my chest but when I thought about it, I realised I'd probably have snitched on her, too. Or I would have, before I'd realised how ill Mum really was. I hadn't had a chance to discuss it with Janie yet.

'You stupid girl,' was all Mum said, levelling her eye-watery gaze at me for a second. For a moment she

74

reminded me of the mum I had when I was a teenager. 'Always taking unnecessary risks. Putting other people in danger.'

She grated her gaze from me to Janie and back again. Janie's head bowed and I felt the burn of her guilt.

'Janie,' said Mum. 'You're driving whether you like it or not. Even though on this occasion Annette could, because we're in the car with her. But she can sit in the front seat next to you since she's the only one who knows where we're going, although why we're even bothering I don't know.' She paused to cough, gripping the dog with one arm, her other hand on the car roof. Janie glanced at me, scared. 'I should have put my thick cardi on,' Mum said then, dabbing her mouth with a tissue. 'It's colder than I thought.' She glared at me.

'I'll fetch it for you.' Romy wagged her tail uncertainly and followed close at my heels. In the porch I stroked her head and bit my lip. *Fucking* Mum. *Fucking* Janie. *Fucking* me.

Unclenching my fists I grabbed Mum's woolly off the peg. Pulled the door shut and turned the key in the lock.

Mum had installed herself on the back seat of the car with Poppy on her lap, her bag on the seat next to her. She gazed straight ahead as I handed her the cardigan.

I miss my mountains. I want to go back to Ireland.

I walked around the back of the car and opened the other door, Romy behind me.

'Hop in.' But Romy planted her feet on the drive and stared at me obstinately. 'Come on, Romy, hop in.' Hair blew across the side of my face. Romy panted, anxious.

I wonder if you can get auction deposits back.

I tried to push Romy onto the seat next to Mum but she resisted.

'You'll have to put her in the boot,' said Mum, looking ahead.

'What, why? There's plenty of room next to you.'

'She sheds horribly. And she'll only get Poppy excited.'

'Perhaps you'd like me to go in the boot as well?'

75

Janie, in the driving seat, craned her neck back over her shoulder.

'Put her in the boot, Annette. You can take the cover-thing off and leave it behind the fence. She'll be all right in the back, quite comfy I should think. More room to stretch out and you'll be able to keep an eye on her in the make-up mirror.'

Mum tutted loudly. 'All this fuss over a dog.' (The *hypocrisy*!) 'Just put her in the boot, Annette. Mind the picnic basket's fastened closed.'

Mum's lips were disappearing further into her mouth. If I didn't make a decision quickly she'd haul herself out of the car and declare that she wasn't going anywhere, and then what would I do? It was unlikely Janie'd consent to a day out with only me, especially as we were both meant to be looking after Mum.

'Oh, all right!'

I shoved the back door shut. 'Mind your head,' I told Romy as I lifted the cover out. To my surprise she jumped straight in, immediately shoving her head over the back of the seat, panting at Poppy. The small dog scrabbled about on Mum's lap, yipping up at Romy.

'Sit down Poppy, there's a good girl,' Mum's voice was strained.

'Lie down, Romy. Good girl.'

I closed the boot carefully and installed myself in the passenger seat next to Janie. After I'd buckled myself in I thought about shouting, 'Is every-body hap-py?' as our dad used to when we were setting off on a journey. But I suspected nobody was, so for once I kept my mouth shut.

16

Janie, now

Annette said the road past the lake would be more scenic than the bypass, but she still refused to say where they were going. Janie could've done without the hassle of a magical mystery tour on her first full day back home. Not really home though, she corrected herself.

Childhood home, to Janie, was the Victorian semi-detached in the south of the city. They'd spent their childhoods on the nearby common, making friends with the horses. Or playing in the woods at the park on the other side of the river. In the days when they let children take rowing boats out on the lake and not expect them to wear a life-vest. But best of all were the hot summer days at the lido. Entrance fee was tuppence and they would stand in an endless, snaking queue of unaccompanied children waiting to get in. The changing rooms were slippery and echoing. The corridor led directly out to the pool's blue depths and the sky was a matching shade of cobalt. At the end of the long afternoons, Annette would be frustrated with Janie's efforts to drag off her wet swimming costume and pull dry clothes onto her chilled, damp body in time for them to reach the ice-cream hut before it closed. More than once Annette made her walk home wearing her wet swimsuit as underwear, water flowering in patches on her thin summer dress and her thighs chafing.

Reflections of the lake glimmered in the wing mirrors and Janie recalled the time Nicholas lifted her up with him onto the top tier of the fountain at the lido and she'd been thrilled at his attentions. The water fizzled under her bottom and she laughed. But then Nicholas clambered down and walked away, leaving her up there on her own. She must have been five. Older children climbed up. They surrounded her and splashed each other. Later they all descended and ran off to jump in the pool at the deep end. Janie was scared, shivering and coughing snot. Unable to move. It was such a long way down to the paddling pool below.

She wiped a hand over her eyes as she drove.

'What's up with you?' Annette asked.

'Nothing,' she said. Glancing sideways she noticed the frown between her sister's eyes.

In the rear-view mirror it looked as though their mother was nodding off. The Jack Russell sat alert on her lap, panting, tongue hanging out. Romy must have been asleep in the boot.

At the roundabout to Rookery Lane, Janie remembered it was Annette who had rescued her from the fountain, coaxing her down with big-sister hands on Janie's waist. Once her feet had touched the floor of the paddling pool she'd clung tightly to Annette, her forehead buried in her sister's bony chest. Nicholas had sat, laughing, on the wall of the paddling pool with his two best friends.

'I was going to get her down,' he insisted when Annette turned her hysterical sister around for him to see. 'Eventually, honest I was. But I was doing her a favour – she's such a sissy and she needs toughening up.'

The memory flooded in so strongly, Janie felt

disassociated from her present self. Through the darkness of the sunglasses she'd plonked on her nose she watched her adult hands performing the everyday tasks of driving – allowing the steering wheel to slip through them as she straightened the car's trajectory after turning right onto Brant Road, according to Annette's instructions; shifting gears, pulling on the handbrake at the traffic lights. They climbed a winding hill and turned back on themselves into Bracebridge Heath.

'It'll be quicker going along the top road,' Annette said. She tapped a finger to the side of her nose.

'For goodness' sake, where on earth are we going?' Janie finally snapped. Annette was no longer the big sister she turned to for rescue. Now she was an ageing, annoying girl-woman who had never had the kinds of responsibilities Janie had, and therefore still wanted to play childish games.

'That's for me to know and you to find out!'

'Oh, Annette, why don't you grow up?'

She hadn't thought she'd spoken loudly enough for Annette to hear but the downturned shape of Annette's mouth when she glanced over again told Janie she had. *Oh, this is hard.* The small injustices of childhood lay just beneath the surface, along with their unbreakable sisterly bond.

'Okay,' she decided to play along. 'Are we nearly there yet?'

'Might be, might not be.'

'Hmm. So which way do I go at the junction?'

'Turn left. I think. . . '

'Well, you'd better let me know pretty quickly, there's a car behind me,' Janie's hands gripped the wheel tighter. 'Hurry up!' A line of oncoming cars whooshed past them on their right.

Annette had a sheet of paper spread out on her lap. Janie eased down into first, her foot on the clutch.

'Hurry up.' The car behind them tooted. 'Oh, fuck off.'

'Whoo-hoo, get you!' Annette took her sweet time deciding on the direction, sticking her left arm out of the passenger window with a two-fingered sign at the car behind.

'Go right,' she said, grinning.

Janie indicated and took the right turn when the oncoming traffic allowed. The other car's horn blared as it roared past behind them.

'You want to be careful,' Janie said. 'There's such a thing as road-rage, you know. Probably not in Ireland where you come from, but they're a belligerent lot out here in rural Lincolnshire. You don't want to get on the wrong side of them. Which way now?'

'Keep going.' They covered a few more miles. In the rear-view mirror Janie could see a snippet of her mother's reflection, fully asleep, head tilted back and mouth a dark cavern. Coldness lapped in her stomach; she wanted to ask Annette about Mum's condition, but she couldn't bring herself to. She got the feeling Annette was protecting her.

Annette had gone quiet, the lines of her face tensed.

'What's up?' Janie said at last.

'You'll see.' Annette bit her thumbnail. 'I've done something big, Janie.'

Annette was always doing something "big". They waited at a railway crossing. Amber lights flashed and a flimsy barrier came down on either side of the road. Janie felt the rattle of the approaching train.

'Something big and probably stupid. It was an impulse; I couldn't help myself at the time but now I'm wondering how the fuck it's going to work. And what you and Mum are going to say.'

The train roared by – carriage after industrial carriage – so Janie didn't hear what Annette said next. The barrier on their side rose. Janie inched forward across the tracks. She heard a snort from the back of the car, Mum, awake. Flicking her eyes between the road and the mirror Janie only now noticed how thin her mother's hair had become – Dad used to call it her crowning glory. Oddly, her thick brows had not turned grey. Poppy licked her mistress's face. Romy appeared above the seat, one of her ears folded backwards.

Mum fumbled with the bottle of fruit-flavoured water she took out of her voluminous handbag and, having wrested the lid off, took a sip just as Janie drove over a bump.

'Damn,' Mum said, dabbing her embroidered t-shirt with a tissue. 'This top was clean-on this morning.'

'Sorry, Mum.' A flush of heat came to Janie's cheeks. Annette nudged her.

'Always were clumsy, you.'

'That's enough, Annette,' came from the back seat.

'Oh, for God's sake,' said Annette. She went silent for a moment. Then she said, 'Look, Janie. Look at the narrowboats on the river. Remember when we used to imagine living on one of those?'

'Yeah, I do. Hang on a minute – this looks familiar. This bridge with the traffic lights. I've been here before, haven't I?'

She brought the car to a stop at the lights. After a couple of seconds a stream of traffic came towards them and passed on the other side of the road. When the lights changed again, Janie's hands visibly trembled on the wheel. She struggled to hold them steady.

'Why did you bring me back here?'

'I've got something to show you,' Annette's tone was higher than before. 'Keep going, past the sugar beet factory. Okay, slow down. Hang on, wait for this tractor to pass, we need to make a right turn here.'

She unfolded a clutch of papers on her lap. Janie glanced down and saw an auction house logo at the top of the first page. Her heart took a dive, leaving her dizzy.

'Okay, it's just here.'

Janie crunched the gears. But she couldn't stay still in the middle of the road, so she forced herself to check the mirrors and turn the wheel to move the car in the direction Annette indicated. They drove down a stony track. Janie couldn't pinpoint what her feelings were. A stamp on the top sheet of paper proclaimed the word "Sold". An emotion seeped through: anger, she thought.

'This building here, look, and the outbuildings.' Annette's voice was even smaller. 'And all this land, I assume.'

'What have you done?' said Janie.

'Uhm. I bought it for us – it's an old railway station, look, see the remains of the track? I know you like railway stations. So I bought it for you.'

Janie's mouth had dried.

'Well, for *us*,' Annette amended. 'Except I could only afford to pay the deposit and about a quarter more. But there's quite a lot more than that, unfortunately. So you'll need to pay the balance with your half of the money from Catmally. If that's okay?'

Janie nearly choked. Annette gave her a thump between the shoulder blades, and for a moment she was a child again.

Choking on a boiled sweet. It must have been just after Christmas or Easter because they never had sweets in the house otherwise. As darkness enveloped her then, it was as if their living room had spun around her. She'd flailed her arms, memorising items of their everyday lives one by one. First the central heating boiler in the middle of the wall facing the window. Dad had installed the great white beast to replace the old Aga. There was a purple stain of melted plastic on top, from the hairbrush Mum had placed there after finishing Annette's plaits – Janie could see Mum placing the hairbrush down quite clearly. The fish tank on the wall between the dining nook and Mum's favourite armchair seemed to flash coloured lights. The fish swam madly around in circles as Janie fought for breath. The mouldering stain on the wallpaper at the edge of the sash window throbbed – wallpaper peeled away in front of her panicked eyes. The tatty bed-settee which had an arm that wouldn't fix back into position burned a deeper red. Nicholas screamed for their mother. But Mum was on the toilet and shouted down that she'd be as quick as she could.

Annette saved the day, or rather Janie's life, with a massive thump to her back. The bruise lasted weeks. Once Janie had caught her breath she lay on the floor and screamed blue murder. Mum finally burst into the room, her skirt caught up in her knickers. She assessed the situation with eyes that whipped from one child to the other. Janie on the floor, screaming. Nicholas with his knuckles clenched at his chin and snot pouring down his face. Annette standing by, trying to explain that she'd had to thump Janie on the back to stop her from choking. But Mum only heard the word thump. She didn't notice the ejected boiled sweet which clung to the sole of her sandal as she raised her foot and aimed a kick at Annette's bum. Still not listening, she whacked her older daughter around the head with the flat of her hand...

Now Janie felt pain between her shoulder blades, as she had then.

'Ouch! Fucking hell. Why did you hit me?'

'Really! Is that language entirely necessary?' The voice came from the seat behind, frail but determined.

'I didn't know what else to do. You didn't seem to be breathing, what was I supposed to do – let you die?'

'I wasn't going to die. Don't be ridiculous. Why on earth would I have died? Ouch, it really hurts.' Janie coughed. 'What the fuck, Annette?'

'I give up,' said their mother. 'I've obviously got no say at all over you girls – you clearly don't respect me at all. Are there any toilets here? My bladder's bursting.'

'I'll have a look.' Annette got out of the car, grunting as she pressed down with her hand on the headrest of her seat. Her floaty, Indian-cotton dress slipped off a thin shoulder and as she leaned forward the curve of her spine became more prominent. She flexed her back before moving to open their mother's door. Poppy's panting increased as Annette helped Mum out. She opened the boot for Romy, and the car shuddered as she slammed it shut again. When Mum had brushed herself down, the two women waited on the gravel a second, glancing enquiringly at Janie. She didn't move, and Mum said something Janie couldn't hear. The two of them walked haltingly away from the car, Annette's arm looped through Mum's. The dogs ran in circles ahead of them.

Janie remained where she was. She observed her hands on the wheel and noted the whiteness of her knuckles. She breathed and experienced the pain in her back and in her chest, too; felt displaced from her own body. She wanted to wake up and go home to Catmally. *My beautiful railway station home in the mountains.* The loss was physical. In the distance and through a blur of water she could see the two women and the two dogs exploring the buildings on the neglected, scrubby land. Annette had said that she'd put a deposit on this place. Annette was expecting her, Janie, to pay the balance. However much that was.

She ought to drive away. She should leave her sister and mother behind. Go back to Scotland. But where would she live?

Not for the first time, the idea of travelling like Allegra tempted her. But her wandering would be aimless, not focussed as Allegra's was. Focussed by youth and a hopeful future. Janie had no idea – *no idea* – what she wanted to do with her life. Except that her wish at this point, after all the trauma of the separation and the move – was only to be safe. To be home. But she couldn't go back to Catmally because it wasn't her home anymore.

Juliet's flat in Edinburgh came to mind. It had felt like a haven when she went there after Catmally. But she was too young – or old – or young – to run to her children for safety and nurture. And they were too young to feel responsible for her. And Juliet had a partner now, who wouldn't take kindly to a long-term uninvited guest.

She lifted her face and blinked away the veil of water. *Right,* she said to herself, sniffing hard. *Right.*

One by one she prised her fingers from the steering wheel. She'd been holding on so tightly they hurt and now she cradled her hands in her lap. When the joints felt loose enough, she fumbled in the glove compartment where she found a packet of tissues. Mopped her eyes and nose. Flexed her neck by turning her head from one side to the other, then forced herself to take in her surroundings. *Right.* A sob fought its way up. She blew her nose. *Right.*

She battled off helplessness. Annette should *never* have taken a decision that depended on Janie's compliance. A decision that left Janie with no choice but to pay up or walk away and that would cause Annette to lose her deposit – but that was the situation.

She *sort of* understood what Annette had tried to do. But buy a property together? Live together – here? Did she mean Mum as well? After all, Mum was the reason they were here. But what had possessed Annette to think they could all live together in the wilds of Lincolnshire? Her shoulders rippled with an involuntary shudder.

Perhaps she'd seized on the idea because it was a disused railway station. Janie could just hear her thinking, *Oh, Janie will love this. She thought living in a station was great.* But that hadn't been the point of Catmally at all. It'd been the house itself she and Paul had fallen in love with. And the land and the surrounding mountains. Later they had loved the fact it was a working platform. Trains stopped outside their front door at regular hours with passengers hopping on for Glasgow or, across the tracks, Oban. Juliet, Allegra and Billy were their very own *Railway Children.*

Here, there were no trains. A huge factory stood only a few hundred metres from the property's boundary. And the surrounding landscape was flat. *Flat.* Janie's hand flew up to her mouth. She kicked the car door open. *Breathe, breathe.*

Mum and Annette had disappeared around the corner of the main building. Romy and Poppy galloped along the edge of a wire mesh fence in the distance, barking. Beyond the fence, vermillion poppies bowed amongst the green leaves of potato plants that stretched as far as Janie could see. On the horizon she spotted a copse of trees. She imagined walking between the lines of potato plants until she reached the trees. She imagined curling herself into the fragrant mulch at the base of the strongest tree in the forest.

She breathed into her hands, then spread her fingertips beneath her eyes and across her cheeks, wiping away the water that had gathered on them.

17

Justin, 1972

It was touch and go whether Justin would be able to play the festival. He had a cold that wouldn't go away – lost his voice completely for a while. Worrying about why he hadn't seen much of his girlfriend lately. It was almost a relief when a note was pushed under his door while he was asleep, telling him she'd decided to elope with another man.

At the end of his second week of illness his mother arrived. Said he needed to come home for a rest. She promised to make him one of her potions which would be bound to induce his voice back. Annie's work as a physicist didn't stop her believing in herbal remedies. His brothers used to take him into the meadows that backed onto their home to collect ingredients for her medicinal experimentations.

'Home' was a dilapidated mansion in Norfolk that had lain empty for years when his parents gained permission from the landowner to explore it (at their own risk, he'd said). At the end of the war, only three sons into their plethora of boys, they had stopped their battered old car at the gates one day on their way back from taking the boys to see the pillboxes at Heacham beach. The key to the gates had been long lost and Pa had climbed over, while Annie managed to squeeze the youngest boy through the gap into his waiting arms. Next the two older boys helped their mother climb up and Pa caught her on the other side. Finally, Joshua and Felix had pushed and pulled each other over like two interlinked figures making their way up a lollipop stick. Emerging from a tunnel of trees which seemed to be holding hands with their branches locked together, the family walked into a clearing of light.

Ivy strangled the walls and the windows of their future home, and the door had been boarded over. But Pa, with the help of his enthusiastic sons (Annie was by this time sitting on a fallen tree-trunk feeding baby Rowan) wrestled the planks from the door. He shone the torch he had brought on the lock while Felix did something with the corkscrew part of his penknife. The door reluctantly creaked open. Inside, they found broken glass, crumbling plaster and a hole in the roof which allowed a stream of light to filter in. The boys whooped in delight and set off up the winding staircase to cries of 'Be careful!' and 'Stick to the edges of the stairs,' from Pa. Felix had often told in the years since of how he reached the upper landing and saw his mother walking into the house with the sleeping one-year-old in her arms. He said she stood in the middle of the floor, the ray of light shining on her mousy-blonde hair. And he said he saw the way his mother and father looked at each other and the slow smiles that dawned on their faces. He knew then, he said. He knew exactly what they were thinking.

They sold their newly-built detached house on an estate and bought the dilapidated mansion for a song. This was actually partly true – the landowner knew Annie from her amateur jazz singing at a club close to where they'd lived in Kings Lynn. He asked her to sing for him at a family wedding as part of the deal they made on the mansion. Pa got a year-long sabbatical from his job as an engineer and spent that time making the house habitable. They also had another new baby by the end of the year. A boy – Finlay.

A decade later, Annie wrote and illustrated the story of how her family had rescued the house from decay. She published the children's book at her own expense, and had five hundred copies printed and sold as a fundraiser to help families who were homeless. Justin later found a copy on eBay for his niece, Ivy.

Justin was Annie's youngest child, and most unexpected – she hadn't even realised she was pregnant until two months before he was born.

'Come on, ducky,' she coaxed in his sick-room twenty-two years later, lowering herself onto the edge of his bedsit camp-bed. From somewhere she extracted a soft cloth and pressed it to his forehead. It smelt of lavender and flooded his mind with thoughts of home. 'I have some annual leave so I can stay at home and look after you. A week of Meadows air will do you the world of good. You can lie in the garden on my sun lounger; it swings and has a canopy. You can watch the birds in the apple tree and listen to Pa on his violin. Or perhaps not – he's only been playing it a few weeks. I'll feed you borage soup. You know you love it.'

He made a face.

'That's better,' she said. 'A smile, or something resembling one anyway. All right, tomato soup then. But it will have to be tomatoes from our own garden, otherwise the magic won't work.'

For a Scientist, Annie was amazingly superstitious. 'Also, Finlay's home for a few days with his girlfriend. You'll love Alice. She's a clever girl – one of my students, you know.'

Finlay was Justin's next brother up, but there was still almost five years between them. His mother's steel-grey hair brushed his face as she leaned over to kiss his forehead. Her wrinkles crinkled in a particular way that told him she was worried. *I must be quite ill.*

'You're definitely coming home with me,' she told him in her firmest voice. 'I've decided. We'll soon have your voice back and you *will* play that festival, I promise you. And anyway, I need someone to help me stuff envelopes. I have a new campaign on the go to get people working in our community garden once a week. We're trying to provide a monthly vegetable box for local families who are struggling at the moment.'

———

Thanks to a health-inducing week at home, Justin did make it to the stage at the festival. When he met Annette in the empty folk tent, he was still shaky from his illness. At first his voice wouldn't come out properly. Then he saw the rain-drenched girl in a polythene poncho, shimmering in the light from the door. Justin's fingers continued to strum the strings of his guitar but his mind had gone elsewhere, to an alternative reality in which his fingers were separating the damp strands of this girl's hair instead.

The girlfriend who had recently left him had a delicate nose that turned up at the tip, and jet-black hair that contrasted strongly with her porcelain skin. She was voluptuous and sexy. He'd thought she was his type. He'd been led to believe by his brothers that one always had a type. But this girl was nothing like that. She was thin for a start, almost boyish in figure. And when she turned slightly in the light he noticed the curvature of her spine, outlined in raindrops on the shimmering polythene which seemed to him the most fetching outfit he'd ever seen. She wore her straw-coloured hair in plaits that hung either side of her narrow face. She had wide, dark blue eyes and her nose curved down at the end rather than upwards. Her lips were also slightly downturned at the corners, as if she wasn't the type to pretend to feel anything she didn't. But there was something about her that made his heart clench. He stuttered over his lyrics and forgot the words, so he played a few soft chords and picked out a series of melodic notes before launching into the next verse, his voice strengthening

90

as he sneaked glances at her. She was younger than him, but he felt a connection.

Don't want to have to remember
The peace I never rendered,
All the hearts I never mended.

He sensed a sadness about her, too – similar to the one that underlined his perception of the world. He had an urge to fix it. Mend her heart.

It must have been the illness, making him hallucinate. She was just a girl who'd wandered in by mistake. Or perhaps it was the music. The deep, resonant chords his hands were playing. Full of yearning.

Between each verse he played extra bars so he had longer to think. Extend the moments the intriguing girl would sit in front of him. Ellen, his ex-girlfriend, had never inspired him like this. He was happiest with her when he lost himself during sex. They'd tried to do ordinary things together – Sunday drinks at a country pub, the theatre or a midweek film, but they didn't share the same tastes and they got bored in each other's every-day company. He tried to interest her in the causes he'd imbibed with his mother's milk: fairness, equal rights – justice for all. Boycotting Barclays Bank and oranges from South Africa.   Demonstrations against the Vietnam War. But she'd chosen to go shopping while he went on demonstrations and at the time he hadn't thought he'd minded. She said she liked him being a *rebel* but had no interest in becoming one herself. When he'd taken Ellen to meet Annie, he knew his mother was disappointed.   Her attempts at conversation with his girlfriend had been unproductive.

'She wears a lot of make-up, doesn't she?' Was the only – untypical – remark she made afterwards. Whereas she never stopped praising the accomplishments of Finlay's girl, Alice.

This girl, sitting cross-legged on the floor leaning against a straw bale – he could see her lying on her stomach on the front lawn at The Meadows. Wearing a cheesecloth dress and waving her bare feet around (he added a straw in the corner of her mouth to complete the picture). He knew Annie would like her, too. All the time Justin was having these thoughts he continued to add verses to his song, more-or-less made up on the spot, just to keep her there.

Finally he had to finish because his throat didn't want to produce any more sounds and he needed to save it for later. He brought the music to a gentle close. Once he'd propped the guitar safely on its stand he closed his eyes to stop tears from falling. He sat with his palms upturned on his lap, the way his mother had taught him during his anxious childhood.

The girl's voice blared through his meditations.

'That was all right, that.' A smile tugged at his lips. After a slight pause she added, 'Yeah, not bad at all as a matter of fact.'

He opened his eyes and allowed the smile to spread across his face. Their eyes met. She looked somehow hurt. She reminded him of a bird, a squawky one. *That was all right, that.* A laugh bubbled in his throat. He made sure his voice came out steady.

'Come in later if you fancy it,' he said. 'I'm on at about four. Thanks for listening to my practice session.'

The rows of straw bales were crowded with people, boys and girls squashed up next to each other. They wore Afghan coats, leather jackets and various colours of fake fur. They had thick beards, long, damp manes, and afros of incredible heights. Plenty of glistening polythene ponchos hung out to dry on the tent poles. The smell in the confined space was musty and faintly reminiscent of the cheese his mother made from unpasteurised milk sold by a local farm back in Norfolk. He breathed in. Out again. And in again until he was used to the smell. He was careful not to pay close attention to any faces as he settled himself on the stool.

He wasn't conceited enough to believe all the people had come in to see him. The tent was a dry space out of the rain and he guessed there could be worse places to go if you weren't a fan of Heads, Hands and Feet who would be on the main stage. Still, he was grateful for a full audience. If it had been only her again. . .

He owed it to them to acknowledge their presence. It was one of his things: he began with the back row, nodding and smiling at each audience member. He moved his gaze from the right to almost the middle on the front row and then from the left to the person in the actual middle. He'd known all along that it was her, sitting directly in front of him.

'Hello again,' he said. And played the first chord.

18

Janie, now and then

Sold by Auction. The sign on the old railway gates had slipped down at one corner. Janie shuddered, and as the tremor ran through her she thought of her late dog, Riley, shaking off river water.

So this was to be it. She scanned the field to her right. It was within the boundary fence, and she supposed it must be part of the property. Ahead of her stood a huge barn that looked as if it needed some repairs. With massive, arched doors adorning its front, the building reminded her of the engine shed on *Ivor the Engine*. Billy's toddler-giggles filled her mind and she could almost feel his wriggling body within the curve of her arm as they sat watching his favourite programme while the girls were at school. She turned back and counted breaths, taking a proper look at the house.

A cluster of silver birches swayed next to it, by a rough patch of what could euphemistically be called a lawn, edged with straggling roses. A towering apple tree at one corner partially obscured a black-painted wooden shed, dried blossom from the tree drifting as far as the drive on which

Janie stood. A brick shed peeped out from behind the house on the left-hand side. A tiled-roofed structure butted up against the house, sheltering three stone steps that led up to an antique wooden door with carved panels and scratched blue paint, attached by decorative iron hinges.

Janie found herself imagining a rustic table, set beneath the solid gazebo, fairy lights strung under its roof. Cars would need to be driven right around the other side of the house if their owners required them to be parked in the garage she could see jutting out from behind it on the right. But the garage could be converted into extra accommodation...

Annette and Mum reappeared on the far side of the house near a patio and a greenhouse and a couple more outbuildings. A rampant patch of brambles reached as far as the boundary fence, where the potato fields ranged to the woods on the other side.

Annette's stick-insect figure waved madly at Janie, her other hand positioned beneath Mum's elbow. Mum had her handbag wedged under her arm, keeping her chin down, probably being careful not to trip on the uneven ground. Janie could see, even from where she was, that the flagstones edging the house were greyed and broken.

Mum looked up, but not at Janie. She stopped and pointed at something – two free-standing brick buildings and beyond them a squat, low structure at the end of a broad pathway. Janie realised it was the old railway platform. The larger building with the boarded-up windows might have once been a ticket office. Annette appeared to examine the free-standing outhouse and led Mum forward.

Annette's good with her, Janie thought. She watched her sister and mother test the outbuilding door. After some apparent effort on Annette's part, she wrenched it open. Mum disappeared inside, Annette attempting to take her handbag from her but Mum pulled it back inside. Annette made an open-handed gesture towards Janie.

Janie shrugged and managed a smile. She walked forward

a few steps and peered down at the gully which still contained a few bars of railway tracks. Following it with her eyes, she saw that further on, the extinct track ran close to the patio beside the house, and she imagined passengers standing on the platform. She turned back to examine the house.

A square, two-story building with windows that resembled impenetrable eyes seeming to gaze coldly back at Janie. She shuddered.   Artistic plasterwork formed an intricate decoration above each of the windows. The exterior of the house had once been painted white but the colour had mostly worn off. She thought of Paul's abstract landscapes, now most recently seascapes. He scumbled dry, white paint over the surface to denote a sea-mist. A hoar.

Whore. Vanessa's face reared into her mind. Whore. Why did she come back?

Then

She'd meant to give Paul an ultimatum all those years ago. The children were in bed and the last train of the night had rattled by. Encountering Vanessa in the kitchen, conveniently around the time Paul came in from his studio, she said coldly: 'Wait.'

The back door was pushed open, grinding on the step as usual. Janie observed the warning in Vanessa's eyes as Paul lurched in, murmuring something in his throat.   Janie stepped forward and placed her hand flat on Paul's chest. His gaze searched hers, then his body slackened, his weight slumped onto her hand before she could get her planned ultimatum out.   He began blubbering and apologising. Vanessa stood, calcified.

I thought you didn't want me anymore, lass, Paul sobbed. *I love you, Janie.* Later, she let him have sex with her, and surprised herself with an explosive orgasm.

Vanessa left their home and went to claim her prestigious award (she hadn't been lying about that).   Janie and Paul resumed marital relations until they both became too busy again, and got caught up with other things.

Two years ago, when their beloved dog had to be put down, they turned to each other for comfort, and their relationship was rejuvenated once again. Juliet was by then in her final year of university, Allegra in her first, and Billy in his last year of school.

Janie decided to begin hosting lucky-dip dinner parties again, like in their early years at Catmally. Self-consciously, she took out invitation cards on Tuesdays, and handed them to selected passengers from the 7am and 8am trains in both directions. It was a lottery discovering who they would end up with around the table on the Friday night, as they required no RSVP.

She remembered gazing at Paul, laughing and gesticulating down the other end of the table with the woman who owned the felting shop at Taynuilt, and feeling triumphant. He was the same Paul she'd fallen in love with, albeit with thinner hair and a portlier belly. But his ageing shape perfectly matched her own thickened waist and sagging breasts. The story of their marriage illustrated by their bodies. She felt a flush of desire and loosened the button at her neck. Their troubles were over, she thought. They had made it through the rapids...

...Until Vanessa reappeared at the School of Art, this time as a tutor.

Now

'Are you not even coming over to have a look, then?' Annette bellowed at Janie across the crazy paving.

'I suppose I may as well, now I'm here.' Janie took a deep breath. Picked her way across the gravel, danced between the overgrown weeds and the odd stray potato plant that had pushed its way up through the broken flagstones. Stepping over the handles of an upturned, rusted wheelbarrow that had suddenly appeared through the weeds, she came to a standstill beside Annette. Her sister grinned.

Something nudged Janie hard in the back of the legs.

'What the fuck?' But it was only Romy, backing off in a prancing display of acrobatics.

'C'mere you,' Annette ruffled her dog's ears. 'Where's that Poppy, then? You'd better not 'ave lost me mum's dog. Go on, off you go and don't come back 'til you've found her.'

Clanking from the outhouse. Janie had forgotten all about their mum. Thinking about it, Mum was often on the outskirts of her childhood. It was Annette she shared a bedroom with from the day she was born, Annette who sometimes fed her a bottle if Mum was too busy. Annette who used to whisper to her late at night – things she most likely didn't want to hear. But Annette persisted. She could have ignored Janie and just got on with being a teenager when Janie wanted to remain a child, but she didn't. She kept on trying to include her. Janie studied Annette properly for the first time since she'd arrived at Mum's and she found she could see right through her, back into the past. To the morning they did their first grown-up thing together. Precipitating Annette's expulsion from the family.

Mum sent the toilet door crashing outwards and almost fell over the step as she emerged. Annette rushed forward to catch her, and Janie again marvelled at her own dissociation.

'Good job I had some tissue in my bag,' said Mum. She appeared thin and old, but she was only eighty – an age that didn't seem such a long way off now Janie was in her fifties. She knew a hill farmer in her nineties who looked ten years younger than Mum. The hill farmer was open-hearted, a talented musician – Janie'd been to lots of Ceilidhs in her barn. But Mum was *ill*. Janie felt sick.

'Also, the toilet won't flush. Probably no water in the tank. You can't see a bucket of water round here anywhere, can you?'

They began to look around, as if a bucket of water might

magically appear. Poppy came crashing through the nettles behind the outhouses, a dead rat dangling from both sides of her mouth – its eyes like shrivelled currants and lips peeled back from its teeth. Poppy tossed it in the air ecstatically and ran to grab it again. A horrendous smell reached Janie. She grasped Mum's arm as they stepped backwards in tandem.

'Give it 'ere, ye little horror,' Annette rushed forward. She prised the rat from Poppy's jaws, using one hand to force the terrier's mouth open. Snatching the dead animal, she tossed it into the toilet and jammed the door shut again.

'Now it's really going to stink in there,' laughing like a witch. 'Would you happen to have any wet-wipes in your bag, Mother? I've got essence of dead rat on me hand.'

They made a halting, exploratory journey around the outside of the house, peering into windows at the empty rooms inside. Wooden floors, the odd board splintered, and a pile of plaster in one corner of the largest room. Moving beyond the house, Annette and Janie used their combined strength to tug open the garage door, which scraped along the ground due to a listing hinge. Inside they discovered some old-but-still-useable garden furniture amongst the debris of cardboard boxes and broken bicycles. They stared around at the cobwebs and a set of oily footprints on the cracked, concrete floor.

'That door'll need fixing,' said Annette. She gave Janie a sly grin. Janie struggled to hold in the smile that tugged at the corners of her mouth. Felt the bubble of excitement in her chest. She saw Mum notice, and watched an invisible weight rise off the old woman's shoulders. She decided to play her part.

'Give us a hand with this stuff, then,' she said to Annette. Pushing off a pile of old newspapers, they carried out the plastic table and chairs as if they had every right in the world.

'Not there – under here,' said Janie, backing into the shade under the carport (she already preferred to think of it as a gazebo). She understood instinctively that there would be parts of the property that she and Annette would each make their own. Her fingers had become white by the time she unhooked them from the underside of the table. She wiped her hands on her pale linen dress, leaving grey streaks down the front.

'Have you got those wipes again please, Mum?'

Mum fished out another few from her bag. Janie cleaned first her hands and then the table, so they could lay the picnic food out on it.

Tired, they ate the sandwiches Annette had made and drank tea from the flask, before sitting back in the cleaned-off chairs, looking out from the shade at the blue sky beyond the gazebo. Mum removed her cardigan and after a while her eyelids drooped. Janie snuck a glance at her mother's skeletal upper arms, flesh dangling off them. Flushing, she met Annette's eyes. Annette gave a brief nod.

The dogs had by now ensconced themselves under the table. Bees murmured in the roses. A sense of wellbeing started to replace Janie's anxiety.

Yes, this is how it will be. Squinting upwards, she pictured fairy lights dangling from the metal framework above – the ones she'd rescued from the refurbished coal shed at Catmally Station. She examined possessively the cracked blue-painted wooden door, stood up and brushed a trail of dust from it. The door was filthier than she'd thought.

'Damn, look at my hands.'

Mum jolted awake, fished in her bag and laid the packet of wipes on the table.

'Thanks,' said Janie, tucking the soiled wipe into the dog-poo bag Annette had earlier torn off the roll for exactly that purpose. 'Sorry to wake you, Mum.'

Her mother uttered a sort of growl. 'I was only resting my eyes.'

They didn't have a key yet, but Annette said a woman from the agency would be meeting them there later and Janie would have to sign some papers and provide her bank details, if she agreed, and the agency woman would make a phone call.

'I knew you'd have your driving licence on you, so you'll be able to provide photographic ID,' Annette said. 'Though you might have to go into their office later so they can take a certified copy.'

Perhaps it was a good thing Annette'd made the decision without her. If she'd been presented with the idea as an abstract concept, Janie would have said no way. *Move back to Lincolnshire? To Bardney? You must be crazy.* But it was a home she wanted, a sense of belonging, purpose – and she could see that this *could* be home, with all the potential for live-in guests and community feel that she was used to.

Mum retrieved a packet of mint humbugs from her bag and while they each sucked on a sweet, Janie struggled to remain annoyed with the landscape for being so flat. *No mountains.* She mentally cursed the absence of lochs. Insisted to herself she couldn't live without water nearby. *But there's the river just around the corner from here. The Witham.* Next, she reminded herself how much she detested the ugly bulk of the factory on the other side of the property – but her eyes kept straying over the neglected bricks of the house, imagining them gleaming with fresh white paint again. The garden was overgrown but it was large. And there was a field – a whole field of their own. *Something new always arises out of chaos.*

She could grow things here – build a walled garden, as she had at Catmally. They could take in seaside donkeys – Annette liked animals. There was space all around them – that field of potatoes stretching into the distance and the woods at the back of it. The house was surrounded by at least an acre-and-a-half of its own and there were plenty of outbuildings, a bloody massive barn. *So much potential.* Once she'd coughed up her portion of the money, this would all belong to them – her and Annette.

She placed a hand on her diaphragm, a bird crashing about inside her.

She'd once lost a sister, and now the two of them were here again, in the place their relationship had broken. Janie bore the guilt for what had happened to Annette after the festival, but from the time they were reunited when Janie was nineteen – when her sister had finally got in touch through the family of a school friend – Annette had never blamed her.

Perhaps the place they broke was where they were always supposed to rebuild their fractured lives.

19

Annette, now

Turned out the station house needed quite a lot of work. *General renovation*, was how the surveyor described it. Some roof tiles were missing, and the brickwork needed re-pointing. Oh, and the joists under the dining room floor were rotten, apparently. The building also needed damp-proofing. Personally I'd have been perfectly happy to make do and mend, but Janie said I'd soon change my mind once we moved in.

'Are you serious?' I said. 'Do you not remember the state of that first cottage I lived in after I moved out of my bender on the beach at Lissadel? I don't mind as long as it's got a roof over it. Or most of it. We can always put a bucket under the hole.'

Janie tutted and reminded me she never even saw that cottage. She was too busy living in an un-renovated station house herself, she said, with three small children to look after. She said she was *not* going through that again, and insisted the dirtiest work was done before we moved in.

Only problem was, Janie didn't have an endless supply of money. I'd taken a gamble on her having enough from the sale of Catmally to pay the balance on the property itself and I was lucky. But she insisted on keeping ten bloody grand aside in case her kids ever needed any help – because apparently *that bastard* Paul ploughed his half straight into his purpose-built artist apartment.

'Why do you need to give them money anyway?' I said. 'Can't they stand on their own fricking feet? It's not as if anybody ever gave *me* any money to help me out.'

I swallowed hard. Would I have behaved any differently if I'd had financial help? I couldn't honestly say I would've.

And since *I* didn't have kids, maybe I should stop criticising Janie.

'Yes, well.' Janie pursed her lips. 'Me neither. But it's *my* decision what I do for my own kids. It's the one thing I have a choice in and I'm keeping that ten grand aside.'

She glared at me. Me and Nicholas used to call that her *Paddington Bear* stare. I didn't want to get her riled up again over my impulsive purchase, she'd already had a mini-meltdown when we got back to Mum's that first afternoon. '*I've signed my potential future away. I could have done anything. I could've had some space to make a choice. Now it's all gone and I'm just as trapped with you as I was within my marriage. Only I didn't even* choose *this!*' Blah, blah, blah.

I caught Mum's tired eye. She looked like she could hardly carry her head on her neck. I'd tried to get her to have breakfast in her armchair but she'd refused, stubborn old mare. We were all sitting round the table. She must've wondered why life had blessed her with this rerun of teenage tantrums and hormonal daughters just when she needed a bit of quiet.

'Fair enough then. But I've no idea how we're going to afford to get those repairs done.' I buttoned my lips at the warning flaring in Janie's eyes.

Janie concentrated on peeling the price sticker off a hardback notebook. She must have bought it when she went out to get supplies before breakfast. She used to have a stack of similar notebooks on the shelf above her bunkbed, alongside that collection of glass animals she was so fond of.

The first Christmas I had my job at Woolworths, I bought her an Indian fabric-covered journal that had a silver lock and key. She loved it and hugged me for the first time since she was about eight.

'What're you writing?' I asked timidly, after a few seconds of her scribbling away. I stabbed the last flakes of my croissant with the tip of my finger. Romy nudged my leg and looked up at me, panting.

'No,' the word came out automatically. 'Go lie down with Poppy.' She gave me a look as if to say what, that rangy creature? Poppy's adoration of Romy was still in no way mutual.

'Oh, just ideas,' said Janie, tapping the pen on her teeth. 'How we could get the money, for the floor and the roof tiles at least.'

The garden's resident blackbird let out a sudden musical trill on the bird table just outside the back door. Romy and Poppy raised their heads from their paws, alert, and as if it was aware of the indoor predators the bird flew off. Mum made a muted sound as she pushed herself stiffly out of her chair at the table, and me and Janie caught each other's eye and leaned forward at the same moment. Mum started to collect the plates, her hands shaking. She'd hardly eaten anything, the pills she had to take made her feel sick.

'Leave that,' I said. 'I'll do it.'

She thanked me. I watched her hold onto the furniture as she made her slow way to her armchair. She hadn't had her shower yet and was still in her dressing gown. The white side of her hair was flattened while the wing of black on the right stood up proud from its grey background. For some reason her messy hair seemed even more discomforting than her slowness in getting dressed. *Where's me smart, on-the-ball mum gone?*

She should've done something after our dad died, I thought, watching her settle into the chair. Gone on a cruise, or a trekking holiday in the Amazonian jungle. She was perfectly fit at the time. But she stayed here in her very nice house thank you very much, and went nowhere apart from visiting Janie's family every year before Christmas and Nicholas for a few days after. That one time she visited me in Ireland I tried to persuade her to buy a cottage in Sligo. 'There's a church, obviously,' I said. 'It's a very Catholic community, you'd be right at home.' But she was having none of it. From the kitchen where I went to wash up I could see her sitting tight-jawed in her armchair with the morning's newspaper still folded on her lap. It was depressing.

Janie's voice jolted me back into the present.

'Nicholas.'

'You what?'

'We should ask Nicholas for the money to do the repairs. It's basically his fault we've ended up buying the place, anyway.'

I liked that she included me in her team. She would always take Nicholas's side when we were kids. *Ha.*

'Yeah, you're right.' I dried my hands and moved back to the table. 'It's all Nicholas's fault. He should be made to pay.'

I spoke playfully, but I meant it all the same. I still couldn't quite believe I'd left my rural Irish idyll behind – on the orders of my big brother – after so many years of it being my home. I'd left all my friends behind, too. But another part of me was excited and glad I'd made such a rash decision. Bardney Station was a big place. There was that enormous barn, for a start. We could upcycle old bow-tops, use them for weddings and proms. That would mean we'd have to keep a few horses, too. Ha.

'You don't have to ask Nicholas for the extra money,' came

our mother's weak voice from the armchair. She submitted to a coughing fit before trying to sit up straighter. In my view from the kitchen end of the room she looked a lot worse than the day before and I felt a qualm in my stomach. Her bony hand smoothed the folded newspaper on her lap.

'What was that you said, Mum?'

'I said you don't need to ask Nicholas for the money. Why don't you try asking me instead?'

Janie glanced quickly at me and answered before I had a chance to speak.

'We can't do that,' she said. 'You don't have very much, do you? Only your pension.'

She paused and I could see her thinking – *and this house.* It would take a while to sell the house though, wouldn't it? And prepare the new place to a standard that would make it habitable for Mum. Still, me stomach fluttered with excitement. It looked like my plan was coming to fruition.

'I have savings,' Mum said. Her voice wavered. 'You would only have inherited the money when I'm gone, anyway. Listen, girls, come over here, please.'

It felt weird, her calling us girls. I hung the towel on the back of a chair and moved over to join Janie on the settee. She was still holding the notebook, stroking the cover like it was a small animal.

'When your dad got ill,' said Mum. 'He made me promise not to leave any money to Nicholas, only to you two. It sounds mean, but as your father said, he really doesn't need it. He doesn't have any children and he'll have a massive pension when he leaves the RAF. We funded his attempt at a business start-up before he went in, and we never got any of that back.' She must have read the look on my face. 'I know,' she said. 'Don't think we weren't both aware of how we indulged him. He was too young to handle that much money at the time.'

I opened my mouth to speak but she lifted a freckle-backed hand to silence me.

'He was our only son and all that.' She turned to Janie. 'Perhaps you were spoilt too, to some extent.'

Janie bristled but again Mum raised the hand.

'Yes, yes. I know you were resentful that we moved house during your first term at university. You've never forgiven me for that, have you?'

Janie frowned, a blush spreading over her face. She pulled at the neck of her t-shirt and the red tide flooded downwards until it disappeared out of sight beneath the sapphire cotton. My younger sister, in the middle of her menopause. I caught her eye and winked, wanting to make her laugh.

'At least they gave you their new address when they moved.'

For a moment, I thought I'd made a mistake. Then Janie tried to smother a snigger before letting it out. After a second or two Mum and I joined in, Mum coughing again. Reaching to the top of the small cabinet beside her chair, she grasped her water bottle. She took a sip and pushed the mouthpiece back in again with difficulty. I noticed how her hands trembled.

'As for you, Annette,'

Oh no, I thought. Don't dredge up the past right now. I know I made mistakes but I've paid for them, haven't I? And in more ways than you know. Let's just leave the past in the past.

'We were sorry,' she was saying. What was that? 'Your dad and I. We were sorry that you felt you had to leave.' *That you kicked me out, you mean.* 'And we missed you all those years we didn't see you. I just want you to know that.'

Her nostrils flared pink around the edges. That was the closest she came to showing emotion. But we saw it, Janie and me.

She's finally mentioned the elephant in the room – one of them, anyway.

I had a confession to make. But not yet.

'I'm touched and amazed you came all the way from Ireland, Annette, and you from Scotland,' she nodded at Janie. 'I do appreciate it. But goodness, girls.' She jolted as

Poppy creaked up onto her lap and turned full circle before settling down. The dog's torso ballooned and subsided again, her nose resting on her paws. Mum stroked her with papery hands.

'What I was going to say is that Poppy and I are fine. In fact, if you want to know the truth, we're desperate for our house back.'

'Haha, it's a good job we're moving out then, isn't it?' My voice sounded too loud in the quiet room. Romy wagged her tail. I nudged Janie and we both made another attempt at laughing, but for fecks' sake, it was obvious Mum would never be able to manage on her own.

'I'll admit I may need a little help,' Mum's voice had gone even quieter. 'But the beauty of it is that you're moving close by. So I'm happy to contribute my little portion of money for the repairs.'

She sagged back in her seat, grey and apparently exhausted. The skin on the back of my neck tingled.

Later, Janie made some telephone calls and arranged quotes for the necessary work.

———

Janie had gone to meet some builders at *The Station* (our imaginative new name for the place). They'd had an immediate cancellation and said she had to come either that afternoon or the following week. I went out for a walk with the dogs while Mum was having a nap. It was all quiet when we returned. I thought nervously of maybe needing to help her into the shower later, knowing she'd hate that, but she'd seemed especially weak that morning and hadn't been up to it.

I considered what to do with me little bit of free time.

Stretched out on the leather settee with a nice cuppa tea, I fought the urge to get up and check on Mum. Maybe it was all the excitement, but the tingle in my neck had given way to a sick feeling in the pit of my stomach. She'd be fine, I told myself; experience had taught me she could sleep for a good two hours in the afternoon. I decided to take a furtive glance at the tabloid she thought was a cut above the others. I'd found it on her chair-side table, still folded in on itself and looking unread.

'Ah,' I said to the dogs, full of false jollity. 'This is the life, ain't it? I'm just glad none of me friends can see me reading such tat.'

I unfolded the newspaper and almost choked on my tea. There, on the bottom half of the front page, was a blurry photo of Janie when she was thirteen. With Justin, *my* Justin. Janie was mascara-striped from her fit of crying and he was holding her hands. I remembered that was because she'd been trying to kick a bunch of policemen marching her friend's handcuffed brother into a cubicle. Next to it was another picture of Justin. Him as he was now, although not a very nice one. Towering over the photos was an insinuating headline, dominated by his name and casting aspersions on my little sister.

20

Janie, 1972

Janie'd never met a girl like Lara before. A girl who allowed her hair to grow wild and often went to demonstrations with her brother and his friends. Janie normally only mixed with people from school and church – which was mostly the same people. She'd never known any black people, apart from a family in their church who came from Ceylon.

Lara had travelled with her brother and his friends all the way from London. They came in a minibus with a black panther painted on the side. Janie asked if Lara's mother minded, and she looked sad. She said her mother had died of pneumonia the year before. Her brother was eighteen and he'd fought to keep Lara from being placed in a children's home. He was in charge of her now and they could do what they wanted.

'What about your dad?' Janie asked.

'He got deported.' Lara spoke matter-of-factly, but the look on her face wasn't matter-of-fact.

Janie hesitated, before asking 'What does deported mean?'

'He got sent back to Trinidad.' Lara plucked a piece of straw and began shredding it with her thumbnails. 'The pigs accused him of being a trouble-causer *just* because he was standing up for his rights. It's meant to be a free country and the last time I looked there was no law that says you can't demonstrate.' She sounded like she was saying what someone had told her to say. Her lip curled up at one corner. 'The pigs didn't touch our mum though, because she was white, like you.'

'Pigs...? Oh.' Janie realised she was talking about the police. Lara would think she was *so* dim. Janie remembered Dad and Mum discussing the news on TV a while ago. Janie had been sitting at the table painting new outfits onto her *Dolly Designer* figures. She glanced up and saw the footage of crowds of black people marching with banners in London. Dad had muttered about black power. It'd all seemed so far away from Lincoln. Janie fiddled with the glass zebra in her hands without looking up. She could feel Lara's gaze on her, as if Lara was waiting for her to understand.

'Yeah, the pigs are awful,' she said at last.

Lara laughed. But she had a fierce glint in her eye.

'It was actually the pigs that killed my mum.'

Janie wasn't sure how to react. A sick, falling-away feeling settled with a thump in her stomach. She swallowed a fresh rush of nausea. 'What do you mean? They deliberately gave her pneumonia?'

It would have had to be some sort of injection, surely? Only Lara had said the pigs *didn't* touch her mum. *So how did they do it?* Janie wished she'd listened to Annette more often, she'd probably have understood everything better.

'No, silly.'

Janie felt her cheeks burning. Lara smiled, but in a way that made Janie feel uncomfortable. She felt it best to admit to being ignorant.

'How did they do it, then?'

Lara seemed satisfied by the question.

'When they deported my dad, my mum had to work twice as hard to put food on the table. That was why she got ill. Because she couldn't cope with all the work and all the worry. It started with a cold and then it turned into flu. But she kept going to work. She collapsed at work and they took her to hospital and then we found out she had pneumonia.' Lara swiped at her cheek where a tear sat, poised to run. 'When I saw her, she had a mask over her face to help her breathe but it didn't do any good. She was dead a week later.'

An icicle settled in Janie's chest. Imagine something that horrible happening to your mum! It was so awful she grabbed Lara's hand and pressed the zebra into it.

'Here, you can have this to keep the elephant company. I can easily get another one, my sister works at Woolworths.'

'Thanks,' said Lara. She wiped her face roughly with the edge of her sleeve. She examined the zebra for a second and slipped it into the pocket on her denim bag where she'd put the other animal.

'Anyway, Fergus says I should be angry rather than sad about our mum. He says anger is more fruitful than grief.'

She shook her head as if to clear it of sorrow. Then a smile settled on her face again. Janie smiled back. She couldn't stop staring at Lara. In the light from the doorway her afro, like a halo, glinted with highlights of red-gold. Lara leaned back on her hands.

'What're you looking at?'

'Your hair. It's a lovely colour.' Janie paused. 'What did your mum look like?' She wasn't sure if it was appropriate to ask. But Lara didn't seem to mind.

'She was Irish. She had pale skin and dark red hair. That's where I get my red from.' Lara looked much younger then. She sat forward and pulled at a spiral of her hair which she stretched out for Janie to examine more closely.

'It's gorgeous,' Janie said. 'Really long, too. It's amazing.' She stroked a finger along the length of hair. She thought about how Lara's mum must once have brushed it for her the way her own mother used to brush hers.

'Do you have one of those afro combs?'

'Yes. Here, look.' Lara took an amber comb from her denim bag and teased it through her hair. 'Sometimes I tie my hair up in this scarf.' She pulled a length of patterned orange silk from her bag, which she proceeded to wind round her hair, leaving the tassels dangling at the back of her head. 'Your hair's lovely, too. I bet it'll be pleated when you let it out of the plaits.'

'It will be,' said Janie. 'I'll show you.' She unfastened the bands from the ends of her plaits and ran her fingers through her hair. She could feel it, silky and rippled like waves. She was unused to doing girly stuff with a friend. She and Sally usually talked about animals. Lara ran the wide-toothed comb through Janie's hair a few times.

'See, using a comb like this stops it going frizzy. You should get one.'

Janie felt excited. 'I think I will.'

The crash tent had mostly emptied. Through the flaps she could see that the sky outside had brightened slightly. Although she was enjoying her time with Lara, Janie partly regretted not going to the folk tent with Annette. She had a sort of roller-coaster feeling in her belly like she was going over a bump. It seemed a long time since Annette had left – how long did a folk singer sing for? Her legs were cramped from sitting cross-legged so long. She wondered what time Annette would come back. She and Lara exchanged smiles again but Janie thought they were both becoming edgy.

'I wonder where my sister is.'

'I wonder where my brother is, too. He said he was bringing us some food but I suppose we could go out on our own and explore?' Lara felt in her pocket and Janie heard the jingling of coins. 'I have some money.'

Janie would have loved to. She imagined wandering through the crowds with her new friend. They could link arms so as not to become separated. But what if they got lost and couldn't find their way back to the crash tent? And anyway, Annette had made her promise she would stay there.

'Better not,' she made a face to show what a pain it was. 'I promised my sister I wouldn't leave.'

Lara frowned. 'But she never said she'd be this long. And neither did my brother. I'm hungry. If nobody shows up soon I'm off for a walk anyway. But it's up to you whether or not you come with me.'

Janie felt a gap opening, but she couldn't think of anything to say to close it. She twisted her hands around each other. Lara was giving her what Janie's dad called the cold shoulder. To distract herself, she fiddled with the remaining glass animals in her pocket, the giraffe – her favourite – the pony and the poodle. She was considering getting up and going to stand by the tent door to wait for Annette, when Lara's brother arrived back, his arm linked with his girlfriend's. There were now five other people with them. They all had darker skin than Lara and Fergus. Janie felt the odd one out as they moved towards her en masse and crowded into the small space between the straw bales. They all seemed to be talking at the same time. Janie edged backwards, straw prickling through her jumper sleeves. It didn't stop her nostrils tingling at the appetising, savoury smell they'd brought with them though.

'What's up with you two, then?' Fergus glanced from one to the other of the girls. 'You're quiet. Had a fight or somefink?'

'Not really.' Lara tossed her head, the tassels on her scarf shimmering. 'We were getting fed up of waiting for you, if you want to know the truth. We're bored, aren't we, Janie?'

Janie gave Lara a grateful smile, warm inside that they were friends again. Fergus winked at her.

'Is that so?'

He and his friends had so much energy, laughing and joking. His girlfriend, Althea, opened a hessian bag and started handing out food in cardboard cartons that were wrapped in paper. She also distributed wooden forks between them all.

'It took us ages to find something this delicious,' she told the girls. 'Jerk chicken. Never mind hot-dogs, man. You won't taste anything finer than this, I promise you.'

'Yummy.' Lara began tearing at the paper and Janie followed suit. 'What do you think, Janie? This is traditional West Indian food. That's where my dad comes from.'

Spices zinged in the back of Janie's throat and the chicken melted on her tongue. 'Oh gosh, this is lovely. Mmm. You're right, Althea. Much better than hot dogs. *Or* fish and chips.' Everyone laughed. They drank ginger beer. Janie embarrassed herself by allowing a burp to escape.

'Oops, pardon,' she said. More jokes and a cheer.

'Right, now then.' Fergus rubbed his hands together. 'We're going out to watch the Average White Band in a minute.' He glanced around the half-empty tent as if looking for something. Janie's hands clenched under her jumper sleeves, anticipating what he'd say next.

'You coming with us, Janie? Where's your sister, by the way?'

'I don't know,' she said in a small voice. 'I thought she'd be back by now.'

The rest of the group had stood and were gathering their things, shrugging their coats and jackets back on. One of Fergus's friends collected the empty food packaging.

Janie didn't want to be left in the tent by herself. What if something had happened to Annette and she never came back? More likely Annette would have forgotten the promise she'd forced out of Janie. Perhaps she'd also gone to watch the Average White Band and Janie would find her there and Annette would act cross as a way of hiding her guilt for deserting Janie.

'Are you coming?' Lara was wearing her beautiful Afghan coat. She raised one eyebrow at Janie and held out her hand.

'It looks like your sister's forgotten you. Sorry,' she added, probably having seen the stupid tears springing to Janie's eyes. 'We'll find her out there, I expect. Look, you don't want to wait in here on your own, do you?' She jerked her chin in the direction of a snoring figure laying a few straw bales away. His mouth was open and there was a dribble of sick down the side of his face. His jumper had ridden up to reveal a dough-coloured, hairy belly. Janie shuddered.

'No.' She struggled up and pushed her arms into her parka sleeves. 'I don't.'

Lara helped her on with her coat. Fergus and all the others had pushed their way out of the door.

'Come on then.' Lara picked up Janie's bag and handed it to her. 'This is going to be fun. The Average White Band is one of my favourites. I'm sure we'll find your sister. We don't want to be stuck in here, do we?' She jumped up and down and yelped, startling Janie. 'This is a festival, man.' Lara sounded like her brother. Janie felt a thrill of excitement. Sally would never *believe* the people Janie'd been hanging out with. And Janie was the *only* one who'd seen Roxy Music. Sally would be *so* jealous and so would everybody else at school when they all found out. She heard Althea saying to Fergus that she was happy Lara had found a friend her own age, it was a shame she'd been forced to grow up too soon.

'Let's go listen to some *music*!' Lara grabbed Janie's hand. Her hair flew around her face as Lara pulled her along the top of one straw bale to another. Janie loved her new, wild friend. She felt as if her real life was just beginning.

Annette would be proud that she'd finally stopped being such a sissy.

21

Janie, 1972

They screeched the song lyrics and jumped up and down to the music, aiming the word *sister* at each other. The Average White Band were *amazing*! Janie didn't care about the rain or that she still hadn't found Annette. Her sister would be furious, but she didn't care about that either. Annette should have come straight back after the folk singer. If she had they might be dancing up and down together now.

Althea snaked her hips to the music. Her black velvet trousers clung to her bottom and swayed loose around her lower legs. Fergus grasped her waist, his hands moving with her wriggling body and slipping beneath her belted woollen jacket. Janie couldn't help imagining what he was touching. His lips fastened themselves to Althea's forehead.

Althea's cropped hair outlined her head. When the stage lights swung round it was topped by a crown of crystal raindrops. The light also picked out the perfect stretch of her neck. She was the most beautiful woman in the world. Janie's eyes kept returning to the entwined dancers as their bodies moved closer and closer together until they writhed in unity. Despite the rain, she felt hot.

Her own hair was plastered to her forehead and the silken ripples Lara had combed out in the tent were waterlogged and felt heavy as they flapped up and down on her shoulders. She probably had panda rings around her eyes, too, but so what? This was the best evening of her life. In blurry motion she watched Fergus's friends passing a thick, stinky cigarette around. One of the tall men – Vincent, she thought he was called, caught her eye as she accidentally nudged his arm.

'You want some of this, gorgeous?'

She shook her head, spraying raindrops. That nervous, rolling feeling in her stomach returned. Vincent had dangerous eyes. His lips peeled back from his teeth as he smiled but the smile didn't reach upwards. Janie moved away and continued to dance with Lara but her movements felt more forced. She made certain to keep Lara in her vision all the time. What would she do if they became separated?

Where was Annette?

Mum and Dad probably hadn't really given their permission for Janie, or even Annette, to come to the festival. It was the first time in her life she'd ever done anything this bad.

Panting for breath, she and Lara came to a stop at the end of the song, leaning forward with their hands on their knees.

'I'm so glad I found you here,' Lara straightened and took both Janie's hands. Her eyes sparkled. 'It's cool hanging out with my brother and all the rest but it's not the same as having a friend my own age.' Her lips spread into a wide grin.

'I'm so happy too.' Janie gave Lara's hands a shake. 'I've never done anything like this before.'

Imagine what Lara would think if she knew Janie still played with *dolls*. When she got home she would place them all in the suitcase on top of the wardrobe. Elsie and Debra and Rosalie, who she'd had since she was two. She would buy records with her pocket money from now on. The

Average White Band and Roxy Music for a start. And she and Lara would write letters to each other and maybe one day Janie could visit London. Lara had already written Janie's address down in a little notebook she carried in her bag and she'd torn out a page for Janie with her own address on.

'Which is your favourite member of the band?' Lara asked. 'Mine's Alan Gorrie. The singer on the right-hand side, there look. It's a pity we can't get closer, isn't it?'

'I like the saxophone player,' Janie decided on the spot. 'I like his long hair.' She blushed, hoping the rain masked it. 'Do you think they're keeping dry up there, under the polythene?'

'They'll be dryer than us at least,' Lara said. 'And they all have long hair. You could take your pick. They all have beards, too. Which beard do you like best?'

They played this game for a while, *which beard, which shirt, which pair of jeans* – shouting over the music, swaying and sometimes holding hands as they danced. Suddenly the band announced their final song. 'Nooo,' Janie and Lara shrieked. 'Don't go.' Janie was going to burst.

The crowd milled around, creating confusion as some left the stage area and others arrived in preparation for Rory Gallagher. Lara's brother and his friends got together in a huddle. The huge sheets of polythene above the stage sounded like beating wings. Janie craned her neck to see the tops of the metal towers holding the lights. They seemed to be swaying but that might have been her dizziness. She brought her chin down again and the ground lurched. Laughing, she grabbed on to Lara, an anchor in a sea of unfamiliarity. But uncertainty made her head swim again.

Where's Annette?

Fergus disentangled himself from his girlfriend and pulled Lara closer to him. He ran his eyes over Janie and back to Lara again.

'Hey girls. We're going over to the Giants of Tomorrow tent.'

Janie was still holding onto Lara, her arm stretched. She

ventured an attempt at a joke, 'Giants of tomorrow? Are they small at the moment?'

'Yeah, maybe they're the goblins of today!'

'You girls really are comedians aren't you?' He glanced at Althea and she nodded.

'Maybe we should drop you both off in the crash tent. It's past your bedtimes, anyway.' He winked at Janie. 'Your sister might be looking for you.'

She felt hopeful and disappointed at the same time. She wanted Annette but. . .

'Nah, man, let them come, yeah?' the pupils of Vincent's eyes were huge. Janie shivered and looked away but she could feel his eyes on her and her skin prickled. Unconsciously, her fingers slipped down Lara's arm and clung to the fur cuff of her sleeve.

Lara was threatening to bubble over with excitement.

'No! Fergus, don't be mean. We want to see the giants of tomorrow too, don't we, Janie? Maybe they're on stilts. . .' she put a hand over her mouth and exploded in giggles. Now that Janie looked at her from a static position, Lara's pupils seemed dilated, too. Or was she only imagining it? Perhaps she'd half-noticed Lara accepting the joint from Vincent when they were dancing, and hadn't wanted to see. She let go of her new friend's sleeve and rubbed her own arm. A rush of longing swept over her for Annette. *Where is she?* Maybe Annette was tramping around in her wellies, pushing her way through crowds of people, calling Janie's name. But it was so noisy Janie would never hear her. Janie bit her lip. She stared hard at Fergus, hoping he would insist they returned to the safe space where Janie might find her sister. Maybe she could at least ask him to show her the way back and then it was up to Lara whether she stayed with Janie or went off with her brother. She watched Althea speaking in Fergus's ear, plucking up the courage to ask him. But he looked to have made a decision.

'Okay then, I give in,' he said. 'You can come with us,

but you'll probably be disappointed. And you have to behave yourselves, we've got a bit of business to attend to. Now look, it's getting really crowded around here. Keep your eyes on us. Hold onto each other and don't get lost in the crowd.'

'Yeah! Cool, man.' Lara seemed more than ever a stranger. Her hair was escaping and she pulled the scarf from her head, pretending to lasso Janie with the long rope of silk. Her corkscrew hair sprang in every direction, given life by the rain.   Janie stepped back and bumped into two or three close-packed people who nudged her in return, in a friendly way, but for a second the sky pressed down on her and she felt alone and tiny. Her dolls were at home, tucked in at the end of her bed. They suddenly seemed appealing company. At home they would've had their Saturday night fish and chips and would be watching *The Generation Game*. Annette would have gone out with Mary, after the inevitable argument about what time she'd be home.

The music blaring between different live bands paused and the speakers crackled for another announcement – she'd heard several throughout the day.   Annette had told her earlier that the voice was John Peel from the radio. *Would* Simon (said the announcement) – *that's* Simon Ostridge – *come to the release tent please? Your friend* Richard *is having a bad trip.*

A bad trip. She had an idea that was something to do with drugs.

Mum and Dad would be frantic. Especially if they knew she'd lost Annette. Janie stuck close to Lara's side as she had no choice but to follow Fergus and his friends through the jam-packed crowd. If she recognised the crash tent she could dive inside it, no doubt to find an angry-yet-relieved Annette waiting for her, but it would be worth it to *not* hear her own name called over the speakers. She wouldn't know where to find the release tent anyway, or even what it was.

'I don't want to be stuck in no boring crash tent,' said Lara, as if she could read Janie's thoughts. She grabbed Janie's hand again. 'Hey, look over there – foam fight!'

Lara was right. White foam was being pumped from a massive tube attached to a machine on a lorry. The lorry had parked a distance away from the prison-style metal perimeter fence. Foam flew high in the air and spurted outwards into the crowd. People had started charging into the middle of it. They grabbed handfuls and flung it into each other's faces. Janie saw a man strip naked. She watched, her eyes stretching wider and wider at the sight of his *thing* swinging from side to side while he ran into the foam. Then he slipped in the mud and fell flat on his face. Foam enveloped him. When it felt like he'd really been down too long (perhaps he'd drowned in the foam?) he scrambled onto his hands and knees and crawled out, mud and foam plastered all over his body and face. Janie felt sick.

'Come on!' shouted Lara. She dragged Janie along with her, towards the giant custard-pie foam pit.

'No,' Janie tried to shout out. 'I don't want to!' but Lara wasn't listening. Janie pulled back, digging the heels of her wellingtons into the mud until the feet of her boots were completely covered, but still she was dragged forward.

'Stop it, I don't want to.'

Someone grabbed her parka hood. She was being pulled both ways, thinking she might choke. But Fergus's hand reached past her and grabbed Lara's hood as well. Lara was pulled up short. Fergus let go of Janie and gave her a curt nod. His tone was furious when he spoke to his sister.

'You know what, Lara? I'm getting sick of your defiance. I told you to stay close behind me and what do you go and do? The exact opposite! I've a good mind to give you a good hiding...' but Althea appeared at his side. She grasped his hand and pulled it down between them.

'No need for that, baby.'

Janie, who'd been on the point of tears, swallowed them down. Fergus was scary but Althea sounded so tender with her boyfriend. What must it be like to love someone like that? She was struck by the fact Fergus wasn't much older than Annette, yet he was fully responsible for Lara. With no Mum and Dad at home, it must be hard. She knew Annette found it frustrating when she was left in charge of her and she played up because it was funny to test Annette's limits. Janie examined Fergus from a new perspective. He must often want to get on with his own stuff instead of having to think about his sister.

A short distance away the white foam continued spraying from the machine. People were going crazy; the noise was astonishing! But Fergus didn't seem to notice how fun it could be.

'Give your brother a break, hey, honey?' Althea said in a low voice to Lara. She must spend a lot of time soothing tensions between them. 'Now, you want us to show you the way back to that crash tent with all the straw in, or are you coming with us?'

The crash tent, please, Janie mouthed.

Lara's lower lip trembled. 'With you,' she said in a sullen voice.

'Okay then,' Althea spoke as if she was Lara's mother. 'You come on now and don't get into any more trouble, huh? How about you Janie – you want to come with us or shall I take you back and see if we can find your sister?'

Lara's eyes fixed on Janie, pleading. She looked so lonely Janie took pity on her. She gave Lara a reassuring smile, despite the swishy feeling inside her.

'I'll come with you.'

'Thanks,' Lara's gratitude made Janie feel warm. 'And I'm sorry for trying to force you to do that.' She jerked her chin back at the foam. 'Sometimes I get overexcited and I just kind of want to do something stupid. It helps me forget bad things. Do you know what I mean?'

'Yeah, 'course I do. I get overexcited as well. My mum's always telling me...' *Poor Lara.* Janie couldn't imagine not having a mother.

'Don't stop,' Lara tugged Janie's sleeve. She linked her arm through Janie's and pulled her close as they walked behind the others. 'Tell me about your mum. What does she say about you?'

'Oh. Just that I get overexcited and it will end in tears.' Janie's cheeks burned. She felt childish in comparison to motherless Lara.

'You two wait over here a minute,' Fergus directed them to a row of straw bales outside the *Giants* tent. He pushed his sister down onto one. Janie shuffled up close beside her. Lara opened her mouth to protest at being manhandled by Fergus but a look from her brother made her shut it again.

'Have you still got your animals?' Janie asked, to distract her. She closed her fingers around the pony in her pocket and brought it out with a whinnying sound to make Lara laugh. 'I know they're babyish, but I love them. I'm going to buy a special box to keep them in.'

Lara sniffed. 'Velvet-lined?'

'Yeah, velvet-lined.'

'What colour velvet?'

'Hmm.' Janie considered. 'Midnight blue, I think.'

'Mine will be rose-red,' Lara decided. 'What will your box be made of – carved wood or embossed metal?'

'Oh, let me see... carved wood. Dark-stained.' Teak, like the wall cabinet in the living room.

'Mine will be embossed metal. Pewter, which is darker than silver. They sell boxes like that at Walthamstow market. You should come and stay with us and I'll take you. You'd love all the market stalls; they sell everything from boring stuff like dishcloths and cleaning liquids to all sorts of amazing clothes. You know, like Indian saris and African headdresses? Paintings and handicrafts, too. Like the boxes we're going to have. And wooden animals. You could get some wooden animals to go with your glass collection.'

Janie's mouth had fallen open. 'That would be so brilliant. Would you really like me to come?' She couldn't imagine anything more exciting than going to stay with a friend in London. What would Sally say? On the other hand, Mum would never let her stay in the flat of a girl who lived with her older brother and no parents. And it was London and Lara was black so Dad would mutter about the riots on TV. Her parents were so *square*.

22

Janie, 1972

What had happened to Fergus and the others? Janie scanned the flux of moving figures so intently it was like looking into a floodlit kaleidoscope. The sky had turned ominously dark. She stopped searching and closed her eyes. When she opened them again she spotted Fergus and his friends, standing with some others against the tent wall. Janie strained to see more clearly. She counted three extra black men and two other black women as well as a young white man and an older white woman with rats' tails for hair. Vincent leaned in angrily towards one of the strangers. Janie saw Fergus handing out sheets of paper, about the size of her school exercise books.

'What are they doing?' she asked Lara.

'What?' Lara screwed up her eyes and followed Janie's pointing finger. 'Oh, those are Fergus's newsletters.'

'Newsletters? What about?'

'Just information he's gathered. He's carrying on our dad's work.'

'But I thought your dad. . .' Janie bit off her words. The glass pony dug into her palm.

'Yeah, my dad got deported,' Lara sounded out of breath. 'Like I said, he was only sticking up for his rights. You wouldn't understand, Janie. You don't know what it's like to be black. The pigs are on your back all the time, especially boys like Fergus. What do you expect him to do?'

Janie slipped the pony back in her pocket and jammed her hands up her coat sleeves, suddenly feeling cold. Lara was right, she didn't understand. Where had her friend's sudden anger come from?

'I'm sorry,' Lara tucked her chin into her neck. 'I shouldn't have shouted. It's not your fault.'

'It's okay.'

But Janie *really* wished Annette would descend on her at that moment. She could shout in her face and give her a Chinese burn and Janie wouldn't care. Her fingers played around her wrist where there was still a faint red mark from the one Annette gave her when she wouldn't get up that morning – so many hours ago. Another day. Another *life*. It was night-time and she hadn't seen her sister for hours and hours. Her breath hitched and a sob broke loose.

'Aw, don't cry.' Lara put her arm around Janie's shoulder. 'You'll get used to my bad temper. I don't mean anything by it, honestly. Here, d'you want to borrow my hanky? I haven't used it, so it's perfectly clean.'

'Thanks,' Janie noticed her hand shaking as she took the hanky from Lara. When this happened at home Mum would make her have a drink of water or put the telly on to distract her. Or she'd open the high cupboard in the kitchen and lift the biscuit tin down. '*You can have two*,' Mum would say, when normally they were only allowed biscuits at teatime. '*Your blood sugar must be getting low*.' And it always helped. But there were no biscuits now and no Mum to comfort her and this time the hand started shaking harder and harder. It had never shaken that badly before. She scrunched the

hanky in her fist and bumped it against her nose. *Focus,*
Mum would say. *Look, here's your horse book. Which one's
your favourite? That foal on page twenty, isn't it?* But Mum's
words fell out of her head and there were too many people
and too much movement and noise to focus on anything.
Cold water tingled in her brain and trickled down into her
face and neck. Ice froze in her chest. She tried to keep her
thoughts straight. *Annette.*

Janie had lost her *forever.* Annette must have returned to
the crash tent – eventually – and found Janie wasn't there.
So now she must be wandering the vast fields, packed full of
people, in the darkness – searching for Janie and calling her
name. Annette would be frantic. At home their parents had
probably called the police, Annette would get arrested. It was
all Janie's fault.

Janie couldn't stop crying. She'd soaked the hanky and
Lara would be cross. She wanted *Annette.* She wanted *Mum.*
She just wanted to go home.

Help, I can't breathe!

'Hey girls, what's going on – what's the matter with her?
Lara, what happened?'

'Aww, Janie, it's all right, don't worry.'

'Janie! Stop it, calm down. You're getting yourself into a
state. Janie!'

'What the hell's the matter with her? Calm her down for
heaven's sake, we're drawing attention.'

'Janie, Janie!'

All those voices calling her name but none of them
Annette. Janie was scared of Fergus, she'd seen the way he
would have hit his sister if Althea hadn't stopped him. They
were all crowding around her now, Fergus and Althea and
Vincent with his sinister smile, and the others. She threw
herself around and fought for escape.

'Let me go!'

'Janie! Now what's all this, honey? Stop crying and tell us
what the problem is.'

Someone – she thought Althea – was trying to pull her into a hug but she lashed out and pushed her away. Tried to shove her way out of the protective circle and make a break for freedom – to *find Annette*. Her eyes were blind with tears and she knew she was being stupid but that only made it worse. She couldn't stop. She couldn't breathe. She needed to get *out* and crawl into a hole and close her eyes and never wake up. She kept flailing her arms and bawling, because it was somehow comforting to do that and put off the embarrassment as long as possible.

Soothing voices and gentle hands turned to shouts of anger and rough jostling. Through swollen eyes she saw Lara fall. Panic screamed in her head as the sheltering wall was torn apart by aggressive hands and she became aware of black uniforms: coppers with hats and truncheons. Now she reached out for Lara and Althea, for those who felt familiar amidst this new sense of dissonance, but someone had hold of her arm. She called her friend's name, forcing it from her clogged throat but Lara didn't seem to hear. Close by, she heard a dull crack. A shout of pain, almost in her ear. Something warm and wet touched her. What was that? *What was that?* Blood sprayed onto her hand. She swung around and saw Fergus being dragged away through the crowd. A gash on his forehead spilled dark liquid into one of his eyes. 'Lara,' he called, his heels ploughing runnels in the mud. 'Lara!' Althea screamed and tried to run after him but she was grabbed and held in place. Janie's stomach curdled.

A policewoman had hold of her. 'Stop fighting, love,' she said. 'You're safe now, we've got you. You're all right.'

23

Annette, 1972

He sang *Suzanne*; surely only for me. I jammed my hands between my knees because I didn't know what else to do with them. He said it was a Leonard Cohen song and I resolved there and then to rush straight to the record section before I started work next Saturday. I'd grab myself a Leonard Cohen record. I'd probably drive Janie mad playing it over and over in our room, but she'd better keep her mouth shut because I wouldn't want any interruptions to the thoughts I'd be having about Justin Christian.

When he finished his set, some people left to go and listen to Average White Band and some moved closer to the front to wait for the next folk act. Two or three girls pushed their way in front of me to get their autograph books signed by Justin. I wasn't sure what to do next. I knew Janie'd be all right because she was with that girl, Lara. And they'd said Lara's brother was bringing them food so I needn't worry about her getting hungry.

I fiddled with the end of my plait; resisted the urge to pop it in my mouth. Mum said I'd get a hairball in my stomach and die if I sucked my hair. Instead I brushed it over the veins that showed faintly under the skin of my hand, pretending I was painting a portrait of Justin Christian. My legs were cold and I wished I'd worn my jeans. Not least because straw was bloody scratchy to sit on – it must've made a criss-cross pattern on the backs of my thighs. I didn't want to look and draw attention to the goose-pimples I was sure were also there.

The last of the laughing girls got her book signed. I noticed how patiently Justin dealt with them and gave each one a big smile. At the same time I just knew he was strongly aware of me waiting in the background. *Good things come to those who wait*, as Mum was always saying. And it was true, 'cause he stepped towards me after the girls left. They gave me funny looks and one of them nudged into me as she passed, no doubt jealous. Not surprising, really. I righted myself but it still felt like there was a stormy sea in my head as my feet carried me forwards and our hands did a kind of dance before they met in the air and shook each other, quite formally.

24

Justin, now

Justin sat with his head in his hands. Chants of "pervert" and "paedophile" came from the street outside, and the rocking of the bus only made his already-delicate insides feel worse. Andy emerged from the bathroom, looking sicker than Justin felt. *Remember what you always do*, he told himself, studying his shaking hands on the table. *Look Andy directly in the eyes*. Andy dabbed at his face with one of the seemingly-endless supply (who kept replacing them?) of rolled flannels from the bathroom, rinsed it again and squeezed it over the kitchenette sink, before folding it in two and laying it on the draining board with apparent great care. Finally, he turned to face Justin.

'Don't forget you have an appointment in twenty minutes, Boss.' He folded his arms across his stomach.

Sliding out from the seat, Justin reached forward to grasp Andy's elbows in his two hands and manoeuvred his face in front of him, to ensure Andy had to look him in the eye.

'Speak to me,' he said in a voice more confident than he felt.

133

While he held Andy's gaze, he was at the same time nudging his way through a crowd at the Great Western Express Festival. Annette was holding his hand and he had his guitar slung across his back. Average White Band were setting up on the main stage. From the corner of his eye he was aware of a fresh sprinkling of raindrops on Annette's hair. She felt light as a feather in his grip, an elfin presence. Perhaps they were under a bewitchment – it was the only way he could explain what was happening. . .

In the present Andy coughed and allowed his gaze to drop from Justin's face.

'It's not you, Mr C. I don't believe a word those bastards say about you. They're afraid you're going to win, and they'll do whatever it takes to knock you down and trample all over you.'

Justin let go of Andy's elbows and the driver rubbed his hands over his face.

'You can explain the truth of the story behind that headline or not, sir,' Andy continued. 'It's up to you. I didn't run into the bathroom because of you. It was the headline itself. It brought back some horrible memories, that's all.'

Justin waited, angling his head to show he was listening. Outside, the crowd seemed to have organised themselves into a single chant, sing-song and with a flawless rhythm that as a musician he couldn't help but admire. *'Don't let him in! Paedos mustn't win!'* Standing there, he'd begun to tap his fingers along to the rhythm on the tabletop, before he realised what he was doing, and curled his fingers into his palm.

Out of the blue, it occurred to him that he didn't have to put up with this. Politics had become a bitter game of obfuscation and muck-throwing. He pictured his allotment and the fresh, wholesome vegetables and fruit he made sure Ivy got for her baby. Precious Olivia. What a world to bring her into. *The world has become | A huge experiment, gone wrong. . .* Perhaps music was the path he *should* have taken to try and get his ideas across after all. Was it too late? His phone was going mad, on the table. He was surprised his team hadn't sent in bodyguards to extract him from the bus and explain himself.

'Will you be going over to the hotel for your meeting, sir?' Andy straightened his back. Justin could see rawness on Andy's face – it hadn't been there before this whole thing with the headlines. He made a decision. *Fuck the meeting.*

'Actually no, I'm not, Andy. Sit down a minute while I pour you a coffee, will you? And I'll have another one myself as well. Here you go. Now, if you'll excuse me a moment while I just let my secretary know I'm cancelling the meeting. And my appearance this afternoon, too, for that matter.' He sat at the table opposite Andy, clicking away on the touchscreen phone that had taken him so long to get used to. 'There, that's done. Now, are the doors of the bus securely locked? No-one can get in from the other side?'

Andy snapped his jaw shut. He must be astonished that Justin was cancelling an appearance in a safe seat.

'They are, sir.'

'Good. It's not that mob outside I'm bothered about, you know. In fact. . . ' Justin reached over and drew back the curtain. 'There. Let them gawp at me as much as they want, and lose their voices chanting stupid slogans. I've got nothing to be ashamed of.'

'Of course not, Mr C.' Andy took a sip of black coffee. Justin believed in his friend's sincerity.

'I just don't want any of my lot from the hotel coming in and interrupting us,' Justin said. 'Now, tell me what got you so upset when you saw the headline. You mentioned it brought back horrible memories?'

Andy placed his cup on the table. 'My daughter, sir.'

'You don't have to call me sir,' Justin said. 'Call me Justin. Or Mr C, if you prefer. I didn't know you had any children. What happened to your daughter?'

The white-knuckled man had reared up to the window again, but Justin fought every self-protective instinct and ignored him.

'What happened to your daughter?' he asked Andy again.

'She disappeared. Ten years ago.' Andy picked at his crisp, white shirt sleeve and chewed his lower lip. The man outside had fallen back from the bus window and was rubbing his elbow, casting angry glances at Justin. As he turned and bent his head to examine whatever was causing his discomfort, with his back to Justin – the newspaper tucked under his arm – Justin noticed a swastika tattooed on the back of his neck.

'Disappeared,' Andy said. 'She was only four. We were shopping in a supermarket and my wife and I got into a mild argument about whether we should allow her a brand of sugary cereal. She'd had a sleepover at her grannie's – my mother's – and been given it there. We discovered later that Lucy had taken a box off to the checkout, all by herself. The checkout assistant asked the people in the queue who Lucy belonged to and a woman who'd just finished packing her shopping claimed her. Witnesses said Lucy went with her under her own steam. The woman paid for the box of cereal and let Lucy carry it out of the shop.'

Justin swallowed. 'And – what? I mean, there were witnesses and yet you never saw your daughter again?' It was incomprehensible. 'What about CCTV?'

'The camera outside the shop didn't get a clear picture of the woman, only a back view. It picked up the registration number of the car Lucy got into with her – quite willingly, it seems – but it turned out to be a rental. She travelled with Lucy to Dover, where she boarded a ferry.' Andy rubbed his face. 'Records showed she carried a child's passport as well as her own. The car was returned to a sister-company in France and the police said the woman could have taken Lucy anywhere in Europe, or beyond.' Andy pushed his hair back with a shaking hand. 'But what made it worse – if anything could make something so terrible worse, sir – Mr C – before the police had even searched through the CCTV footage, the newspapers got hold of my photo and tried to make out *I* had something to do with Lucy's disappearance. It nearly broke my wife and me.'

'I'm so sorry,' Justin said, feeling sick. 'No wonder the headline upset you.' He wanted to begin making promises about enhancing the powers of police to search for stolen children abroad, but realised they'd be empty. And suddenly, something crumpled inside him. He might never be in a position to do that, anyway. Andy's story moved him deeply. Love, family, caring for each other and anyone more vulnerable than yourself; that was what counted, not scoring political points. The thing inside him that had crinkled and curled up on itself opened out again, transformed. A plant bearing new flowers. *Can it really be this easy to decide?* He patted Andy's hand, and stood up.

'I'll do everything I can to help you find Lucy again,' he said. 'I promise you. I have a contact in a charity based in France that works on cases like this. Right now,' he told his friend, 'I'm going outside to make a statement.'

Andy coughed. 'Shouldn't you wait for your personal secretary and your press secretary to advise you on what to say, first?'

'No,' Justin said. 'God, no. I know what they'd say.' He collected the clean, ironed (Andy's doing, as he knew Justin never bothered) shirt from the hanger in the nook outside his bed-cubicle and shrugged it on over his white t-shirt. He gave Andy one of his crooked grins and cast his eyes over the interior of the bus.

'I feel like I've just had an epiphany.' He left the top two buttons of his shirt unfastened, symbolic of the decision he'd unwittingly made. 'This won't take long. Best put another pot of coffee on, and how about that slice of toast you promised me – in fact make it two – I think I'm going to need it after this. Wish me luck!'

He put his hand up as Andy ventured to protest, and moved carefully past the rows of seats, his legs like jelly. He made sure to straighten his back, tie or no tie. He waited in the lobby of the bus until Andy pressed the button to open the doors. Straightening his shoulders again, and looking the crowd directly in their eyes, he opened his mouth to speak.

25

Annette, 1972

We held on for much longer than you normally do when shaking hands.

'Great of you to come back and see me again,' he said. 'I thought you would've had enough of me earlier.'

'It's okay,' I said. 'I wasn't doing anything else in particular.' A muscle in his cheek flickered and I realised how mean that sounded but it was too late to take it back. I coughed nervously.

'Are you all right?'

I discovered I was still gripping his hand, while holding my other over my mouth. I nodded.

'Just a frog in my throat.'

'Maybe it's the straw. Are you allergic?' I shook my head. Somehow we were holding hands in the normal way now, our arms hanging down between our two bodies. I didn't see any reason to let go. A group were setting up their instruments and while we stood there, people pushed in through the main entrance, raindrops splashing off their hair and coats as they shook them and stamped mud off their feet. Without any discussion, Justin and I made our way out into the rain, which seemed to be easing off again. He had his guitar on his back and I could feel it bumping gently against my right shoulder as we picked our way through the crowds and between stalls selling t-shirts and badges. Briefly, I thought about Janie, but she'd be pigging whatever food Lara's brother had brought them by now. Probably even finished and having another nap among the straw bales. Janie often acted sluggish after dinner. She'd be okay for another half-hour or so, I reasoned.

'Do you want to get a drink?' Justin asked, fastening my fingers more securely in his as we negotiated an obstacle course of prone bodies and makeshift tents.

'All right.'

We made our way through an opening in a crowd of rockers, which closed behind us like the Red Sea. Or was it the Dead Sea? The pungent smell of sweat and smoke filled my nostrils as we broke out the other side.

A tickle rippled through my stomach when I glanced sideways at Justin and I could feel the corners of my mouth turning upwards. I couldn't believe this was happening – after everything I'd gone through to get to this festival – here I was holding hands with one of the musicians! I'd be able to point out his name on the programme and make up a story for all the girls at school. I didn't dare hope I might ever be able to see him again.

'I know the best van to go to,' he said. 'We can get a hot dog as well, if you like.'

'Yeah, ta.' I grinned, gave his hand an involuntary squeeze. He squeezed mine in return, and I saw a blush creeping over his face, but only from the corner of my eye. I was careful not to look at him directly. Concentrating too hard on unfamiliar sensations, I slipped in the mud at the edge of a path that had been worn through the grass on the way to the stage.

'Are you okay?' Justin grabbed my elbow.

'Hmm, apart from all this bloody mud spattered up my legs

and all over the back of me skirt. Damn. Look!' I craned my neck to assess the damage.

'I am looking,' Justin said appreciatively.

'Oi, cheeky bugger!' I gave him a playful slap on his arm. Rain had turned the sleeve of his denim jacket a darker blue and it suited the colour of his eyes. It was my turn to blush as I grabbed hold of his arm while I brushed the back of my skirt with my other hand.

'Look,' he said, and I strained to hear as the music became louder with a change of wind direction. A roar of applause filled the air before the gust of wind blew back the other way and it was quiet enough to hear again. This time I noticed a change in his voice that sent fresh shivers up my spine. 'Forget about the hot dog van, there's a massive queue.' I followed the line of his gaze. 'Come back to my tent with me, if you want. There's a tea urn in the main marquee and some food as well, if you're hungry. I can help you dry off.'

'Yeah, all right then.' I had this weird feeling, like the air around us had gone sort of quiet, even though there were loads of people streaming around. I managed to keep my foot inside my welly as I pulled it out of the mud and I shivered, but not from the cold, although the backs of my legs felt damp and uncomfortable. *Should've worn me bloody jeans*, I thought, yet again. Justin brushed a strand of hair away from his face, then it didn't matter anymore about my chilly legs. All I could think was how I wanted to kiss him.

'You're shivering,' he said. 'Come on.' He guided me through a gap between two large market tents. Another round of applause blew over to us from the main stage. Justin must've noticed I had my ear cocked.

'Did you want to go and see the band?' he asked.

'Nah, it's fine. I'd rather go and have a look at where you musicians stay.' *And have a snog.* I leaned into him a bit closer and he slid his arm across my shoulders. 'Me mate Mary's a massive fan of Average White Band, though,' I couldn't resist adding. For some reason this made him stop.

Pulled short, I nearly tripped over again, and more mud splashed my legs.

'Damn!'

'Sorry, it's just – I was wondering – how old are you, Annette? Sorry, I need to ask, that's all.'

'Why, got wicked plans for me, have you?' I must've been blushing. *I wish* . . . I looked him directly in the eye.

'Er, uhm, no. It's not *that*, well, I didn't mean. . . anyway, how old are you? I just need to know before. . . before I take you to my tent.'

'Yeah, okay, I get it. You don't want to be accused of being a child abductor. Anyhow I'm sixteen, nearly seventeen. I could get married if I wanted, so you needn't worry. Oops,' seeing doubt flash across his face – 'don't worry, I'm not going to propose.'

An extra-strong gust of wind blew a spray of raindrops off a flap of polythene nearby. The cold shock on my face made me gasp. Justin smiled and removed his arm from my shoulder.

'Here,' he used his thumbs to wipe drops from under my eyes. 'That's better.'

'Ah well,' I said, recovering. 'I never had a wash this morning – got up too early – so it's a good thing. I did have a bath last night, though,' I added too quickly, and bit my tongue to stop myself saying anything else stupid. He laughed.

'Come on, you.' I had that same weird feeling – like I'd known him ages. We set off again, past some black guys handing out leaflets. I pushed down a small surge of guilt about leaving Janie.

'Are you okay?' Justin must have felt my tension.

I slid my arm around his waist, under the bulk of the guitar. His body felt thin, tenderness turned my insides liquid.

Yeah. Yeah, I am.' I wanted that snog so badly it was hard not to blurt it out.

'You sure you don't want to stay and watch the band?'

'No. I want to be with you.' We both fell quiet as we crossed another intersection between tents.

'It's in there.' His hand shook as he pointed.

We didn't get a hot dog, or even a cup of tea.

'I don't usually do this kind of thing the first time I meet a girl, I promise you,' Justin broke away from me a moment and looked deep into my eyes. His chest was bare and I buried my fingers in the small thicket of hair between his button-like nipples.

'Me neither.' I kissed him again, brushed silky hair away from his face with the side of my hand. 'Not with boys – I mean men.' Justin was twenty-two. 'You're only my second, if you want to know.' It was hard not to tell him everything, but at the same time I felt there was too much air in my lungs. *Stop talking, Annette.*

'Oh,' Justin moaned. My insides flipped. This foreplay was driving me insane – I wanted him in me, right away. We were lying on the thin mattress he'd dragged down from his narrow camp bed. My hip had knocked against the bed's metal leg and felt sore, but I didn't want to break the intensity by saying anything.

'What are you doing?' The loss of his body pressed against mine left me bereft. Leaning over me, continuing his kisses, his right hand rifled furiously in a rucksack half-under the bed. I reached out and tried to pull him down again.

'Annette, wait. We've got to be careful.'

'What do you mean?'

'I'm looking for a Johnny.' He turned his gaze on the rucksack and let go of me so he could use both hands to start tossing things out of it. 'Damn. I remember now. Bloody hell.'

My body felt cold without him. That grammar school boy hadn't used a rubber. I was sure it would be okay. You had to

143

have sex a few times before you could get pregnant, anyway, right?

'I gave them to a mate,' Justin sounded devastated, kneeling upright. He groaned. 'I didn't know I was going to meet you, did I? And I never thought... Oh, Annette. We can't. I want to so much but we can't do it.' He lay down beside me again, stroking my face. The muscles of his face tightened like he was about to cry. Another wave of tenderness rolled through me. We had to do this, we *had* to. I wanted it to remember him by, guessing life would go back to boring-normal and I might never get a chance to see him again – not until I could escape from home. Mum and Dad would go mad and ground me forever for what I'd done.

I stroked his face in return, fixing a reassuring smile on mine.

'It's okay, I'm on the Pill, silly,' I lied.

26

Annette, 1972

He'd moaned as he came. Being new to the business of sex, I didn't know anything about orgasms but at least it didn't hurt like it had with the grammar school boy. Sitting up afterwards, Justin trailed a finger down the back of my neck inside my open blouse and across the top of my imperfect spine, traced my scar.

'You're so beautiful.'

I laughed. 'A likely story,' but it caught in my throat and I was compelled to turn my head and kiss him.

'Mmm.' He grabbed his t-shirt and pulled it over his head, inserting his arms into the sleeves in one fluid action. I searched ineffectually for my jumper, but he quickly gathered up his denim jacket and drew it around my shoulders instead, feeling in the upper pocket at the same time, like he was trying to fondle me through the fabric.

'Oi,' it tickled. I laughed again and slapped his hand away. 'Cheeky!' I started fastening my blouse.

'Just getting these,' Justin held up a pouch of tobacco and a packet of papers. 'There should be some matches in one of the other pockets. Can you?'

It felt intimate fumbling around in his pockets. I discovered a plectrum, the stub of a pencil and a cotton handkerchief which felt stiff in places. Normally this would have disgusted me but because it was Justin – because the skin of my upper thigh also felt stiff where his stuff was drying on me – it didn't seem to matter. I marvelled at myself. The matches were in another pocket, along with a sheet of paper which, when I took it out and opened it proved to be song lyrics and guitar chords, jotted in pencil. Probably the pencil from the first pocket. I felt they belonged together so I retrieved the pencil and rolled it inside the notebook page, slipping them back into the folds of denim.

'That was the song you were singing at the rehearsal, wasn't it? The one about wanting to render peace and stuff.' Justin nodded. A wavelet lapped inside me, not just desire: affection. I hardly knew him, but it didn't make a difference. He smiled at me. Lit the roll-up and handed it to me first. Breathing it in, the nicotine went straight to my head. I started to imagine how we could become boyfriend-and-girlfriend, but it seemed unlikely what with me still being at school and him a travelling musician. He must do this kind of thing all the time. Just wait 'til I was able to describe it in detail to Mary, who was bound to act all squeamish.

'I've often wondered about going into politics,' Justin said, bringing me back into the present. 'I'd really like to make a difference, you know, to the world. Help people.'

I patted his thigh, suctioned to mine by the wetness that'd come out of us. His pale skin looked vulnerable beneath a layer of hairs. I felt another shiver, deep inside me.

'Don't you think you can make a difference through music? I mean, look at Bob Dylan and all them.' I handed him the roll-up. He took a drag and held it in a moment, before exploding in a cacophony of coughing.

'You okay?' I patted his back. His skin felt hot under the thin cotton of his t-shirt. He carried on coughing, until I started to get worried. 'You okay?' I asked again. He had a sheen of sweat on his forehead.

He nodded, still spluttering, handed me back the cigarette. I looked at it and it didn't seem like such a good idea anymore. I stubbed it out on the metal leg of the camp bed and checked carefully to make sure it was properly dead.

'Are you sure you're all right?'

'Yeah, I'm fine, honestly. Don't worry. I've had a chest infection, that's all. But I'm better now. Hey, listen. I never even bought you that hot dog I promised. And I really need a drink. I bet you do, too. Let's get dressed and go and find something to eat.' He looked shy. I nodded and tried to play it cool. The grammar school boy had described me as "heavy", when I asked if we were going to see each other again.

'Yeah, I'm definitely hungry.' As we separated from each other and I fished around the floor for my jumper and skirt, I was aware of a poised moment: as if, for perhaps a whole second, everything had stopped. The noises of people; the rain and the wind; the bongo drum and the band on the main stage, as well as performers in the Giants of the Future marquee, which was closer by. Nothing. In that moment I remembered Janie, and realised it had been a long, long time since I'd left her. Dread flooded me. Almost at the same moment I heard an announcement over the tannoy, which had been releasing intermittent messages throughout the day. As I took it in I understood what the amplified voice was saying. It was asking for me. For *Annette Woods* to go to the Release tent, where her sister Janie Woods was waiting for her.

I froze. Couldn't believe they would call my name out, in public. That Janie would do that to me. Humiliated at being caught in such a compromising position, I went mad.

'Annette, what are you doing?' I'd scrambled onto my knees

and was throwing clothes about, grabbing the corner of the mattress with both hands, trying to find things underneath it. Where were my socks, my jumper; my knickers? I elbowed Justin out of the way and heaved the mattress back onto the bed. Pounced and dragged on my skirt, pulled my jumper on over my blouse, the buttons done up wrong. The call for me to go to the release tent was repeated over the tannoy. *Shit.* Found my knickers and hopped into them, almost falling over. Could only find one sock. Where were my bag and my furry coat? Justin pulled his jeans on and shrugged into his jacket – the jacket that only moments before had kept me warm and smelled of him. *There it was*, I grabbed my bag, my coat was under it. Justin stared at me, concern in his eyes. He kept trying to place his hand on my arm and calm me down, but I kept batting him off.

'Annette, is it you they're asking for? Is Janie Woods your sister? Annette, talk to me!'

'Yes, she *is* my sister!' I yelled. 'She's thirteen years old and a right cry-baby, and now she'll tell my mum and dad what I did and they're never going to forgive me for this! I'm in so much trouble.'

I pulled away from him – he'd got hold of my arms and was trying to do a special thing he had with his eyes to make me focus on him, only moments before I'd found it intoxicating – and batted my way out of the tent. Well, I tried to, but the canvas ties seemed to be knotted and I couldn't undo them. My bag slipped down my arm and I shifted it up onto my back again, my arms flailing at the tent doorway.

'Help me, I can't get out!'

'It's okay, Annette, calm down. I'll help you.' For a second his voice grounded me but as soon as the door opened I tried to set off again. I wanted to throw myself into the crowd.

'Where is it?' I screeched. 'I don't know the way to the *Release* tent. Janie'll be having a meltdown, I've got to get to her.'

Justin looked white with the shock of my temper. I wanted

to calm myself but I couldn't, not with the thought of Mum and Dad looming over me.

'Stop. Wait here,' Justin's voice was firm. 'I mean it, don't go anywhere. I'm going to find out where the Release tent is and take you there.'

I stood helplessly, hunched over as he slipped through the flaps into the larger tent next to his. I sank into a crouch, hugging my knees. When he came out again he grasped my arm and pulled me upright.

'Come on, I know where it is. You'll be reunited with your sister in no time. Just hold onto me and I'll get you there.' His voice was so kind I could feel my face crumpling again.

He held my arm as he manoeuvred me through the crowds, and steadied me when I slipped in the mud. But his hands felt impersonal and different to when they were touching me in his tent. I felt sad, so sad that I'd ruined everything. Why couldn't I have stayed calm when I heard my name called instead of going mad and ranting at him?

'This way,' Justin said into my ear, grabbing me and pulling me back. He'd let go of my arm for a sec to forge a path through a tight knot of people blocking the way forward, and I'd started to wander off in the opposite direction. I felt dizzy. I always got like that when I was hungry – a bit like Janie, only she was the one who got away with the tantrums. Justin slid his hand through my arm again. 'Nearly there.'

The Release tent was big and crowded but I spotted Janie straight away, sitting at a table on her own. She looked at me slyly from the corners of her reddened eyes when I hurried over, stomping my feet; one welly looser because of having no sock on. She'd have known I was going to scream at her. Justin hung back, but he was taking it all in and his presence behind me felt comforting. Janie put her hands up as if afraid of me, but when it came down to it I only wanted to cry. Janie was safe, but she'd ruined the beautiful time I'd had with Justin and I didn't think he'd ever forgive me. Why should he? None of it was his fault.

'Are you the sister?' A woman wearing a sailor-top like the ones in *The Sound of Music* hurried over from an opposite corner, where I could just see a girl with an afro, wearing an Afghan coat – it was Janie's friend Lara – disappearing into a makeshift booth, shadowed by a policewoman. *What the bloody hell had happened*? Sailor-suit closed her lips tight. She must have seen the way Janie flinched when I arrived. I flicked my plait over my shoulder.

'Yeah. My name's Annette.' Sniffing, I tried to swallow the snot and phlegm in the back of my throat. The woman looked me up and down with a disgusted expression on her face.

'And you left your underage sister alone for...' she consulted her watch. 'Almost three hours?'

I stuck out my chin. 'You seem to know better than me. I lost track of the time. That's all.'

She looked me up and down again, taking in my back-to-front skirt (which I only noticed when her eyes lingered on it – at least it explained why my clothing had felt so odd on the rush over there) and my hastily-pulled-on jumper, my jacket hanging off one shoulder. I realised that my eyeliner and mascara must also be smudged like Janie's. I must have looked a right sight.

'Well, we've called your parents. They've had to go to a lot of trouble because of you. They're on their way over now and will be taking you both home. Come and wait here, please.'

All the breath went out of me and I bent over double. This was the worst day of my life. All the anger and shame I'd taken out on Justin drained down my body, into my legs and over the tops of my welly boots. I just wanted to be back in his arms, lying on his narrow mattress, smiling at each other after what I was convinced would be the best sex of my life. Noticing a photographer prowling around with one of those big cameras (he was probably from the *Echo*) I turned my face away but from the corner of my eye I saw the flash light up a knot of people coming in the entrance. I clutched myself around the waist, struggling for breath. Disgusted, I reminded myself of Janie, hyperventilating and having a meltdown. *Justin*, I wanted to screech. As if he'd heard my silent scream, I saw him taking a step towards me but the woman – who hadn't even introduced herself – put her hand up and a bobby stepped in front of him and stopped him coming over.

It was probably a good thing. He'd never look at me again the way he had in his tent. He was a grown man, and I was only a hysterical schoolgirl – my behaviour had proved that.

27

Janie, now

When the builders had left, Janie stood in the centre of what would become the sitting room – or communal room as she preferred to think of it – and turned around on the spot, lifted her arms like a ballerina on the music box she once rescued from a Flea Market for Juliet. The felt-maker from Taynuilt who'd bought Catmally would probably be making her lunch at this moment in Janie's former kitchen: sunshine-yellow and looking directly out onto the platform. The regular passengers would be waiting for the three o'clock train to Glasgow.

Janie felt a lurch of panic that she would never, ever look out at that view again, with the opposite platform backed by a wall of trees and behind them the steep rise of the mountains. And neither would her children, who were brought up at Catmally. Where would they think of as home, now?

Her hands shook. She stared at them. *Think of something nice.* She focussed on the walls surrounding her, picturing them (after the holes had been filled) painted slate blue, with the deep skirting boards, the dado rail and the plaster cornices (which needed to be repaired – expensive – Janie had it all written down) picked out in brilliant white. The ceiling should be painted cream and the old wooden floorboards stripped down and the grain brought out with cherry-tinted varnish. There was a nice fireplace (wood burning stove or open fire? Annette would probably vote open), and an original wooden surround that ought to be decorated in white gloss. You could fit three decent sofas in the room.

The house was too big for the three of them, though Mum would need a downstairs room. They could take in lodgers, perhaps even become foster carers? But she didn't think Annette would have the patience for children.

Homeless youths though, perhaps. Refugees waiting for their asylum claims to be heard, that had worked well at Catmally. *Gypsies, tramps and thieves* – she imagined Annette saying. But Janie would know what she meant. There must be grants and schemes available. Janie was used to sharing her home with strangers and Annette had lived communally for years. Janie's heart beat a little faster. *This could work, it could really work.* She could get help landscaping the garden – approach the Council, or the Probation service. Get local schoolchildren involved. She rubbed her hands together, the shaking of her limbs lessened, and plans tumbled over each other in her mind.

She took out her new notebook and jotted a few things down. Then she moved into the kitchen and switched on the kettle she'd brought along, dropped a peppermint teabag into a mug. There was nowhere to sit so she leant against a dilapidated cabinet and held the mug directly beneath her nose, breathed in the decongestant steam. She felt as much a wreck as the house. She needed to sort herself out. Don't let *that Paul* win, Mum had remarked, apparently noticing Janie's red eyes as she came out of the bathroom that morning. *You can be more of a woman without him than you were with him.* Mum sometimes came out with gems of wisdom. Pity they'd been few and far between in Janie's adult life.

She carried her tea into the garden. Thank God it was May and not November, as it had been when she moved into Catmally. At least she'd be able to spend a lot of time outdoors while the filthy work was done inside. The trees surrounding the scrubland that currently passed as a lawn – she'd get some grass seeds sown next time she drove out here, probably tomorrow – had burst into leaf. And the blue sky was the colour of possibility. She might even paint her new bedroom in that exact shade. Warm blue, the colour of possibility *and* hope. Her eyes wandered and she planned where she would build the wall for her kitchen garden, use the bricks from one of the derelict outbuildings. There was a load of cardboard in the garage, it would come in useful for laying out her no-dig beds. She could just picture a row of sweet corn over by the fence to the potato field, sashaying and whispering in the breeze. It would be all right, she promised herself. *Everything will be all right.*

Making ready to go back inside, her toe in its canvas slip-on caught against something half-buried in a tuft of grass. After sipping the last of her peppermint tea, she transferred the mug to her left hand and fished amongst the coarse blades with her right. Soil embedded itself under her fingernails, pristine from lack of recent garden work. It was satisfying to see them return to what she thought of as their natural state. She levered the object carefully from the soil, already having worked out what it was, and knowing it could easily break. The one she'd had in her pocket at the festival – just down the road, hard to believe as that was – had broken. Or rather, she'd snapped its neck in two when she was scared and having a meltdown. When she'd got a crowd of people who'd only been trying to look after her, who'd given her the best time of her life, into trouble. Big trouble. To her enduring shame.

She brought the glass giraffe out from its burial ground and closed her eyes as she turned it over in her hand. The same fingers, more than forty years older, that'd snapped her childhood treasure in two, explored this other glass giraffe tenderly. It must have once belonged to another child – possibly a girl of a similar age to herself, who lived in the house she now owned, at the same time as she was having a meltdown in a field not far away. When she was dragged away from Lara by the police: the stickiness of Fergus's blood on her. This felt like the same giraffe, made whole again. Like a sign that she was supposed to have come back.

28

Janie, 1972

'*Laraaa*,' Janie screamed, struggling in the policewoman's arms.

'It's all right, love. We've got you now, you're safe,' said the pig.

'Let go of me! I want Lara!'

'Don't worry, love. We'll find Lara for you.'

The gap between Janie and her friend widened and filled with struggling bodies. Pigs and people with black skin, and a few hippies that had got involved, seemingly protesting. She couldn't see Lara anymore, nor Althea. She'd lost sight of Fergus with his bleeding head, being dragged backwards, his heels ploughing mud. She rubbed her hand, tainted with Fergus's blood, furiously against her parka, over and over. She couldn't understand what had just happened – all she knew was the woman pig was threading her arm beneath both of hers, behind her back – as though she was injured and couldn't walk. The pig pulled her along so fast she had to almost run, clumsy in her Wellington boots. The pig spoke urgently into her radio but Janie couldn't make out what she was saying. She stopped talking and shoved the radio into a pocket on her uniform jacket.

'Come on, love, we'd best get you out of here and see if we can find your mum and dad, eh?'

What? Her mum and dad... didn't these people know she was here – had been here – with Annette? No, of course they didn't. It can't have been Annette that called them. A howl escaped her and she felt so miserable she could die. Where was Annette? Where *was* she?

Abruptly, the pig jerked Janie to one side of the path and a moment later she saw why. Amongst the music, crowd noise and shouting from the chaos she'd been dragged away from (Lara, where was Lara?) she heard what sounded like thunder, then she saw it was a troop of uniformed policemen and policewomen – pigs! – charging in their general direction, brandishing truncheons. Janie screamed.

'You're all right now, love,' Pig-woman said into her ear, pig-breath hot and tickling her neck. Janie shuddered, sobbing. 'You can stop making such a fuss,' her captor continued. 'We'll soon deal with that lot back there, don't worry.'

The herd of pigs charged past them, scattering hippies and rockers to either side of the path. Panting, Janie understood what was happening. *Lara!* She had to go and make sure her friend was okay. It was all her fault – Janie's – she now realised why the police had arrived in the first place. It was because *she* had been making such a fuss. They'd thought she was being hurt. Mum always said if you cry wolf, one day someone's going to believe you. Or was it no-one would believe you because you cried wolf too often? No, *no!* She had to stop them. They'd hit Fergus on the head with a truncheon. Lara had fallen into the mud – she'd seen with her own eyes, why hadn't she made the pigs listen? Lara might be crushed to death or at the very least her beautiful coat would be ruined and it would all be Janie's fault. She felt herself beginning to hyperventilate again, but focussed on the horror of what she'd done. On the knowledge that she had to sort it out. *She* had to stop this. She needed to go and tell the charging pigs that Fergus, Althea and Lara had done nothing wrong.

Janie broke away and dived into a huddle of hippies standing nearby. Amongst the Afghan coats and cheesecloth dresses she caught snatches of phrases such as 'Hey, man,' 'that was heavy,' and 'I thought we were gonna get busted, then!' They didn't seem to notice her. The light from a lantern hanging off a tent roof half-dazzled her, but she spotted the WPC turning a corner, searching for her. She wouldn't expect Janie to head back in the direction of the trouble she believed she'd rescued her from. Janie pushed her way out of the huddle and set off back along the path, sure this was the way the WPC had propelled her. . .

A firm hand grasped her arm and she let out a yelp. It was the same old pig. She was joined by another bobby, grabbing her arm on the other side. They didn't look too friendly. Janie whimpered with shock and pain, but she gulped it down and tried to think about what Annette would do if the pigs got hold of *her*. Stick her chin in the air; that was what she'd do. Mum was always saying Annette acted haughtily. Annette would give them some lip, as well.

'Get your bloody hands off me,' she let out, stopping short at the word pigs, which was what she'd been meaning to say. She needed a poo suddenly, quite badly.

'You're a cheeky little monkey, you, aren't you?' the WPC said, looking as if she was smiling. Bloody cheek.

'Spoilt little madam if you ask me,' the bobby said. 'Come on, let's deliver her to the Release tent and then we can get on with catching some proper criminals, like those bastards back there.'

Janie hoped they had a toilet at the Release tent, whatever that was. All day she'd heard announcements over the speakers asking this person or that person to go there. She felt powerless. Her feet dragged and she kept tripping. By the time they got into a less crowded area she could hardly stand on her own two legs. Off to one side she could see the lights and hear the noise from the foam fight and her insides gripped. If her arms hadn't been held prisoner she would have folded over herself, mourning Lara and the fun they would have still been having together if Janie hadn't been such a sissy. She hoped the Release tent wasn't too far away because she needed a wee now as well, and she didn't think she could hold it in much longer.

'Wouldn't be surprised if her mam was a druggy or something,' she heard the bobby say to the WPC. 'Bloody hippies, they should get their kids taken off 'em.'

'I wouldn't cast aspersions if I were you,' the WPC answered. 'You can get in trouble for that these days, you know. Come on, Cheeky Monkey, we're almost there. You can have a nice cup of hot chocolate if you're good, and we can find your mum and dad and get them to take you home.'

Janie started to cry again, but silently this time. Hot tears soaked her face. She supposed the make-up Annette had applied would have washed away and she must look stupid and babyish, which is what Annette usually called her. No wonder the pigs were treating her like a little kid. Mum and Dad were going to be so angry. Mum would say she'd never trust her again and Dad would seal his lips into a thin line and refuse to speak to her. And as for Annette – when they got hold of her, (if she was ever found) they were going to *kill* her.

The Release tent was crowded and had what looked like a DJ station in one corner. She was escorted to a plastic toilet in its own freestanding cubicle. When she flushed, blue liquid poured into the speckled grey bowl. The smell made her gag and she washed her hands hurriedly and pushed the door open to escape, without drying them.

'Here you are, ducky,' said a woman with frizzy, grey hair and wearing a navy-blue sailor-suit with white piping around the collar. She looked like the children on *The Sound of Music*, only with hairs on her chin. 'You sit here. Would you like a hot drink and we can have a little chat?' Janie found herself nodding. She was so tired.

Not long afterwards she was sitting at a table against the canvas wall, sipping from a plastic mug of lukewarm hot chocolate, telling Sailor-woman her parents' names and reciting their telephone number.

The pig who'd captured her came and sat opposite at the table, next to Sailor-woman. The WPC carried a notebook and a tiny pencil. She screwed up her eyes at Janie.

'All right, now?'

Janie narrowed her eyes back. 'Mm-huh.'

'Okey-dokey. Right.' She tapped the miniature pencil on the open page of her tall, narrow notebook, which Janie noticed opened vertically. 'So. We need to talk about what happened to you back there.'

Janie's insides clenched again. 'What do you mean?'

Pig tapped the mini-pencil on her teeth instead of the notebook.

'Back there, where we rescued you from. You were screaming and struggling. In danger.' She paused. Janie snapped her lips together, tight. She considered saying no comment, because she knew they could take whatever you said and use it against you. Worse still, against Fergus and Althea. But before she had a chance, Pig had another go at her.

'They were trying to kidnap you, am I right?'

Janie unsealed her lips. 'Who?'

Pig's mouth dropped open. 'You know who I mean, what are you playing at, silly girl?' she raised her eyebrows at Sailor-woman and looked back at Janie as if she was some kind of ninny.

'I don't,' Janie said. Deadly serious. She had to be careful not to get her friend's brother into any more trouble. 'Nobody tried to kidnap me. I was with my friends.'

160

'Your friends, what do you mean? Where were your friends? You weren't with any friends when we rescued you. You were with that bunch of... with, well, you know what was happening. You were surrounded by a crowd of people who did not look like your friends, and you were screaming.'

'It was my fault,' said Janie sadly. 'I didn't mean to get anyone into trouble.'

'What do you mean? It wasn't *your* fault.' Pig chewed the end of her stupid pencil and did a different funny-eyebrow thing to Sailor-woman. Sailor-woman patted Janie's hand.

'It's all right. Drink your drink, ducky,' she said.

Janie raised the mug to her lips but her hand was shaking and it was difficult to drink. She lowered the mug again. Half-closing her eyes, she saw Lara falling into the mud, and Fergus dragged away, calling his sister's name.

'They bashed him,' despite her best efforts, her voice was thin and high. 'They bashed him. You lot, you pigs. You bashed Fergus on the head with a stick – I mean with a truncheon. You made him bleed. His blood got on me! It was *your* fault, not mine! What happened to Lara?'

Chocolate spilled out of the mug onto the Formica table. A defensive expression crossed Pig's face; she couldn't deny it. Janie fixed her with a hard, angry stare. Sailor-woman was looking at Pig in a less friendly way now.

'He was acting aggressively,' Pig said.

Janie struggled hard to control her breathing. She gazed at the spreading patch of chocolate on the table. Snatched up one of the biscuits from the plate someone had put in front of them and nibbled it slowly, as Mum had taught her to do when her blood sugar was low. There was no point arguing with the policewoman. The main thing she needed to do was make sure Fergus, Althea and Lara were not in trouble because of her.

'Well?' Pig said.

Janie unclenched her hands. Biscuit crumbs fell into the spilt chocolate and slowly dissolved.

'They were looking after me because... Well, my sister...'
It was no good, she was going to have to drop Annette in it.
She hadn't told Sailor-woman or the police about her sister
up to now, only said she had been at the festival with friends.
Even allowed them to call a false name "Mary" over the
speakers, adding "Whiteband" when put on the spot for a
surname. Now she needed to tell them the truth.

'Yes?' prompted Sailor-woman.

'I met my friend Lara, she was the girl who fell down in
the mud –' She gave her opponent another hard stare, 'in the
crash tent. Lara is here with her older brother and I'm here
– I was here – with my older sister.' Pig threw herself back in
her chair at this revelation, slapping the notebook down on
her knees and letting out a huff of breath. Sailor-woman only
raised two eyebrows of her own and scrabbled for a new sheet
of paper.

'Give us your sister's name, ducky,' she said. 'Her proper
name, this time. And we'll get the DJ to put a call out for her
over the speakers. No wonder *Mary Whiteband* never turned
up to collect you, hey?' When she sniggered it sounded like a
lamb calling for its mother. Janie watched her hand the
sheet of paper with Annette's name on to a young man in a
knitted tank-top who took it over to the other corner of the
busy marquee. Within a few moments she heard Annette's
name being called out, and imagined it travelling over the
tops of tents and people and bands before it reached Annette,
wherever she might be. Janie could hardly remember her
sister's face, the day seemed to have gone on forever. She
rubbed her sore eyes. Didn't have the energy anymore to
worry about Annette's reaction when she was summoned to
the release tent. She transferred her attention back to Pig.

'Anyway,' she continued, 'my sister said I had to go with
her, but I wanted to stay with Lara and then my sister didn't
come back, so Lara's brother and his girlfriend said I could
go with them.' She drew in a snot-blocked breath. 'They were
looking after me!' She leaned forward over the table and

162

looked Pig hard in the eyes again. 'And *you* beat them up!' she shouted it so loudly that several heads in the tent turned towards them. A hurrying woman whose bell bottom hems were soaked in mud paused, a clipboard under her arm, her lips pursed in an unspoken question, directed silently at the WPC.

'All right, all *right*,' W. *Pig* Constable raised her hands in the air as if she was surrendering. 'Perhaps we acted hastily. We only had your safety in mind. After all, you didn't look as if you belonged in that group, and you were screaming. We were *rescuing* you. You ought to be grateful, you silly girl.'

She didn't sound in the least bit guilty about hurting Lara's brother. Another wave of fury surged in Janie's chest.

'I am *not* a silly girl,' she forced her mouth to say, her fingers clenched tightly into fists. 'But I know what *you* are. You're a racist, that's what.' It suddenly felt as if Annette had invaded her head. Leaning so far across her upper body was almost lying in the spilt chocolate (and she didn't care) she added: 'A racist pig.'

There was a shocked silence, as if the whole festival had heard what Janie had said, but in reality the silence was only in Janie's head. Everyone else carried on as normal, except the WPC, who pushed her chair backwards and stood up.

'That's it,' she said. 'You're not a very nice little girl, I'm afraid, and I'm sorry we rescued you. I should have left you where you were. Clearly the wrong sort of company has rubbed off on you.' Her eyes flicked over the backs of Janie's hands, curled into fists on the table. Janie glanced down and noticed how grubby her skin was. She drew in a sharp breath, but bit her lips together to stop herself saying anything else. The policewoman stomped away and was soon swallowed by a throng at the entrance to the marquee. Sailor-woman frowned so hard a deep ravine appeared in her forehead, making it look cut in two.

'Why don't you finish the last bit of your hot chocolate, ducky?' she said. 'It's always sweeter at the bottom of the cup. Hopefully your sister will be here soon, and your parents must be on their way by now as well.' Janie shuddered at the thought of the look she knew would be on her mother's face. And *Annette*. But she raised the mug to her lips and sipped at the cold sweetness, her brain racing, wondering if Lara would ever allow her to say sorry for what she'd done.

Sailor-woman patted her shoulder. 'You'll be all right here on your own for a moment, won't you? It looks like I might be needed over there. Just stay here now, won't you? Promise me?'

Janie's racing brain took a moment to process what Sailor-woman had said, but by that time the social worker had risen from her seat and was moving away. Janie gripped her mug, sticky with spilt liquid, feeling abandoned. Her eyes roved the constant movement of people in the shadow-decorated tent interior until she pinpointed the white piping on the navy top and followed the direction it was heading in.

Lara!

Lara. Standing by the marquee door with Althea, who was holding her close. A policewoman – different from Janie's captor – stood next to Lara on her other side. Lara looked defiant, but underneath, scared and miserable. Janie's view of her became blocked by the back of Sailor-woman and she found herself leaping to her feet, the final dregs of her now-cold drink oozing onto the table. She screamed Lara's name.

'Lara, *Lara*. Lara, I'm sorry!'

But Althea had tightened her arm around Lara, leading her away, and Lara, her head having whipped round at the sound of Janie's wail, cast hateful looks back over her shoulder. It hurt, but Janie knew it was her own fault. She'd ruined *everything*. Destroyed her friend's *life*. She still had Lara's address in her pocket; she'd try and make things right again. It must be possible. It *must* be. They'd had the beginnings of a real friendship before Janie broke it, just like she'd broken the glass giraffe. Standing alone, shaking and sobbing, she closed her fingers around the precious slip of paper, not even caring about the dismembered, once-favourite animal. What Mum was constantly saying hit home for the very first time: her behaviour had as much effect on others as it did on herself. Trying to calm herself, she made a promise that she would never, ever again allow one of her stupid tantrums to take her over like that.

29

Annette, now and then

Now

Feeling cold despite the sunshine, I grabbed me jacket from the peg in Mum's porch and stood outside the house to have a smoke. My mobile was in the coat pocket and I turned it over repeatedly, trying to pluck up the courage to call him. He'd be going mad. Not on the outside, but he would inside. He didn't deserve this.

I hadn't actually spoken to Justin for years but we diligently kept up-to-date with each other's contact details in case we ever needed to be in touch. The last time was when he'd texted to let me know about. . . well, it was the second thing I wanted to put out of my mind. The aspect of my secret that added insult to injury, so to speak.

What could I do about *this* crisis, though? One thing was for sure, I couldn't let his career be put in jeopardy over a lie, even if it was just an implied one. Justin knew nothing about Janie when I agreed to go with him to his tent at the festival. And he was caring enough to go with me to fetch her when they called my name over the tannoy, even though I went mad at him. He could easily have stayed out of it and then this wouldn't be happening now. He tried to help, just like I'd observed him doing from a distance all these years.

I took a furious puff of my ciggie, wondering what time Janie would be home. I tried hard to conjure a tangible memory of my real home, back in Ireland, but it was like one of those fairytales where everything goes up in a puff of smoke. The Wicked Witch had magicked the memory of my home away. Only trouble was, I didn't know which one of us was the witch – me, Mum or Janie.

I took the last few drags of my roll-up, holding the smoke in my lungs. My head swam. Pain flared in my fingertips as the ciggie burned down to my skin. *Damn!* I let go of the glowing stub and ground it with the heel of the loosely-fitting Birkenstocks I was wearing – Janie's, probably – into the mossy concrete outside Mum's front door. Someone should probably give the front path a clean, I thought. The fence at the end was looking rickety as well. Bending to retrieve the tab from the ground set me off coughing. I shuffled over to the bin in Janie's stupid clogs and dumped the tab in it, checking to make sure it was definitely out – I could imagine the look on Nicholas's face if I set Mum's place on fire. Then I grabbed my phone and scrolled down until I found Justin, pressed *call* without thinking about it too much. It rang eight times, then clicked into voicemail. I felt sick as I heard his voice again, after so many years, saying he wasn't available right now but I should leave a message and he'd get back to me as soon as he could. It sucked me backwards to when I had to get in touch with him before, more than two years after the festival.

Then

He'd already changed his name to Justin Citizen by then and was no longer a practising musician – said he didn't have time.

He worked in a legal aid office. Turned out he lived not far away from me in North London (where I had a room in a squat) but by that time I was about to move on – which was why I needed to see him. I was no longer the naïve lass who'd slept with him at the festival. A bit of a hard bitch, as a matter of fact. How I saw myself, anyway. A fighter. That was why the tears that stung my eyes surprised me. I wiped them away on my sleeve, hoping he hadn't noticed, but of course he had. His face was open still, just as I remembered it. Pain flared in my chest. *Those blue eyes*, so familiar.

'You look different,' he said once we'd sat down in the café on the green – as good a place as any for our meeting. Both of us over-stirred our teas.

Yeah, hard-faced, you mean, I thought. Well, I'd had to be, hadn't I? About to turn nineteen, I was making the second-most-ginormous decision of my life. I'd known I'd be able to make up my mind as soon as I saw him, and I wasn't let down by the memories. That he was a decent bloke. We'd been sitting there a few minutes before I turned around, confused, thinking I could hear *Suzanne* playing on the tinny radio on the counter, whereas it was actually a song by The Beatles.

We small-talked for a few minutes more, before he told me about how his career-plan had changed in the Release tent at the festival. Reminded me of the commotion we'd heard that turned out to be a young black man, Lara's brother, being brought in by the police. *Dragged* in. He had a bandage around his head and you could see blood seeping through it. At that moment Lara burst out of a canvas booth and threw herself against her brother's body. Then Janie started screaming, hurling herself towards the policeman who had his forearm across the front of the brother's neck. 'You pig, you pig,' she was shouting. I had to check it was really her. I was so gobsmacked I couldn't move but Justin dodged between two coppers and took hold of her arms, trying to get her to look in his eyes in that way he had. Trying to calm her. That bloody photographer got a snap of the two of them like that. I hoped to God the photo would never make it into the Echo.

In the café Justin told me he'd heard Janie sobbing, things like 'I've got to sort this out,' and 'They were only looking after me.' He said he quickly put two-and-two together and offered to arrange legal representation for Lara's brother. He'd said goodbye to me then but I was too ashamed of myself to meet those blue eyes of his. 'I'll call you,' I heard him say just before he turned to demand the use of a telephone for a solicitor. By that time Janie'd attached herself to me like a limpet.

I never saw Justin again after he went marching off with a policeman, but I remember an article in a national paper a month or so later, with Justin's photo included. It had been taken in the Release tent and showed him looking angry and waving his arms around. The headline read *Just-in-time for justice. Christian values at a pop festival.* The police'd had the nerve to try and prosecute Lara's brother, Fergus, for getting in the way of their truncheon, but Justin made sure justice prevailed.

In the café I swallowed at the sight of his safe, reassuring hands curving around the white porcelain and burned inside with deep regret I hadn't got in touch with him sooner. At what we'd both missed out on. He said he was planning to get into politics, but first wanted to do something in "real life". I wanted to cry, but not because my life was bloody difficult. He was so *good*. I wondered how it might have been between us if I hadn't rejected his phone call (he'd looked up my parents' phone number and address in the local telephone directory after the festival). He told me in the café that he'd only wanted to make sure I was all right. I never got to see any of the letters he said he'd sent – apparently there were three – what did Mum do with them? I put the phone down the one time I heard his voice, too ashamed of the childish way I'd behaved at the festival. And things were bad at home at the time. He told me he'd rung again but a woman answered and said I wasn't available, and not to call anymore.

I wouldn't have spoken to him anyway. My lack of control had convinced me I really *was* a child, and it was obvious he was too mature for me. I should just let him get on with his life, unknowing of the course mine was about to take.

Less than two months later I was living in London, washing pots in a restaurant, but it felt too late to get back in touch by then. I'd let my chance pass me by.

'So what have you been doing with yourself?' Justin asked, giving me that intent gaze. I'd run out of questions to ask him. 'It's really nice to see you. Thank you for tracking me down, I always...' He left the sentence hanging. I chewed my lip and studied the way his eyelashes cast shadows on the tops of his cheeks. His soft brown hair was shorter than I remembered. Outside on the grass a flock of pigeons suddenly swooped down from the trees. A bell pinged as the café door was pushed open by a big man in a black donkey-jacket, and crashed closed, over-hard, behind him. Justin and I followed the man with our eyes as he trod heavily across to the counter. His hands were oil-stained and the smell of cigarette smoke drifted around. I couldn't speak. Justin turned his attention back to me.

'You said you've been living in London, too.' He gave me a big smile, looking directly into my face. I met his eyes but I was the first to drop my gaze. I lowered my cup gently to the table, it was no use prevaricating any longer. But I struggled to speak – I twisted my hands together, searching for the right words. Eventually I managed to force something out.

'Uhm, err. There's something I really wanted to talk to you about.'

I tried not to let feelings get in the way of my decision. My plan would be best for everyone concerned. And it would be easier to carry it out now, than later on.

30

Justin, now

The door hissed as it closed behind him, sealing him into the bus again. The sound erased the details of what he'd just said to the people outside. Cameras flashing in his eyes – judgements, criticisms – he'd be so glad to be finished with all that. *What a relief.* He pictured his allotment. Perhaps he would travel – freely – not under someone else's orders. Perhaps he'd spend longer with his guitar in his sunshine-filled kitchen in the mornings. Maybe he'd finally get to have that talk with Ivy that he'd been planning for so long. Would his niece be disappointed in him for what he'd just done? He hoped not. That would be the worst.

'Mr C,' Andy's voice broke through his thoughts. 'Mr C, come away from the door, won't you?' Justin's vision returned to what was in front of his eyes rather than the recesses of his mind. Fists hammered on the sealed door of the bus. Lenses pushed up to the glass, flashing. Flashing. 'I've pulled all the curtains across in here,' Andy said. 'And I've turned off your phone, to give you a break for a while. But we won't have long before your colleagues come for you. You were supposed to be at the meeting ten minutes ago and, err. . . the hyenas. . . ' he cocked his head at the clamour in the street, 'won't waste any time in letting them know what you've said. That's if they haven't already watched a live broadcast of your speech. Tell you what, sir. . . Justin.' Andy took Justin by the shoulders and steered him into a seat. Fatherly, he pulled the seatbelt across his friend's body and clicked it into place. 'Let's get out of here. Let's just bloody go. I'll take you wherever you want to be.'

His allotment, his parents' place in the centre of the woods. . . a desert island?

'But right now, let's just get out of here and find somewhere quiet to stop and have a proper breakfast. Eggs, toast, mushrooms, vegetarian sausages and a fresh pot of coffee – the lot. But we need to be quick. I know a back-route out of these streets, and if we can get away before anyone thinks to follow us, we might be able to evade them. You ready, Justin?'

Andy was already in the driving seat, starting the engine. Justin couldn't see out of the side windows, but he imagined the chaos that must be happening outside. Sure enough, the flashing cameras had formed a barricade at the front of the bus, trying to prevent it from leaving. But Andy was determined. One of the reporters clung valiantly to a wing mirror as the bus pulled out, dropping like a weighted sack as Andy wove from side-to-side, leaving the mirror slightly wonky. Justin hoped the young man hadn't injured himself. The crowd parted as the bus ploughed forward and Justin imagined them racing for their cars to drive in its wake, impatiently shouting at other drivers to get out of their way. He closed his eyes.

What he saw behind his eyelids surprised him. He was picking his way between close-packed tents at a crowded music festival, holding the hand of a girl who made him feel different in every way from how he'd ever felt before. He opened his eyes to the bus's dim interior, flickers of light at the edges of the curtains, then closed them again, the better to immerse himself in his thoughts.

She filled his mind now. The photo of him with her sister in the paper had revitalised his few, vivid memories of her. Her fury and fear at the announcement over the speaker, of the simple and moving evening they'd spent together before that, the tenderness he'd felt. Being convinced he'd fallen in love.

In reality, it had been the meeting in the café that had changed his life. The agreement they'd made. Maybe now was a good time to catch up – he was, after all, in the middle of an emergency. It wouldn't be breaking their agreement. He needed someone. It was hard to admit, but he did. The bus engine took on a deeper tone and vibrated through his body. His eyes jerked open again.

'Hold on tight, Boss,' Andy called over a screech of brakes and the crunching of gears. The bus had swung hard left and when he was planted firmly in his seat again Justin could see through the front window that they were on a narrow one-way street, climbing a steep incline. The bus slowed while Andy negotiated their passage through a corridor of parked cars. Justin heard the roar of car engines in the distance, apparently going in another direction as the sound died away. He tugged the curtains open and breathed. It was a clear day with a blue sky.

He'd leave London. Hide himself away – not because he was afraid to be seen but because he was sick of urbanity, of being expected to keep up appearances and towing the party line. His views were simple and genuine, but he'd been forced to express them through a filter. He was sick of arguing with the people who were supposed to support him.

Yes, he could start again. He had enough savings – maybe even enough to buy a farm, but if not, at least a smallholding. That's what he would do. Up North somewhere. It was lovely around here, for example, and the people were friendly. He felt better for the decisions assailing him like bullets. As if the holes they'd made in everything he'd thought he was aiming for were letting out the badness, as his mother used to say of the boils that he and one of his brothers were prone to suffering during their childhood.

His stomach grumbled. Perhaps after breakfast, he'd get Andy to drive him to his parents' place in Norfolk. His parents were in their nineties, but still perfectly fit and well. Dad spent most of his time in an elaborately fitted-out garden cabin, working on projects for his grandchildren and great-grandchildren, whilst Annie (she hated being called Mum) was still involved in several charitable endeavours. *No*, he couldn't bring the chaos of the press down on his parents' heads, it wouldn't be fair. Anyway, Andy would most likely need to take the bus back to its rightful owners soon. It would be wrong not to.

'Where are we going, Andy, mate?' he had to raise his voice above the strain of the engine.

'There's a valley I know of, up on the moors. It's quiet and not on the tourist trail. Nobody'll think to look for us there.' Andy grunted and changed into a lower gear as the climb became steeper.

'You're amazing,' Justin said. 'How do you know about these places?'

Andy paused before answering. 'Used to go up there to think after our Lucy disappeared.'

'I forgot you come from around here,' Justin said, still having to shout above the engine. It felt wrong that way, so he unstrapped himself and moved to the front of the bus, where he sat directly behind Andy. Leaning forward, he patted him on the shoulder. 'I'm so sorry, Andy. It must be difficult to cope with not knowing where Lucy ended up, but my friend in France might be able to help.'

He leaned back and crossed his arms over his chest. The girl was probably living a happy life somewhere, but unaware of who her true parents were. Although perhaps she had buried memories of her early life that she was unable to trust. A pain gripped Justin and he wrapped one arm

174

around his stomach.   It was a while before he could straighten in his seat.

'Don't forget your seatbelt, Mr C,' Andy caught his boss's eye in the rear-view mirror. 'It's about twenty minutes' drive from here, and it doesn't look as if anyone's following us, so we should at least get to eat our breakfast in peace.'

He'd probably mistaken Justin's discomfort for hunger.

An hour later, Andy had set up the long, sturdy campaigning table and chairs on the grass outside the bus.

'There you go,' he said.   'The full vegetarian English breakfast.' They had a wonderful view over the valley. Justin had taken advantage of the chance to doze, laid flat out on the grass while Andy was cooking the breakfast, and felt a whole lot better than when he'd woken up with a hangover earlier. Was it really the same day? The gig in the pub the night before felt so long ago, too. Stretching and clicking his fingers, he tested himself to see if he minded about his momentous, and possibly ridiculously-handled step down from politics – from Leadership of the Opposition, for Christ's sake. But no, he didn't. He bloody well didn't. Astonishing. All he could think about was freedom.

'Hang on a minute,' said Andy, picking up Justin's plate and setting it down at one end of the table. 'Grab your chair and bring it over here. I'll sit at the other end. Let's dine like lords, shall we?' Andy settled himself in his chair. They both realised at the same time that the coffee pot and orange juice, in the centre of the table, were too far away for either of them to reach. Justin put up his hand.

'You stay there. You've been a lifesaver today, Andy. Time you had a chance to relax. No, I insist. You don't work for me anymore, remember? From now on we're just friends.' He poured the coffee and carried it to the other end of the table. Placing it carefully in front of his mate he added, 'And I hope we'll remain so. I know you'll be working for someone else but, well, this is some adventure we've shared, isn't it? Want any more toast?' Laughing, he slid the toast rack down the length of the table and Andy caught it before it fell over the edge.

'This is a good day,' Justin said, swallowing a mouthful of thickly buttered toast, just the way he liked it. 'A bloody good day. Can't believe I carried on so long. It wasn't doing any good, that's the waste of it. What good is being well-meaning? There are other ways to help people. I should have realised before now, I'm better off out of it.'

A kite circled overhead, sunlight catching the edges of its wings. Justin's eyes filled with tears. *Bloody hell.*

Andy got up to collect the plates.

'You did a lot of good, sir.' He met Justin's damp eyes as he said it, to show the word hadn't slipped out by mistake. 'You brought the possibility of Socialism back into the hearts of the people. Some of them, anyway. Demonstrated how to care – something that's been missing from politics for a long time if you ask me. That's got to be a good thing.' He paused at the doorway to the bus and gave Justin a long look. 'As you said, there are a lot of other ways to make a difference in this world. I don't think we've seen the last of you yet.'

He placed a foot on the step, then turned back and asked, 'Would you like me to bring your guitar out, sir?'

'Oh, go on then,' said Justin.

By late afternoon, only a few cars had passed since they'd parked in the sunken layby and they hadn't been disturbed at all. Shadows crept over the valley, the lowering sun straddling two tall hills opposite. They had folded the table and put it away under the bus. Andy was refreshed from his sleep on the grass after their late breakfast, while Justin had gone inside and had the shower he'd missed that morning. He rehung the spotless white shirt back on a hanger in the tiny wardrobe and put on jeans and a soft blue t-shirt that he'd had since 1994. Searching in his rucksack he found his ancient denim jacket and slipped it on. Tucked around his neck the silk-painted scarf Ivy had made for her Art GCSE (her school year was the first cohort to sit the new exams) and given him for his thirty-eighth birthday. Was there anything he couldn't manage without, that he might still have left in his holdall? He checked once again and stuffed a few extra things into his rucksack. His laptop he wrapped inside a suit jacket – an old one he'd worn to Ivy's graduation. Not as if he needed anything smarter for job applications. . . he laughed at himself at the thought.

'We'd better be heading off, Justin.' Andy emerged from the bathroom, rubbing moisturiser into his hands. 'I've enjoyed today a lot more than I would have if we'd been doing the same old, same old. But if I'm not careful they'll accuse me of stealing the bus – or more likely you of hijacking it. Paint you as the villain and me as the victim. I'll call in and say I'm bringing it back and that I ferried you to Leeds or something. Where d'you actually want me to drop you?'

Crouching on the floor, Justin tightened the drawstring at the neck of his rucksack and buckled the top flap. He straightened, looping his arm through the straps.

'Nowhere, mate. I'm getting off here.'

He put out his hand for Andy to shake, then drew him into a hug. Andy struggled free, looking aghast.

'What. . . what do you mean you're getting off here? We're in the middle of nowhere. I can't leave you here!'

'Oh yes you can,' Justin laughed, making jazz hands and tilting his head. But Andy's expression remained firm.

'I can't, Boss. Don't want to find my mug in the paper again for being the cause of *your* disappearance.'

'Shit, yeah,' said Justin. 'I never thought of that. Let me think. . . No, don't start up the engine yet, I'm not ready. Look, you get in touch with whomever you need to and let them know you're bringing the bus back while I work out what to do.'

After staring at Justin a moment and then nodding, Andy slid out from behind the steering wheel and sat down at the breakfast bar, pulling out his phone. *That's a thought.* Justin had almost forgotten his. He found it in the pocket beside the window next to where he'd been sitting earlier – Andy had switched it off for him while he'd made his resignation speech to the public. No doubt he'd be slaughtered for not doing things properly by his enemies within the Party. Oh well. They could do what they wanted now. Justin shrugged his arms out of the rucksack and rested it on one of the seats across the aisle. As Andy spoke quietly in the background, he turned on his own phone. It detonated in his hand, buzzing and pinging and flashing up notifications, images and messages. But he ignored all that and hit the social media app on which Ivy had urged him to set up an "official" account.

'Hi, Justin here,' he said, holding the front-facing camera on the phone up to his face, taking care to keep only the interior of the bus in shot and not the surrounding countryside. He was recording one of those "live" videos the party encouraged during his rallies when the turnout was good (it was usually too noisy to hear himself speak but the party seemed happy). 'I just wanted to let you all know that I haven't taken today's decision lightly. But I'm really not sure that working from within this *system* is the right way for me to go about things any longer. It's polluted by *spite* and *greed*.' He emphasised the negative words, feeling blood coming to boil in his veins. As he spoke he was mystified to see a constant, upward cascade of *likes* and *hearts* floating in front of his face on the screen. 'And,' he continued, 'I'm not sure it was ever me, to be honest with you. I seemed to find myself in this position by accident and I tried my best to fulfil the needs of the people and the party of which I've been a member my whole life.' Andy had finished speaking on his own phone and was gazing at Justin, the mobile held loosely in his hand. He snapped his mouth shut and made a tea-drinking gesture with his curved finger and thumb, raising one eyebrow. Justin smiled at him and gave him a thumbs-up, forgetting for a moment he was broadcasting live to the nation. To the world. He steadied the phone before his face again.

'Sorry about that. My friend here, Andy – who may I say has been a loyal supporter both to me and to the party – and I sincerely hope his act of friendship to me today will not in any way jeopardise that role – has just offered me a cup of tea.' Smiley faces and laughter emoji streamed upwards on the screen. A shiver went through him, despite the heat of his blood.

'I've been touched and honoured by my reception over and over again throughout the past couple of years. I want to thank *you*, the people, for taking on board the simple values of compassion and consideration for others, so necessary to a functioning society. I hope that you will continue to do so. As you all know, we need to look after each other.'

He paused and swivelled the phone towards the table as Andy placed a mug of black tea down on it in front of him, and turning it back, watched a new flood of smiley faces and teacup emoji deluge the screen. Andy leaned forward and waved into the picture, and the screen went bonkers with pictorial symbols. When Justin could see his own face again, as the emoji dwindled to a steady stream, he continued speaking.

'Finally, I wish to address once again the imprecise and frankly unkind *story* – if you can call it that, which I don't believe you can – about me in the newspapers this morning. The girl in the picture was called Janie, as some of the newspapers cruelly revealed: have they even *thought* what this story might *do* to her *family* today if they came across it unexpectedly?! I very much doubt it. Janie is the sister of a young woman with whom I spent some time at that festival, so long ago. Janie's sister and I lost track of time and Janie's sister, knowing her sibling to be in the care of trustworthy friends, had not realised there was a problem.

If you care to examine the evidence of what happened that day you will discover *what did* cause a problem. But I'm not going into that now. Anyway, I *was* trying to assist Janie when a photographer – for other reasons, nothing to do with young Janie – snapped the picture of us. And that is all. Thank you, and I leave you all with my very good wishes. I intend to stay under the radar for a while, and you can rest assured you will not be seeing me earning (if you can call it *earning*) a ridiculous amount of money appearing at corporate events.' A tide of hearts, flowers and thumbs-up emoji flooded the screen and obscured his face again. 'Thank you very much for listening, and goodbye.'

Justin switched his phone off again, without checking any of the messages clogging his inbox. He needed time to think.

31

Annette, now

No answer. It was no good, I'd have another fag while I decided what to do next. Maybe I should call the newspapers or something – *Hello, Daily Direct it's me, Annette. The sister of Underage Festival Girl. May I speak to the Editor, please? I want to tell them they've got no right printing lies about my sister or about my... Oh sorry, what was that? You knew that already but there's not a damn thing I can do about it? Right, well thanks!*

I stopped rolling the ciggie and tipped the tobacco back into the pouch. I *knew* my voice sounded like a child's. They'd think it was a prank call – that's if I could even get through to anybody in the first place.

Wriggling my shoulders, I attempted to ease my aching back. Also shake off encroaching nausea which was getting hard to ignore. Tried Justin's number one more time but it still went straight to voicemail. *Oh bugger.* I pushed the front door open and slipped off Janie's Birkenstocks. The dogs sat up, alert.

'Shush,' I told them. 'I'm listening out for me mum.' Poppy cocked her head on one side while Romy sank into the down position. 'All right, you can talk amongst yourselves,' I said. 'It's all quiet up there.' She'd been asleep a long while, it'd do her good, I told myself.

I wasn't used to televisions; never had one since I was a kid. After fiddling about with each of Mum's ridiculously complicated remote controls (there were three) I managed to get the bloody thing on. Pressing button after button I found the twenty-four-hour news channel, and if I wanted to see Justin's face, I wasn't disappointed. In a recording from earlier he stood in the doorway of a political tour bus. Emblazoned on the side was a slogan about his support for the plebs rather than the toffs. *He never changed his views.*

If we were both to go back to that day in 1972, but as we were now instead of barely more than kids, we'd probably still have got on just as well. Or fancied each other to bits like we did then. I felt an unfamiliar flutter in the parts of me that hadn't been reached for a while. Romy gave me a suspicious look from the carpet, where she had her nose between her paws.

On the telly Justin was speaking but I couldn't hear what he was saying because a presenter was talking louder than him. She sounded over-excited and kept tripping on her words. But she said the word *resignation* a couple of times. A red strip ran along the bottom of the screen with fast-moving writing in white, which confirmed it. He had, unprecedentedly they said, resigned direct to the public instead of handing in a letter to his party. My mind flashed back to him looking into my eyes as he sang *I don't want to feel I never tried to save the day.* He *had* tried, hadn't he? Yet guilt still wriggled like a worm inside me. Lots of things would have turned out differently if I hadn't gone off with Justin instead of checking on Janie. I ground my hands into my eyes and it was too much for Romy. Panting, she got up from the carpet and shook herself. Came and shoved her nose in my lap.

'Good girl.'

Janie's car pulled into a handy space outside the front gate. After hitting about sixteen different buttons on the remote with panicky fingers, I switched the telly off. My face was wet so I gave it a quick dry on me sleeve and scrambled to my feet just as Janie opened the door into the porch. I had my back to her when she came in, bending to plump Mum's cushions and tidy away her water bottle, which probably needed refreshing. Romy barked and then quietened, getting used to Janie.

'It's going well,' Janie said, behind me. 'I'm coming to terms with it, you'll be pleased to know.' Pause. I folded Mum's crotchet blanket. 'I'm talking about *Bardney*,' Janie revved her voice up a notch when I didn't answer. I heard the strap of her handbag hit the banister.

'Can't you hang your bag in the porch like everyone else?' I snapped, whipping round. God, I sounded like Mum.

Janie was quiet a moment. 'What's got your goat? Oops, sorry. I didn't mean your *actual* goats.'

I took a deep breath through my nose. 'Nothing. Being cooped up here, I suppose. I miss me horses. *And* me goats, in actual fact.' I picked up Mum's bottle and took it to the kitchen. Coming back, I forced an expression that might have passed for a grin.

Janie did a double-take and pulled a face.

'That's just weird, Annette, stop smiling like that. Where's Mum, anyway? She can't still be asleep.'

She kicked her canvas shoes off, and seeing my frown, picked them up and chucked them in the shoe-cupboard. Poppy creaked to her feet and stretched, glancing hopefully towards the porch as if Janie had just thrown a treat. Disappointed, she collapsed on the rug again.

The back of my neck tingled, so sharply it hurt.

'Fuck me,' I said, trying to sound casual. I folded Mum's cardigan and placed it neatly on the back of her chair. 'I forgot. I meant to take her a cup of tea ages ago. Yeah, she has been quiet for a while.'

Light wobbled behind my eyes. I started to head back towards the kitchen. 'I tell you what,' I said. 'I'll put the kettle on while you go and check on her.'

In the kitchen I pinched my cheeks. Told myself it was nothing, the feeling crawling up the back of my neck – only stress. But it reminded me of my premonition about Ponytail-Pete.

'Remind me what your last servant died of,' Janie called out. But she made for the stairs anyway and I held my breath.

Listened to Janie's soft tread up the stairs and her approach to Mum's bedroom, convinced I'd hear a scream, or a cry. But nothing. Just a long moment of silence. Then Janie's feet moving again on the floor above me. I let out my breath and Romy wagged her tail.

'It's all right,' I told her. 'Silly Annette. Too much imagination, that's my trouble.'

Relaxing, I filled the kettle and flicked it on and then went back into the living room to listen out for the murmur of Janie's and Mum's voices as Janie gently woke up Mum. She'd never sleep tonight if she napped any longer. But still nothing. The floor creaked again but I couldn't hear any voices. Maybe Janie was watching Mum sleep, putting off the moment of waking her up. Or. . . What was the sound I just heard? Guttural, unearthly.

'Annette,' Janie called down, not loudly, but breathlessly. The panic that'd been waiting in my chest rose like a wave. Janie's voice sounded strangled.

'Annette, can you come up here, please?'

From the bottom of the stairs I watched Janie come out onto the landing, looking down through the banisters.

'Something's wrong with Mum. Her face is all twisted and she can't speak properly.' Although she was standing still, her hands gripping the rail, it looked like she was on the move, she trembled so hard.

184

Poppy gave out a low whine and darted past my legs, galloping up the stairs ahead of me. I held onto the banister to steady myself, and clung on tightly as I began my own climb that seemed to go on forever.

———

I sat in a waiting room at the hospital while they did some tests on Mum. They kept wheeling her off to one department or another, and after a long day of shocks and worry my back was playing up more than ever. I struggled to keep pace with the formula-one trolley the porters had been pushing her about on and soon the nurses told me to wait until the tests were all finished for the day.

'Go and get yourself a cup of tea, love. It's wet and warm at least. Take the weight off your feet. We'll look after your mum for you.'

I didn't even know if Mum had been aware I was there. She was as quiet as a mouse, and seemed fascinated by the lights streaking overhead as she zoomed along the corridors.

Janie had left to drive home and check on the dogs. She'd stay with them a while and bring some of Mum's things back with her later. She was also going to ring Nicholas. Everything felt unreal. First Justin resigned because of an insinuation that had its roots in something I did, and now this with Mum. Suffering a stroke alone upstairs when I should have been checking on her. Mixed up with it all was the memory of pausing with my hand on the gate at the bottom of the path up to Ponytail-Pete's house that last time. Back then I'd called Dex, and today I sent Janie up instead of me. It was my job, not hers, and I failed. I should have checked on Mum earlier, but instead I put the telly on.

I really wished I could speak to Justin. This was an emergency, wasn't it? Anyway, I'd left him a message and he hadn't got back to me. He was probably angry.

It was time I sorted things out.

I really needed to talk to Mum.

I hoped it wasn't too late.

Almost three hours later I sat in a waiting room once again. I'd rung Janie earlier and told her to wait until they got Mum settled on a ward. I'd grabbed a cheese and pickle sandwich from the booth on the ground floor, before panicking they might have brought Mum back and found me missing. But there was still no news. The blinds on the window had been half-drawn to offset the glare of the lowering sun and now I felt a great longing for a view of fields, of my beloved Irish mountain. It was too hot and the air – the lack of it – felt close. I gnawed on my knuckles as the tea in the plastic cup grew cold on a table beside me. A nurse entered the room. She glanced around – there were only three of us in there and one, an elderly man, was snoozing in a corner. Her gaze settled on me. As she approached, soft-footed, the leather-jacketed young woman with black-kohl eyes sitting near the door sighed loudly. The nurse hesitated as if about to say something, then pressed her lips together and continued towards me.

'You can come and see your mother now, love,' she said. 'She's back from her MRI and they've found a bed for her on the ward. It's this way, I'll show you.'

I'd become so stiff I could hardly move. With difficulty I flexed my back muscles, then gathered my sandwich wrapper and dropped it in a nearby bin. I didn't know what to do with the half-full cup, so I left it where it was.

We followed the blue line along the wall in silence.

Mum was propped up in one of four beds beds in a partitioned-off bay of a large ward. The other three beds contained tiny, silver-haired old ladies. It was the black wing on one side of her head that enabled me to recognise my mother.

The nurse made an effort to smile at us both, before turning and walking back in the direction from which we'd come. I felt abandoned. Creeping closer to the bed, I cleared my throat.

'Hey Mum.'

She didn't answer, but her gaze shifted from the overhead lighting to my face. Her mouth was pulled down at one corner.

'I'm sorry,' I said. *Damn face, wet again.* A paramedic had given me some tissue when I was in the ambulance with Mum; I pulled it out it and dabbed my eyes before blowing my nose. Her eyes stayed on my face. 'Sorry for not checking on you, I mean.'

She opened her mouth and a kind of squeak emerged. Shadows flickered over her face. My heart thudded but I reached for her unresponsive hand and held onto it.

'Yeah, yeah,' I said. 'I know what you're saying – *everything always has to be about you, Annette.* You're probably right. Sorry. I'll let you have your moment of drama, eh?' I sniffed, hard. Blew me nose again.

Mum's hand was limp in mine, it was on the side of her that seemed to have collapsed. I took her hand again and squeezed it anyway. Her eyes looked fierce.

32

Annette, now

'I've got something to tell you, Mum,' I hesitated.

A family walked into the bay and gathered around the bed of the old lady opposite Mum: two teenage girls and a middle-aged couple. There were greetings and low-level laughter, the rustle of cellophane. One of the teenage girls sang "Happy Birthday" in a high voice and the rest of the family joined in after the first line. The woman, perhaps the old lady's daughter, glanced over her shoulder at me and Mum, placed her hand on the shoulder of the youngest girl and made a show of shushing them all. I nodded and looked away. Leaning closer to Mum, I positioned my mouth close to her ear.

'If I don't do it now I never will. . . ' I paused again.

Fuck me, I've kept this inside for so long – hardly even admitted it to myself – it feels like going back to the life of someone else. How do I get the words out? How do I dig up those memories and give life to them again? Involuntarily, I must have squeezed Mum's hand because I thought, was almost certain, I felt an answering squeeze. Her bed was near a window, the sky was growing dull and early-evening lights from houses opposite twinkled through gaps in the blinds. Lives must be going on – ordinary lives like ours had been only this morning, despite Mum's illness. I had to assume she was able to understand everything I said.

'You know at that festival?' I started. Mum blinked, her eyelids moving slowly. 'You know all the trouble... when I left Janie. Yeah? Well, I was with this guy.' I closed my eyes. On the back of my eyelids I saw *her*. She'd always been there, hidden behind a curtain. Now I pulled the curtain back for the first time in years. I saw her laughing face, trusting me.

Nobody knew, once I left London. I lost touch with everyone who'd been involved.

Tell the truth.

With my eyes closed, I conjured up my daughter for Mum.

'She had fair hair, like Janie's when she was a baby. I had an older friend in the squat who knitted some clothes before she was born – cardigans, hat and bootees, you know the kind of thing. She also crocheted me a blanket which I kept for a long time afterwards.' I wouldn't open my eyes, otherwise I'd never get the words out. I could feel Mum's pulse in her fingers – tipper-tapper-fast.

'She smiled for the first time when she was only three weeks old. It was definitely a smile, not wind like everyone always says. It was after I'd fed her. She looked me in the eyes and opened her mouth in this big, wide smile. She did it again and again, too, so I knew it was real.'

I jerked my chin up and braved a glance through narrowed eyes at Mum's face, pulled out of shape by the stroke. She'd been *struck*, and now I was striking her again.

'Are you strong enough, Mum?' I whispered. She was still looking at me and her steadfast gaze told me she was. Wetness lay under her eyes so I placed her hand gently on the bedspread and wiped the leaking moisture away with the edge of my tissue, then noticed a box of man-sized ones on the windowsill. Grabbing a handful, I blew my nose again.

189

This time I couldn't bring myself to take Mum's hand. I wrung mine together as I attempted to get the story out. *Ivy's story.*

'I didn't tell you when I first found out, Mum, because... well, you know the way things were. I'd already let you down over Janie.'

Because you had thrown me out anyway. Told me you'd never trust me again. With the pregnancy, you would have said I'd brought shame on the family. That was why I didn't tell you. I already felt alone and abandoned.

It shocked me, the regret-fuelled fury in my chest.

Mum would've come around to Ivy eventually – would've loved her if she'd known her – but only at the cost of ramming shame down my throat.

Mum's eyes were leaking again and so were mine. I mopped us both dry and continued, now I'd started it was easy.

'I was already living in the squat in London when I had her. I had a job washing pots in a restaurant and they were good to me there. I worked as long as I could before the birth and they made sure I ate at least one good meal a day. I also got milk tokens from the government and once she was born there was the Family Allowance.' The words came tumbling out of me in a hurried whisper. I noticed one or two curious glances from the family across the aisle, but mostly they were concerned with their grandma. The lady in the bed next to Mum's snored loudly and the other two lay inert, flat on their pillows. A nurse arrived to check on one of them. She leaned over Mum, too, to check a monitor at her bedside. I saw her frown before she left again, and I felt the slightest new tingle at the back of my neck. I looked at Mum, but her eyes were still fixed on mine. She wanted me to continue.

'For an hour or two every evening my friend at the squat looked after her so I could put in a shift at the restaurant, and we got by. But it was hard, Mum. Fucking – sorry – bloody hard.'

I paused for another mop of both our faces.

Thunderous-looking clouds had appeared in the gaps between the blinds.

I was a mother. I am a mother.

'Yeah, I know I deprived you of being a grandmother,' I snuffled, thinking I could read Mum's thoughts. It was easier to confide in her now she couldn't talk back. 'But Janie made up for it later. Perfect Janie and her perfect children. *Sorry.* I'm sorry.'

I was proper crying now, and the family opposite had gone quiet and were unabashedly eavesdropping. I scrambled out of my chair, wincing at the pain in my back. Dragging the curtain across, I peeped out to say pointedly, 'If you wouldn't mind. . .' It seemed to do the trick. The family went back into their huddle and I noticed a flush creeping up above the woman's collar before I drew the curtain fully closed.

I hated being in this position. Hated showing my vulnerability. I honestly hadn't minded about Ivy for all those years. And now I did. As if she was new. *She was my baby,* for feck's sake.

Mum made an unintelligible series of noises, and I took them to mean, 'Go on.' So I did. I swallowed snot and continued talking about my daughter.

'She was born the February after I left home. A dainty little thing – only weighed six pounds at birth – like Janie's Allegra. She was quiet, too. She slept in my bed with me, or a mattress on the floor to be precise. Yeah Mum, I know you probably think sleeping with your baby is spoiling her. . .' I sniffed and dabbed again at my nose. I remembered visiting Scotland with Mum one year (years later) when I was over on a visit, and how she went on at Janie for carrying Billy around all the time in a sling. *You'll spoil that baby!*

I was glad I'd kept Ivy close to my body for most of the time I had her. I checked Mum's face. A lopsided frown had appeared between her eyes and her good hand clawed at the air.

'What is it?' I asked, patting the bedspread.

She was trying to say something. I leaned forward again, but I couldn't make out what her rasping sounds meant. It was easier to pick up meaning from the look in her eyes. She wanted me to carry on.

'All right, Mum. I don't know if you remember, but it turned bitter in the middle of the month and that was exactly when I had her. One of my housemates drove me to the hospital in his battered old van. Another came with us – the one who knitted me the baby clothes. She'd also brought some tiny nightgowns and terry nappies, outgrown by her sister's babies. We only just made it to the hospital in time. I was practically giving birth as they got me into the foyer. They shoved me in a wheelchair and rushed me to a delivery room. It didn't take long for her to be born. They kept calling me Mrs Woods even though I told them I wasn't.' I met Mum's sunken eyes. She tried to shake her head on the pillow. I fought the urge to say sorry.

It was her who had asked me to leave home because I was a bad influence on Janie. Janie had some sort of nervous breakdown – not speaking or eating after the festival. I was old enough to look after myself. And so on and so on. I never even finished my A-levels – Mum suggested I'd grown out of school and would be better working for my living. She'd barely spoken to me since the night the police had escorted her and Dad into the Release tent. They'd led them over to where I stood, practically under arrest, next to a sobbing-her-heart-out Janie. Mum enveloped Janie in her arms – *'you poor thing, what has she* done *to you?'* while Dad grabbed my arm and gave me a clip around the ear.

One night, some weeks later, I was getting a glass of milk before going to bed (feeling like a ghost in my own home) and Mum followed me into the kitchen.

'I thought this would help you find a place of your own,' she said in a stiff voice. I looked down at the open envelope she was holding in front of her, containing what looked like a lot of money. A few weeks before I'd have been thrilled and felt I was rich, but instead my reaction was a black well of sadness going deep inside me. I wondered how they'd got that much money together – they must have *really* wanted rid of me.

I couldn't talk to Mary anymore, she seemed so much younger than I felt. I was stuck in an in-between time – too young to respond to Justin's attempts at contact and too old for my school friends. I never told Mary what really happened at the festival. Our new differences began to show; she'd begun to separate herself from me right after the festival, and soon she was best friends with Hilary Townsman.

I left early in the morning, about a week after Mum gave me the money. I'd spent the time since that night in the kitchen selecting clothes and packing them into a suitcase that had mysteriously appeared on the chest of drawers in mine and Janie's bedroom (I recognised it from the top of Mum and Dad's wardrobe). Throughout that week, seven pairs of new knickers and a bra, as well as several pairs of tights, also appeared on the chest of drawers. Janie lay on her side on the top bunk, not saying much to anyone. I was finding it difficult to swallow, like there was a massive obstruction in my throat. On my final morning at home, I vomited, even before partaking of my solitary breakfast. I put it down to nerves. No one was around to see me off.

London seemed the obvious place to go. Arriving at the station that early Monday morning, I got on the first train to leave and sank back gratefully in my seat, trying to feel positive about my new life. I knew there'd be hostels where I could stay until I got myself sorted out with a room. I knew there'd be jobs in shops or in restaurants.

Nothing had been the same since Justin, anyway. I was still ashamed of the way I'd behaved. And once I was in London (and found out about Ivy) I always thought I would contact him eventually, but it never felt like the right time. I could hardly think once she was born.

Taking Mum's hand again, I tried to make sure we had eye contact.

'The squat was no place for a child, Mum. Not with me as her mother. I felt suffocated by the responsibility. I loved her, but I had no patience, and no money, and I didn't know what to do. My friend introduced me to her sister, who had a couple of daughters, but we had nothing in common apart from that. I kept thinking of ringing you and telling you about her – about Ivy, I called my baby Ivy.' My eyesight had blurred and the overhead light made a halo of Mum's thin, white curls, the black streak in her hair like a shadow. '– but I couldn't face what you'd say to me. And you had your hands full with Janie.'

What I'd really wanted was for Mum and Dad to track me down, but that never happened. I thought they'd washed their hands of me.

'There was an eviction notice to get us out of the squat. Most of the housemates decided to go travelling, take the Magic Bus to India. I wanted to go with them but I couldn't imagine doing that with Ivy. She was about fourteen months old by then and she'd just started walking. I didn't know how I was going to be able to afford a place for us both to live in when we got kicked out. My friend was going to India with the others, so I wouldn't even have a babysitter for managing to stay at work.'

You could have come home, I could feel Mum thinking it, and I knew she was right. I could have gone home with my tail between my legs. Mum and Dad *would* have accepted Ivy, their real, live grandchild. I knew that. But I would have never lived it down in Lincoln. And I would have been trapped there. Water pooled beneath Mum's eyes again, and her gaze wandered. Again I wiped the moisture away, along with the dribble at the downturned corner of her mouth. It reminded me of wiping Ivy's grubby little face, her filthy hands, with a damp flannel. She must have built up a good immune system, that kid. The things she put in her mouth. I loved her, but I never had enough patience and I didn't think I was a very good mother.

Mum resumed clawing the air.

'All right,' I said. 'I'll tell you the rest of it. Get it all out in the open, eh?' I stroked the back of her veiny, brown-spotted hand and took a ragged breath.

'I looked in the telephone directory for the name of her father. He'd told me where his family lived, in Norfolk. I spoke to his mother and she gave me his number in London. It turned out he was living more-or-less around the corner from me.'

Mum drew in a rasping breath.

'Yes,' I said. 'I *did* put his name on the birth certificate if you want to know. Yes, he *is* her father. It could only have been him, in case you're wondering.'

It might have been my imagination, but her face looked more at ease.

'We met in a café and I told him about Ivy. He was shocked and disappointed I hadn't let him know earlier. He said he would have helped me look after her and he still would if that was what I wanted, but it was too late for me by that time. I know you'll think I'm bad for saying this, but I wanted freedom from the responsibility. I thought it was only fair I let him know about her, so he could have a choice about what to do. He was training to be a solicitor. He wasn't any more equipped to look after a baby than I was. He offered to marry me though, Mum. He was good like that. He's a good person.'

So what did you do? Mum must have been asking.

'I didn't have Ivy with me the first time we met but I offered to meet him in a park the next day, and bring the baby with me. I had this tattered old Silver Cross pram that I had to keep in the hallway of the squat, and bump it up and down the outside stairs every time I took her out.'

I had a sudden memory of the feel of the rubber handle beneath my hands – the nick in the rubber that meant the cold metal beneath touched a certain spot on the underside of my finger every time I pushed it.

'When he first saw her, she was wearing a pink woollen bonnet and a thick knitted jacket that the health visitor had brought for me. She'd chosen it especially for Ivy from a box of donated clothes at the clinic. Ivy had thick woolly tights on as well, and she was wearing her first pair of shoes. I saved up and bought those for her myself when she started walking. Proper *Clarkes* shoes like you always made us wear. Justin told me she looked just like me, but actually, she looked more like Janie.'

I could have done with a wee, but I mustn't stop now, I thought. I had to finish the story. While Mum's eyes seemed to be focussed on the curtain rail above, her fingers made some faint movements on the bedspread and I took this as my cue to go on.

'Justin, that's his name, Mum. He said he'd come up with a solution if I really didn't feel I was able to carry on looking after Ivy myself. He seemed to think for a long while and then he told me his brother, Finlay, and his wife, Alice, had been trying to have a baby for a long time and it had turned out they couldn't have them. So now they were desperate to adopt. He said he was certain they'd love to bring Ivy up as their own, and that knowing how kind Alice was she probably wouldn't mind me seeing Ivy sometimes if I really wanted to, but it might be better if I pretended I was an auntie or something.

I truly thought I might stay in Ivy's life when I made the decision, Mum. So that's what we did. I gave her away to her true auntie and uncle. She grew up thinking *Justin* was her uncle and she never knew me at all.'

I felt strangely lighter once I'd told her the whole truth. I squeezed Mum's hand again, but there was no response anymore. She appeared to have fallen asleep. I started to push myself up onto my feet, intending to sneak off to the loo before she woke up again, but then the alarm on one of the monitors started blaring in my ear.

33

Annette, now

The shock of Mum's death made me realise I wanted to tell Ivy the truth. At least give her a chance to meet me, if that's what she decided. I knew who *she* was, I'd seen enough media photos of Justin with his "devoted niece and number-one supporter" to be able to look her up and contact her directly if I wanted to, but I thought it would be better coming from him.

Since she already knows and loves him.

Bile curdled in my stomach. I'd deprived myself, deprived Mum, and deprived Ivy of a part of her identity. She was forty-three years old – the little girl I gave away. What would she think of me?

But Justin hadn't answered any of my calls. Christ, I was so angry. It wasn't like me; I'd coped with plenty of difficulties before and managed without bitterness but this time the emotions defeated me. Janie thought I was in shock over Mum. She kept telling me it wasn't my fault. But she didn't know what I'd spoken of that last night.

Over the course of the next weeks I left Justin a few more messages on his mobile, each one snottier than the last. I told him I needed to tie up loose ends and said if he didn't get back to me soon I was going to take matters into my own hands. I'd become obsessed with the idea of Ivy, and of her baby. Maybe meeting them would make sense of things. The only thing that held me back was that I knew I was a mess. I shouldn't let her see me like this.

I didn't have the energy to go for an actual walk, so I leaned against the corner-section of wall from one of the demolished outhouses – left standing at Janie's instruction, because she was planning to rebuild it into part of the boundary for her kitchen garden. Apparently, she'd done a bricklaying course in Scotland, she never ceased to amaze me. I watched as Romy ran in ever-increasing circles on the land that would become a paddock for our rescued horses and donkeys, some distance from the house. We'd convert the barn standing behind it into stabling and perhaps even run a petting zoo to bring in some extra income – if I could get me act together and sort something out. Janie said she had enough on her plate with the human side of things. "Animals" was down to me.

Romy's tongue flapped to one side and her tail streamed like a banner as she galloped around the stony ground, but Poppy only nosed desultorily in the nettles, searching for a suitable place to wee. As soon as she was finished she'd hobble back across the land and in through the kitchen door. She'd flop onto her cushion behind the middle sofa in the living room (or communal room, as Janie called it). I felt like curling up in a dark hole as well. Like Poppy, I seemed to have had the stuffing knocked out of me, and however many pep-talks I gave myself, I couldn't shake off the depression that had descended since me mum died.

———

'Come on, Annette,' Janie said at least once a day. 'We need to start putting our plans for this place into practice before the winter sets in. Contact the Council, seek Lottery funding. We could make this into a home for people who need one, or at least a respite centre of some kind. We've got all this. . .' she opened her arms wide. At the lack of reaction from me she tutted. 'I've got a meeting with a charity that finds rooms for homeless teenagers next week. You could come with me.'

I remained sitting inert, but she started buzzing around the room, tidying away chip shop wrappers from the night before and two or three mugs from the table and windowsill. She bent to pick up my rainbow cardigan, lying under the pegs on the door that opened into the tiled passageway to the carport – sorry, *gazebo*. Now pimped up with raised decking, surrounded by wrought-iron latticework threaded with fairy lights. The gazebo looked out over the back lawn. Janie enjoyed sitting there in the evenings at her reclaimed metal table and chairs.

I couldn't bring myself to join her yet. It reminded me of that time we sat under the carport with Mum.

'I'm off in, Romy,' I pushed away from the wall. Poppy had already skulked inside, having emptied her bladder and done a hard little poo, which I'd pick up later – or Janie would, with her usual air of martyrdom. The sun was too hot for me though, everything felt too much. Romy had a mad gleam in her eye, chasing a butterfly, and I left her to it.

My phone went off in me skirt pocket just as I stepped into the kitchen, almost fell out of my hand as I grabbed it with stiff fingers – I must've caught me mum's arthritis, or maybe it had been shared between me and Poppy – but I managed to snatch it in time to avoid a crash on the stone floor. Seeing the screen I breathed hard, propping my elbows on the kitchen counter and loudly vocalising my annoyance into the phone, not wanting him to know of the relief flooding through me: 'Took your bloody time answering my calls, didn't you?'

'Hello Annette,' Justin said, after a pause. I burst into tears, believe it or not.

'I'm sorry,' he ignored my sobs, or rather spoke between them. 'I've had my phone off for weeks, buried at the bottom of a rucksack, couldn't risk letting myself see any hate messages or being distracted from what I was doing. I got hold of a pay-as-you-go phone to let my family know I was okay – new SIM, of course, blah blah blah. I went off-grid, wild-camping in the Yorkshire Dales. After that I had some detective work to do for a friend who helped me out. Had to go to France...'

I was still trying to get myself under control and didn't answer, so he carried on speaking. 'I'm back in society now and I've only just reunited myself with my smartphone. It didn't occur to me I would have had any messages from you, Annette. I'm sorry. Are you okay, what's happened?'

He sounded so calm I started laughing instead of crying. *What's happened*, he said. What *hadn't* happened? I took a few deep breaths and started sniggering again. A few more breaths before I could speak. Turning on the tap, I filled a glass with water and took a long drink.

'I don't need to tell you about your own resignation,' I began, calmer now. He laughed.

'I'd almost forgotten, I'm more rested than I've been for years. But why should that have upset you?'

Warmth pooled inside me.

'It did feel a bit like my fault,' I said, turning to face the wooden shelves Janie had fitted on the opposite wall. Reclaimed from an abandoned railway carriage found in the barn. I rubbed my back and leaned against the sink. 'Because of the article, you know. The insinuations were awful.'

'That's the media for you,' Justin sounded offhand. 'Anything to stir up anger or hatred. It was only the catalyst for what I did, and I soon put the people right on the story.' His voice sounded the same as ever. I closed my eyes. 'It's no problem,' he continued. 'It wasn't your fault.'

'You're so trusting,' I said. 'Of the people. No wonder they love you.'

I love you, I thought, out of the blue, as if we were resuming where we left off at the festival more than forty years before. But now there was a grown-up Ivy, and a grandchild to take into account.

'My mum died,' I blurted out. 'She had a stroke on the day you resigned.' Feeling in my other pocket, I retrieved a handful of toilet roll and blew my nose.

'I'm sorry to hear that, Annette,' Justin said when I stopped blowing, folding the damp tissue tightly in my hand. I heard Janie's car rolling along the stone track, and Romy barking.

'I take it you reconciled with her, eventually?'

'Yeah,' I said. 'After a few years. But I never told her about Ivy, until after the stroke. And then she died. It felt like the news had killed her. It's been a crap few months, actually.' I refilled the water glass and made my way into the dining room. Pushing the door into the corridor beyond that open with my foot, I headed for the stairs, glancing back at the front door. I didn't want Janie to hear what I was talking about when she came in with the shopping.

'I'm sorry you've had such a bad time,' Justin spoke softly into my ear. 'Would you like to meet up and chat about things?'

I couldn't speak. And while I couldn't speak and was closing my bedroom door behind me just as I heard the front door opening downstairs, Justin said, 'In fact I was thinking it was about time Ivy knew the truth about her parentage.'

Now I couldn't breathe let alone speak. *Great minds think alike.* I dropped heavily onto my bed and lay back against the pillows, my eyes roving the cracked plaster on the wall opposite (I refused to have it prettified the way Janie was doing most other parts of the house). Janie called a greeting up the stairs and my breath filled my lungs again.

'Yeah, I'll be down soon,' I shouted.

'You nearly deafened me,' Justin said, and laughed again, then stopped. 'Do you mind me asking who you're talking to?'

I felt the hilarity bubbling back up. 'Janie,' I told him. 'You remember Janie, don't you?'

He snorted. 'I think I've seen a photo of her somewhere,' I could hear the smile in his voice. 'Possibly in a newspaper.'

I told him Janie and I were now living together. 'Crazy, isn't it? Everything happened so quickly. Our Mum was ill and me brother made me come and look after her. Janie was getting divorced and she had to sell her home in Scotland. It was a railway station, where she lived. Long story short we ended up buying another old railway station, here in Lincolnshire – just down the road from the festival, Justin. Can you believe that? We have a house and a load of outbuildings, and a couple of acres of land. She's all right, as it turns out, Janie. Got loads of ideas for this place. Actually, I don't know what I would've done without her these past months.'

Justin was quiet for a minute. 'You've been having a tough time.'

I was aware I hadn't answered his questions, either of them.

'I want to meet up,' I said. My voice sounded strange and small inside my head. I listened to him breathing for another moment. 'And I want to meet Ivy. I want her to know about us.'

34

Janie, now

The communal room, with its slate-blue walls and deep skirting boards painted cream, looked exactly as she'd imagined. Broken parts of the decorative dado rails and cornices had been recreated to perfection and picked out in brilliant white. The ceiling was smooth and cream and a refurbished, beaded chandelier that Janie had discovered half-buried in one of the sheds now hung from its centre. The joists had been replaced and the old wooden floorboards stripped; their grain brought out with cherry varnish.

In the restored fireplace, a navy-blue wood burning stove glowed, not really necessary at this time of year, even in the evenings, but it was comforting. Three squishy (reclaimed) sofas lined the walls and they'd managed to wedge an armchair into a corner. Janie had found an original Turkish rug (with one tattered corner the only damage) in a junk shop: a perfect centrepiece to the floor.

This late in the year, sunset was noticeably earlier than a few weeks before. From the two windows she could see the cluster of silver birch trees, rattling their penny leaves, and the apple tree, sprouting fruit, its crown set off by the black-painted shed behind it. Recent rain had turned the grass of the regrown lawn luscious, and orange streaked the dusk-blue sky behind the barn opposite.

Late summer, and Janie already sensed the poignancy of autumn, like a premonitory ghost. Or the lingering ghost of her mother.

Almost four months previously, Janie had never even got to say goodbye. She had not even properly acknowledged the severity of her mother's condition, playing along with Mum's stiff upper lip. She couldn't take it in.

Janie nestled in the corner of the sofa opposite the fire, on the phone to Lara.

'I'm sorry I didn't make it down to London. Especially because I know you wanted me to meet your dad, after all these years. How was the visit?'

'It was... strange. I'm happy he finally made it over from Trinidad, but sad I just can't seem to get close to him. I don't think I've ever really got over feeling he deserted us when Mum died. Fergus was more of a dad to me than him.'

Janie thought carefully before she responded. 'You feel he deserted you, even though he was deported?' She tapped her free hand on her knee. Lara's temper might flare if she said the wrong thing.

'Well. I've thought since that he could have appealed or something. To the government, I mean. Or sent for me to be with him. I would have gone. He just seemed to give up on us. And he's done it over and over again since.' There was a pause. Janie put the phone on speaker and set it down on the coffee table she'd picked up from the pre-loved shop in the village. 'Anyway,' Lara said after a moment. 'I don't want to talk about him anymore. How have things been for you since your mum died?'

'I suppose I'm a bit numb. Everything's happened so suddenly and I just feel I need to hide away here for a while, until Annette and I decide what we want to do with this place. This whole plan was supposed to be for the benefit of Mum, after all. Although...'

'You're beginning to think of it as home, aren't you?' Lara asked.

'I suppose I am. I mean, Catmally could never be home again, and I can't have it anyway. It's someone else's now. And I *do* feel I've made a mark on this place. I've already started mulching the soil in preparation for my kitchen garden –' she took a sharp breath, at the sensation of something loosening in her chest. The numbness beginning to melt? 'There's so much hay and manure around here, it's overwhelmingly agricultural,' she continued with new enthusiasm. 'I've started building a wall with bricks left around the property from the demolishing and refurbishing. It's very satisfying. I'm doing what I did at Catmally, I suppose.'

'Starting again?'

'Yeah. Only this time it's a completely blank slate. I have no idea what's going to happen. I mean, there are more options now.'

'As in?'

'Well. I've basically been compensated for having to put all of the money from Catmally into this place by the inheritance from Mum. There was more than we realised... and Nicholas was perfectly happy that Mum left it all to me and Annette – I think he felt guilty for not being there when... But he *has* said he'd like to come and stay with us here whenever he visits Lincoln. Not much reason for him to come back now though, I suppose.'

'Err, his sisters?'

'My family aren't like yours, Lara. You and Fergus have always been close.'

Janie bit her lip to stop it from wobbling.

'You're crying, aren't you?' Lara said.

Janie could hear her friend fiddling with something on the other end of the line. Probably a pen tapping against her desk.

Lara worked from home as a copywriter. One of her children shouted in the background and Lara turned away from the phone to respond. Janie dug her fingers into her rib cage and pulled herself together.

'Anyway,' she said. 'I wondered if you and the girls wanted to come for a visit here some time. Marcus, too, if he fancies it. Billy'll be back from his trip soon and he's coming down again – I only saw him briefly at the funeral. The girls love Billy, don't they? And they might enjoy playing with the dogs.'

Romy, prostrate in front of the wood stove, lifted her chin and cocked an ear enquiringly. Poppy didn't bother to move.

'We've got loads of room. Sorry if I sound desperate!' she laughed but not very convincingly, fearing she'd over-tried Lara's patience. 'Anyway, think about it, won't you? I've got to get off in a minute – loads to do and all that,' (she could perhaps take Romy for another walk) 'but I just wanted to tell you about Annette.'

Lara was shuffling papers in her London flat. 'What about her?'

Janie settled more comfortably again into the corner of the sofa.

'She's gone to meet someone, and. . . this is the best bit, guess what? Okay I'll tell you. It's the *very* bloke she was with at the festival! You know, *the* festival.' Janie and Lara had taken their sons to Glastonbury together a few years previously. 'Apparently Annette's been in touch with him, on and off, all these years. And she's got some big secret to tell me – apparently she told it to Mum the night she died and she *had* been going to tell me the same night but of course after what happened it didn't seem the right time. . . ' she trailed off. There wasn't really much to tell until Annette confided the great piece of news she was being so mysterious about. 'Anyway, I'll let you know when I know. Sorry to ring you when you're obviously still working, Lara. But it was nice to hear your voice and I'll speak to you soon, yeah?' she held her breath to disguise the fact that tears were welling up behind her eyes again, and at least Lara couldn't see her.

'Wait, hang on,' said Lara. 'I've just been looking at the calendar, that's all. How about the end of this month? The girls and I could come for a visit then, and I'll ask Marcus if he wants to come as well – especially if Billy's there. They haven't seen each other for ages. And I always think your Billy's a good influence on my Marcus.'

Janie punched the air. Romy opened one eye, and slowly closed it again.

'Oh, that'd be wonderful, Lara, thank you. It'll be so lovely to see you. Especially here, although I don't suppose this place has got very good memories for you. . . '

'Don't talk rubbish,' Lara said. 'Best thing to do with a bad memory is build something nice on top of it. So thank you for the invite, and I'm looking forward to seeing the old place again, haha.'

Two carefree girls, dancing with abandon in front of a brightly-lit stage, shouting out the words of an Average White Band song.

Sisters. That was the only memory of the festival Janie was going to allow herself from now on. It was the only one she needed. She found herself smiling as she ended the call. Stretching stiff legs, she stood, patting her side and calling Romy to her, knowing Poppy wouldn't want to be bothered this late in the day. Opening the back door, she took a deep breath of evening air and stepped out. The sunset, the trees, the flat land and the wide river that were becoming home beckoned.

35

Justin, now

Justin had rented out his house and was living in a converted camper van. He'd been spending his time working on new songs and making the most of his immense sense of freedom. He might even record an album. His folk songs, to all intents and purposes, consisted of the policies he truly believed in – which he'd previously had to dilute somewhat for the rest of his party. He could say what the fuck he liked now. Ah, *real* freedom!

Jim Robinson had promised him a gig (*best keep it low key, we'll introduce you as a surprise*) at the next party conference, but in the meantime, he'd perform at open mics around the country and rebuild his following. He could perform wherever he pleased, once he came properly out of hiding.

Now he was no longer expected to wear a tie, or even a shirt and "proper" trousers for that matter, he was virtually indistinguishable from other hippie-type men of his age. He'd allowed his beard and hair to grow longer and wore a striped grandad shirt and an embroidered waistcoat from a charity shop in Kings Lynn. The elderly volunteer who'd sold it to him had mistaken him for his oldest brother. Felix lived in a cave nearby during the summer months and transformed himself back into a member of society with a shave and a haircut each winter. Justin felt inordinately pleased by the comparison.

Annie was in the front garden when Justin pulled up outside the wrought-iron gates in his rattling van. She straightened her body, pushing upwards from the soil with gnarled knuckles. He saw the pads strapped to her knees and a gardening fork in her hand. She helped him open the gate and pushed it closed behind the van once he'd driven through, meeting him as he descended from his vehicle. Time melted away every time he was embraced by his mother. He was her youngest child, unexpected baby and the apple of her eye. Annie had to stretch up on tiptoes to reach around his neck.

'You silly boy,' she said as she regained the flats of her feet. 'Could you not have done things properly, for the first time in your life?'

'Sorry, Ma.' Justin hung his head, his lips curling up at the corners.

'Oh, come here,' she said, grasping his two hands in hers. 'It's good to see you, my boy. Now, what is it that you want to talk to your brother and his wife about? They're waiting for you inside, but you've got them all on edge. It's not a repeat of the last time you wanted to talk to them, is it?' she searched his face. 'Justin, it can't be, surely? Not at your age and not at theirs either!'

Justin laughed. 'Of course not, though to be fair it *is* to do with that. It's just that I think the time's come to tell Ivy the truth. For Olivia's sake as much as hers. But I thought it would be kinder to discuss it with Alice and Finlay first. Come inside with me. You can hear what I've got to say, too.'

Alice and Finlay were ensconced in the small sitting room which led off the main hall; the sunlit centre of the house that Justin's mother and father had first walked into with their three oldest sons after breaking the door down in 1945.

209

Light still fell from what had then been a hole in the roof, but Justin's father had filled it with stained glass in a circular frame. Justin paused for a moment, as he always did, to admire the way the many-coloured light fell onto the teardrop beads of the chandelier cleverly strung beneath it, and sprinkled over the walls and floor. Coloured dots also peppered the book-littered surface of the long table, lined with twenty chairs, around which Annie and Alice held community workshops.

'Here you both are! How are you?' As Justin stepped into the sitting room with his mother behind him, his brother and Alice rose from their seats in front of the French windows which led onto the wildflower garden. Silhouetted by sunshine, their outlines appeared more-or-less unaltered from the two that had similarly approached him from the same seats more than forty-one years earlier.

36

Justin, then

Ivy was almost seventeen months old when Justin brought her to The Meadows to meet her new parents. He'd been getting to know his daughter on regular visits with Annette. Their meetings took place either in the squat or at Islington Green. All the while they spent getting to know each other he could feel Annette withdrawing. Not her affection as such, but certainly her engagement with the baby. Annette allowed him to take Ivy back to his tiny flat overnight, to see how she would cope without her mother.

It broke his heart to see Annette's closed-off face. She was still so young, yet quiet and somehow old before her time. Although he believed a child belonged with her mother, it was evident Annette wasn't ready for the responsibility. She was worn-out, desperate. There was no financial safety-net for single mothers and Annette had told him she couldn't take Ivy home to her family. More out of a sense of duty than love for her – she'd become a different girl from the one he'd met at the festival – and before they sealed the commitment to their plan, he asked Annette to marry him. They were at "their" café. She gazed steadily into his eyes – one of the few times she did during those months – and refused.

'You know that isn't what either of us want,' she said. 'But thanks for asking, at least. No, I'm off with me mates on the Magic Bus to India. We leave in a week or two, so we need to complete this process. It's best for Ivy,' she added, evidently registering the undisguised shock on his face. 'The younger she is the more likely she is to forget me and stand a better chance of growing up happy with her new mum and dad. You *are* sure about them, aren't you?'

Alice's soft, rounded cheeks came into his mind. He'd had a massive (platonic) crush on her since his illness, just before he met Annette. Recently, Alice's sadness at her childlessness had spread from inside to out. He saw it in the way she carried her body, in the way she struggled to produce the smile he'd previously taken for granted. Even her voice had lost its stridency and confidence. Finlay was his closest brother. He'd looked after Justin when they were children and made sure he was never left out when his older brothers preferred not to include him. To think he could make both Alice and Finlay happy with the gift of his daughter swelled his chest with combined joy and pain. He was giving up the possibility of Annette, and of the daughter he hadn't even known about. But his beloved brother and sister-in-law would be happy. Alice would smile again. His daughter would be safe and loved, have a better life than either he or Annette could give her.

'Oh believe me, I'm sure,' he said softly. Ivy screwed her head around on its delicate stem and grasped his beard in her small fist. 'Da!' she shouted, pulling harder.

'She says that to everyone,' Annette said quickly, averting her eyes. She stirred spilt sugar on the table with her forefinger.

'Yeah, I expect she does. I didn't think. . . ' Justin peeled the baby's fingers carefully away from his beard. Something dropped like a stone in his stomach. Brief thoughts of keeping

Ivy flitted through his mind, but didn't settle. He swept them away too fast. 'Finlay will be happy when she says that to him. Eventually she'll know what it means.' Giving Ivy the teaspoon from his saucer to play with he spoke over the sound of her tapping. 'We're doing the right thing, Annette. We are. You're very brave, but I knew that already. From the first time I met you.'

If only she'd answered his phone calls and letters in the early days. They could have gone through this whole thing together, learned how to become Ivy's parents. But Alice. . .

'No I'm not,' Annette responded, swallowing hard several times. 'If I was brave, I'd go back to Lincoln. My mum wouldn't be able to resist her in the end. But I'm not brave, I'm being selfish. I want a life of my own and I'm going to have one, so there.' He saw how she avoided looking at the baby, ignoring the tiny hand that offered the spoon to her over the table. Annette roughly brushed away tears and Justin's throat ached.

'I've packed a bag of her things, it's under the pram,' Annette said. 'Today's the day, Justin. I've made up me mind. It's early enough for you to catch a train up to Norfolk this afternoon, isn't it? I just want to know that it's going to be done. Can you arrange for them to meet you there?'

Justin swallowed air. Grasping the table edge with one hand and Ivy with the other he waited until the dizziness passed. 'I haven't even told them about her yet,' he said. 'I didn't want to raise their hopes until I was certain it was going to happen. Couldn't we wait until I've had a chance to prepare them?'

Tears flowed forcefully from Annette's eyes now, her shell had cracked.

'No. It has to be today. Take her to your mother's this afternoon, *please* Justin. I've got things to do, I'm leaving in a couple of weeks.'

She pushed her chair back and stood up.

'You have my PO Box address,' she cleared her throat. 'I

realise I'll have papers to sign and stuff when I get back from India, so you can tell them to get the adoption underway. There's no going back from this, do you understand? I don't want you suddenly deciding to try and keep her yourself and make a mess of it, it wouldn't be fair. Do you promise?'

'Of course,' he said. 'I promise. I want what's best for her as well. And Annette, thank you for putting my name – Finlay's name too – on her birth certificate, it makes things easier.'

Her eyes seemed to burn as she bit her lip.

'Wait,' he reached for her arm, shifting the baby onto his hip as he stood, but too late, his hand slipped away as she moved from the table. 'Wait, can't we at least say goodbye properly?' the air around him reeled. This... this was too sudden. He hadn't expected it to happen so fast.

But she'd already reached the café door. '*Bye, Chickadee,*' he heard her whisper, pausing to blow a kiss to the baby. A bell jingled as the door banged closed behind her. He saw her hand trail over the sparkling hood of the pram (it had been raining earlier) as she walked past in front of the café window. And then she was gone.

37

Justin, now

Half a mile away in the sea, all around the perimeter of Justin's tiny island, he could see hundreds and hundreds of boats. Fishing boats, rowboats, rubber dinghies – lots and lots of dinghies. And there were orange-life-jacketed men, women and children hanging on to the edges and he sobbed as another child went under. Dinghies were sinking, or had already sunk, and empty orange life jackets bobbed on the sea's foam, collecting on the shore until Justin – helplessly perched on a hill in the middle of the island – could barely see over the top of the rapidly-growing orange mountain.

Further out, Justin caught glimpses of the grey bulk of warships, and a few fancy yachts. Even the funnel of a submarine. He fought to regain control of his lungs and called out to the people in the smaller boats closer by. Slowly the people began to hear him. One by one the boats moved closer to the shore and the sailors started helping the people in the water to safety. Justin raised his voice. He spoke about the changes that needed to happen so that nobody fell into the water.

There was wet on his cheeks when he put up his hands to rub away sleep. Still woozy, he sat up and cleared his throat as if about to make a speech, but realising where he was, only mumbled quietly to himself, mouthing some of the sentences he'd said to the angry crowd on the steps of his tour bus in North Yorkshire.

The new Leader of the Opposition was well known for trying to please all of the people, all of the time. Justin feared nothing would change even if his (former) party was elected into government. People were hungry and were losing their homes. Justin needed to *do* something to help.

He stretched and yawned, glancing around the camper van interior. Annie would most likely tramp across the garden soon with a cup of tea and a bowl of muesli, though he was perfectly well-equipped to look after himself. She'd been disappointed when he declined the offer to sleep in his old room. She'd wanted to comfort him when Ivy had stormed away the previous week, snatching her baby from his arms after he'd broken the news that he was her genetic father.

'You're a liar,' she'd cried, while the baby reached to touch the glistening tears on her mother's cheeks. 'You've been lying to me my whole life.' Watching, helpless as she wept, reminded him of the distraught toddler who'd been irrevocably separated from her mother that afternoon in July, 1974. Pushing the pram around Islington Green, the baby's screaming had eventually waned and she'd fallen asleep.

In his parents' house he'd allowed the grown-up Ivy to storm out of the room unchallenged.

Later, she telephoned the house, calmer. After lengthy persuasion she agreed to accompany him to Lincolnshire and, grudgingly, be introduced to her birth mother. She said it was for her daughter's sake.

'I don't want Olivia to have the truth hidden from her the way it was from me. And don't think I'm travelling in that revolting camper van with you, I can't believe you've sunk to such depths Uncle... *Father.*' She'd said from the outset she wouldn't call him Dad. Finlay would always be Dad.

Justin had to smile at her deprecation of his chosen accommodation. If she could only have seen herself, dirty-cheeked and snotty-nosed, in her grubby pram as an infant. With a hippie teenaged mother, living in a squat. Her own daughter was always in clean, top-of-the-range baby clothes, every smear and spillage immediately wiped away. But there was no sense in upsetting Ivy further. He felt protective of Annette, though, and Ivy's potential reaction to her. Annette had been such a child when her daughter was born, but there was something oddly childlike about her still. So different from Alice, the only mother Ivy knew. His guts clenched at the thought of the imminent mother-daughter reunion.

His feet hurt when he stepped down from the bed. Clicking the bones of his spine back into place he reached up to push the skylight open as wide as it would go. It'd be a hot drive to Lincolnshire, and he wished he could have accepted Ivy's reserved offer of an air-conditioned ride in her car, but he wanted to keep his van with him. Perhaps he would stay, for a while at least, at The Station in Bardney. Annette had invited him. She'd said there was a made-to-measure space for his van in the area where the old chicken run had been behind the kitchen, and that they could run an electric wire out of the window for him. Debating whether to make himself a cup of tea at his tiny stove Justin decided against it – he would only end up with two. He used the miniature bathroom before hopping back into bed, where he leaned his head back on his hands and allowed the dream to sweep over him again while he waited for the inevitable visit from his mother.

The people, floundering in a sea of uncertainty. The rich yacht owners and the warships keeping themselves out of reach, refusing to rescue the drowning because it might encourage more and more to try and save themselves. It only needed the right words from him to convince the closer boat owners to offer shelter and repast, to open their hearts to the lost and displaced. What were the words and how could he get them across?

He must have dozed again because he was woken by the van's rocking and Annie clanking her tray down on his compact worktop.

'I don't know how you can live like this,' she grumbled, sloshing tea over the edges of his favourite childhood mug. She poured another for herself, passed him his (it dripped onto his quilt) and hitched herself up until she was perching on the end of his bed. 'Silly boy. No wonder your daughter insists on driving herself to this ill-thought-out reunion of yours.'

Justin sipped his tea. *Your daughter.* 'Do you think it's a bad idea?'

'I didn't say that. It's best to have the truth out in the open. Everything is still as it was – she's always been your daughter after all, and this Annette's. Alice and Finlay were aware this was going to happen one day, Ivy was the only one who didn't know. No. I only wonder whether it wouldn't have been better for Annette to visit Ivy here, first.'

'I have to think of what's best for Annette too, Ma. She's vulnerable at the moment. Her mother's death has hit her hard and I don't think she could face this,' he waved his hand in the general direction of the van's open door. 'Our family, all together. She needs to be on her own turf.'

'Yes, I suppose I can see that,' said his mother. She took another slurp and placed her still-almost-full cup back on the tray. One foot at a time she eased herself off his bed and took hold of the tray (no breakfast then). 'You're probably right. You like her, don't you, son?' she stood, bent slightly, at the door of his van. The tray rattled in her hands. Justin's heart beat extra hard as he met her gaze.

'I always did,' he said.

The week before, in Hunstanton, he'd sat on a promenade bench with Annette. They'd eaten chips and looked out at The Wash. Sun burned through the remnants of mist. Mud-brown sand stretched into the distance.

Annette wore a wide-brimmed hat, said the sun had been getting to her recently, though she'd lived mainly outdoors most of her life. In his mind it seemed a big jump, sitting here, with her now sixty. Her girlish voice seemed unaltered and despite her air of fatigue, she had the same steely determination he remembered.

Scrunching chip wrappers and licking her fingers she stood and put out her hand. Smiling, he folded his packaging in on itself, a few dry chips clinging to the greasy wrapper, and passed it to her, noticed her uneven gait and the way her long skirt flowed around her legs, and the curve in her back as she carried the litter to a bin and crammed it in.

Holidaying families, hunched-shouldered teenagers and old couples who walked painfully slowly, holding hands, all crowded the promenade. They passed backwards and forwards in front of Annette before she was able to dive between them and complete the return journey to their bench.

'So have you spoken to her yet, then?' she asked as she sat, blunt as ever in her approach.

'Not yet. I wanted to see you first.' He regarded his fingers on his lap, gnarling as he aged. The tremor in his right hand was pronounced. He tucked his hands between his knees to hide them, but sensed Annette had noticed.

'Hmm,' she said. 'I hope it's not going to take you too long to get round to it because I've made up me mind. I want her to know who I am. I should've done it years ago and then me mum would've had a chance to get to know her.' She glanced sideways at him.

'I'm going to do it tomorrow, it's prearranged. Wish me luck.' He pressed his shoulder against hers and she leaned into him briefly. The sheen on the wet sand blurred his vision.

'You could always stay over at The Meadows, you know, there are plenty of spare rooms. Ma would be happy to meet you. She says she wants to thank you for giving Finlay and Alice the chance to be parents, and to have her granddaughter in her life. You could meet Ivy tomorrow, after I've told her.'

'That's exactly what I don't want,' Annette said crossly. 'Ivy'd hate to be rushed into meeting me. Give her a chance to think about it and invite her to come to The Station when she's ready. You can book her a hotel in Lincoln if you want – she might like to visit the Cathedral. Me, I'm off back home on the train this afternoon. Janie's picking me up in Lincoln. It's *prearranged*.'

She gave him a sideways smile and he found it amazing that she was able to pre-empt her daughter so effortlessly. She lifted her blue cotton hat to scratch her head and he saw that her hair was quite grey, and she still had freckles on her thin cheeks. He realised the familiarity of her slightly-hooked nose was because Ivy had inherited it from her. He wanted to tell her, but figured she'd find out for herself soon enough.

They sat for a while longer and watched the tide come in, casting nets of foam latticework higher and higher up the beach as it advanced. Annette rolled a cigarette and smoked it. Justin got up, his knees creaking, to fetch them both an ice cream from the kiosk on the seafront.

'Look at you, a proper old hippie you are,' Annette said admiringly. He straightened his waistcoat and smoothed the front of his grandad shirt.

'It's a relief, to be honest,' he said. 'Being able to dress how I want for a change. Anyway, I knew you were coming, didn't I?' he winked at her.

They ate their ice creams and he listened as she told him about The Station, her plans for rescuing animals and Janie's for a community of displaced young people and adults. Warmth sluiced through his body. Perhaps he'd dreamed about the island again for a reason.

Watching her as she talked, it gave him a pain in his chest to see the girl at the festival in her face and her bearing. His whole body ached. He sensed she could still see the boy he was back then, too. He wanted to tell her so many things and yet he also had the urge to simply lay on the floor of a tent with her and say nothing.

38

Festival in Time

Annette, eleven months later

The village centre resembled a theme park for hippies, what
the shopkeepers of Bardney believed hippies were all about,
anyway: tie-dyed, floaty clothes and scarves, rainbow
jumpers, joss sticks and bongs filled every window. There
was even a sword in a stone in the middle of the town square
(I wasn't sure why). The whole thing was a bit twee for me.
But at least the villagers had got behind us. They'd seen the
success of modern music festivals, hence the lack of
injunction this time. Landowners had bent over backwards
to rent out the fields around Tupholme Abbey for this, the
forty-fifth anniversary of the Great Western Express Festival.
They'd even contributed to the surrounding twelve-foot-high
wire fence.

We had marshals, and a pile of yellow 'Can I help you?'
vests instead of hordes of bobbies charging around with
truncheons.

The main stage was ready, as was the Folk Tent, the Giants of the Future tent and the BBC marquee. We even had a crash tent, complete with straw bales and signs warning it would not be suitable for hay fever sufferers. We'd decided not to book a foam machine this time around. Black cloth, attached by technicians to the speaker towers, flapped in the breeze like crow wings and every now and then a harsh sound broke out over the PA system as it was tested.

Otherwise, the festival was as yet unoccupied – a film set. It was all a bit ghostly. Standing in the silence of an empty festival field, I closed my eyes and conjured Genesis on the back of my eyelids – still my all-time favourite band. At least I'd see them this time. Rod Stewart would be making an appearance, too.

We were calling it the *Festival in Time*, Justin's idea. He'd agreed to do one of his speeches – young people loved him and he wanted to continue inspiring them to get involved in politics – but mostly he wanted to perform his set of new songs, the ones he'd spent the past year writing and had recently recorded in The Station Studio – a new-build on the site of the original ticket office. All the proceeds from the album, as well as a percentage of ticket sales, would be distributed amongst local and international charities for those who had been made homeless for one reason or another.

Oh yeah, and I was the fiddle player in his new band. I still went into town to busk on me own sometimes though. It was important to me to keep up my independence. Ivy was fond of reminding me of that, when she rang me or video-messaged so Justin and I could keep in touch with Olivia.

Ivy still struggled to forgive Justin for keeping his identity a secret from her for so long. She said it wouldn't have affected her relationship with Finlay, who would always be her dad. She said she'd trusted Justin utterly and had been his biggest supporter, based on his total (as she'd believed) honesty. It would take a while longer before she could do that again.

Me, I seemed to have escaped without blame, for some reason. You'd think she'd hate me for giving up my baby, but when she found out about my circumstances at the time she couldn't thank me enough. She'd had a wonderful childhood with Alice as her mum and she was sure my lifestyle choices were all very laudable and all that, but she didn't think they would have suited her, growing up. At one point she made a comment about the benefits of running water (it wasn't her fault, it was how she'd been brought up). Her insinuation regarding Justin and me was that at least Olivia had a pair of *normal* grandparents in Alice and Finlay, so she could afford to give the two of us a bit of leeway. Olivia didn't have any other grandparents – Ivy used a sperm donor to get pregnant – so Justin and I turned out to be a useful back-up pair.

It was hard to equate the Ivy I was getting to know with the baby I still saw in flashes of sensory memory. *Snuggling together on our mattress in the squat, easing my tit out of her mouth when she'd fallen asleep. Bathing her in a washing-up bowl in front of the paraffin heater, holding her hands as she learnt to walk on the rough wooden floorboards of our room.* I didn't think I'd done too badly, actually. I'd kept her alive for the first year-and-a-half of her life and carried her through my lonely pregnancy for nine months before that...

Allegra followed Janie out of the antique side-door, both of them placing trays of tea on the tables under the gazebo. Allegra had recently returned from travelling in South-East Asia and had lost the plump girlishness I remembered from the last time I saw her. Tanned and lean, with a certain hardness about her, she reminded me of the young me.

Janie's friend Lara emerged a moment later with a huge plate of sandwiches. Her son, Marcus, was supposedly hard at work with Billy, painting a sign for the petting zoo on the recently-repaired side of the barn which faced the road. No doubt Marcus's sisters were holding the ladder, or washing the paintbrushes, or more likely doing the job the boys were getting paid for themselves, since they both adored Billy. The lads were probably lounging in the hayloft above the stables, playing games on their smartphones or swiping left on Tinder or whatever it was they did these days. The sign, should it ever get painted, would be the first thing the busloads of festival-goers saw as they came round the corner after crossing the bridge over the River Witham.

Festival in Time was family friendly. It would begin tomorrow.

We pulled the chairs out and settled ourselves around one of the tables.

'Better make the most of our last half-hour or so of peace before the rest of the guests arrive,' Janie said. She smiled at her daughter and patted her tanned knee. 'I'm so pleased you made it back in time for this, Allegra.'

'Me too, I wouldn't miss Twenty One Pilots for the world!' Allegra grinned back at her.

'Janie tells me your daughter's coming up tomorrow,' Lara remarked to me.

I still got a thrill when anyone said those two words. 'She is, along with most of Justin's family, I believe. They reserved a load of rooms at the country hotel for tomorrow night. I hope Ivy's got some of those fancy ear defenders for Olivia – don't want my granddaughter bursting an eardrum or anything.'

A donkey let out a startled bray, which echoed against the side of the house.

'Sounds like Nellie,' Janie cocked an ear. 'What's Billy doing to her now? Not making that face at her again I hope, she hates it.' She took a huge bite of local ham.

'What face?' Lara sat back with her own sandwich in her hand. She shook her head as Romy moved to rest her chin on her lap, gazing hopefully at the bread stuffed with our home-grown roast vegetables. Janie's walled "no-dig" kitchen garden had been featured in Lincolnshire's glossy publication for posh people that month. The framed centre photo of Janie with her arms full of broccoli (wearing Andy Pandy dungarees and with a carefully-dabbed streak of mud

225

on her left cheek) had appeared as if by magic on the wall in our entrance hall just the week before.

Romy panted and moved under the table where she watched the floor, hawk-like. I felt a pang for Poppy, who'd died, aged fourteen, on the anniversary of Mum's death.

'Anyway, how do you know it was Nellie?' There were five donkeys altogether.

'Nellie has a particular hitch to her bray,' I said, because Janie still had her mouth full of sandwich. 'And the face Billy pulls is like this,' I stretched my mouth open with my fingers hooked in the sides.

'Wow,' Lara laughed. 'I never knew donkeys were so sensitive. Or so individual for that matter.'

Janie swallowed the last of her sandwich and tapped Lara on the arm. 'That's because you're from London. Speaking of which, look!'

A slick-looking car had pulled onto the stone track, driven by an ageing black man. The car slid past on the other side of the gully containing our sunken garden and I could pick out, through the open windows as he leaned forward to raise a hand in our direction, the long-healed scar on the left side of his head, bare of hair. A stunning older woman with cropped hair and a long neck sat beside him in the passenger seat. The car crept behind the barn and the recording studio, emerging into view again on the approach to the house. It came towards us and purred to a stop level with the front door. Lara jumped to her feet.

'That's... It's Fergus. And isn't that woman Althea? Oh my God. We haven't seen her for years. She went to America, won some sort of reality show there! I knew Fergus and she were still in touch but... What are they both doing here?'

We were all standing now. The front door opened and the Kurdish refugee family who lived in the house with us stood there for a moment, blinking in the sunshine. The little boy, Ali, dragged his father forward to admire the car. Proper imp, he was, Ali. Always asking questions about something or other.   He especially loved being allowed to play inside Justin's van. Inas, his mother, adjusted her floral-patterned headscarf and turned to smile at us.   I waved and she pointed at Ali, shaking her head. *Car mad*, I guessed she was saying. Mind you his dad was the one stroking the bonnet and nodding at whatever Fergus was telling him.

Next, some youngsters staying at The Station as part of a probation project appeared from the bunkhouse sheds at the back of the house. Fergus's car – whatever make it was – had attracted a lot of attention. I had to give it to Fergus, he didn't seem to mind the greasy paw-prints the two lads must've been leaving on its shiny silver surface as they patted it all over. One of the teenaged girls, as well. The other one was talking to Althea. Comparing nose-jewellery, it looked like.

Lara hadn't made it through the gathering admirers yet. She stood motionless on the decking, eyes gleaming. Billy and Marcus and Lara's two daughters arrived from the direction of the barn. The girls threw themselves at their uncle, then stood dumbly in front of the beautiful apparition that was Althea. Fergus gave Marcus a high five and appeared to be listening as Marcus introduced Billy to him. Some of the others crowded in again to ask Fergus more questions about the car. It would be a while before he made it over to talk to his sister.

Janie was smiling in that rare and open way she had, and she looked so like the annoying little sister of my childhood I wanted to give her a Chinese burn.

'I invited them,' she said to Lara. 'I asked Althea if she would come, for old time's sake. She said she'd love to see you again, and perform on the stage she once danced in front of.' Janie put her arm around Lara, who was crying. 'I'm still trying to make it up to you, what happened then. I thought this might finally do it.'

'Idiot,' Lara said, not mincing her words, as usual. 'But thank you, my dear friend.'

Janie hesitated, then removed something from the pocket of her cotton trousers and handed it to Lara. It was a giraffe, made of coloured glass like the ones she used to play with when she was a kid.

'I kept forgetting to give you this. I found it right here, just after we bought this place.'

Lara laughed and kissed Janie on the cheek.

Fergus and Althea broke away from their groupies and started to move towards us. At the same time, I heard the rattle of Justin's camper van pulling in at the gate onto the track. He was back from picking up more guests at the train station in Lincoln. I pushed myself creakily to my feet, brushing crumbs off my floaty cotton skirt onto the decking. It's a good job I was holding the railing at the top of the steps, as I almost tripped over Romy, eager to keep the deck clear of discarded pieces of sandwich. 'Course my clumsiness had nothing to do with my own eagerness to reconnect with Justin. Never see me dependent on a man, you wouldn't.

39

Annette

I walked towards the entrance of our Island, as Justin and I called it (Janie had refused to change the name from The Station) waving to my niece Juliet and her girlfriend, Emily, in the back of the van. Sitting in the middle seat next to Justin was a friend from his politicking days – Andy. An amazing story there. Andy's teenaged daughter Lucy had been abducted as a child and it was Justin who'd managed to get her reunited with her parents. Well, with the help of his brother Rowan's French husband. Xavier worked as a kind of private detective for an international charity that helped find kidnapped children.

All this was the reason Justin had gone off-grid when I was trying to get in touch with him after Janie's photo appeared in the paper. Justin, bless him, was helping Xavier plough through years' worth of birth certificates, passports and residency statuses. Got to witness loads of interviews with suspicious-seeming people who had a child Lucy's age. Even got involved in a couple of stake-outs. Eventually they'd zoned in on a Welsh woman who'd settled in France years before with her four-year-old daughter. Only she wasn't her daughter, it turned out.

All it had taken, in the end, to unlock Lucy's memories of her early life was a recording of her mother singing a song that Lucy had apparently loved from birth. Still it had been hard seeing her clinging to the person she'd learned to believe was her mother, Justin said. He stopped talking for a minute when he noticed I had something in my eye. 'Anyway,' he cleared his throat before carrying on. 'The *officers de police* arrested the woman and marched her into the back of a van.'

I did love it when he spoke in that French accent.

Lucy seemed settled now. A fair-haired girl sitting next to her father, face pressed to the camper window. No doubt she was madly dreaming of her planned introduction to Ed Sheeran at the festival. She can't have been much younger than I was when I met *my* festival hero.

I blew Justin a kiss.

My heart gave a little flutter every time he came home.

The way we live is like
A huge experiment, gone wrong,

The roaring that had erupted after Justin's speech died down, and the field fell silent. Justin strummed the first chords on his guitar before speaking the opening words of the song again, the one that had made me cry in the Folk Tent forty-five years before. Into the chill early-evening air he repeated them once more, pin-drop-softly, then began singing. . .

I don't want it to be this way.
At the end of my life
I don't want to feel
I never tried to save the day.

In the pause that followed he turned to me and beckoned. I hoped nobody noticed my knees wobbling as I walked onto the stage with my fiddle. There was a muted round of applause. As it ebbed I played my soaring notes and then he sang again, Justin Citizen. *My* Justin. He faced me, strumming his guitar and singing, looking deeply into my eyes.

Author's note

Several years ago now (my novels have a long gestation period) when I was still living in Lincoln, Phil and I went out for a drive and found ourselves at a café on a decommissioned railway station platform one Sunday afternoon. The village was Bardney, agricultural home of a former sugar beet factory, set on the banks of the River Witham.

The café is part of Bardney Heritage Centre (https://www.facebook.com/Bardneyheritagecentre/). Full of memorabilia and photographs. I was intrigued by the posters of a 1970s music festival, and the many photos of the event that papered the walls. Hippies and rockers, a main stage with polythene blowing off the speaker towers. Mud and rain. Festival-goers wrapped in polythene and waxed-paper, shelters constructed from straw bales. Roxy Music played their first-ever festival gig there. The line-up on the posters includes Genesis, Wishbone Ash, Nazareth, The Strawbs, Spencer Davis, Lindisfarne and Average White Band, among many others.

Why had I never heard of the *Great Western Express Music Festival*[1] before? I was born and bred in Lincoln, after all. I suppose it was because I was only nine years old at the time. The festival was organised by the Great Western Festival Company and backed by Lord Harlech and Stanley Baker. Worried villagers, landowners and councillors sought a High Court Injunction, to stop the event, without success although it was touch and go. Security arrangements for the festival included a 12ft-high corrugated metal fence with searchlights on top and a 300-strong security force, which consisted of members of the CID, many brought in from outside the area, and some disguised as hippies. Bob Harris and John Peel were the DJs. The weather was appalling and

---

[1] https://concerts.fandom.com/wiki/Great_Western_Express_1972

the festival field was a quagmire. I had to write a book set at this festival!

I might have been only nine at the time of the festival, and my older sister only twelve, but the idea for a novel burst immediately onto a blank page in my mind as I sat in that café. Imagine two sisters like us, though a few years older, one of them determined to go to the festival despite being forbidden to do so by her parents. And imagine the trouble she would get into by dragging her naïve younger sister along. Annette and Janie sprang onto the page, Annette, at least, ready and raring to go.

Around the same time I found out about the festival, a certain Leader of the Opposition was being given a hard time by the press. I was inspired by that politician's basic humanitarian values to create my character of Justin Citizen, a folk singer-turned-politician and the love interest of Annette.

I also took some lines from a poem I wrote when I was eighteen, as the basis for Justin's song that so deeply affected Annette in the book.

There was also the Syrian refugee crisis, the brief period of 'humanisation' of refugees before the language of the press and government turned derogatory. The plight of displaced people haunts Justin's dreams.

Adult Janie's mountain railway home Catmally is inspired by Dalmally Station[2] on the Glasgow to Oban line in the Scottish Highlands. There, in real life, Liz and Graham Whaite are restoring this beautiful sandstone building to its former glory. It's also Liz's 'Heartfelt by Liz' studio, where she runs felt making workshops on the working railway platform. The station is set in a stunning landscape and you can stay in one of the unique and quirky rooms on the active platform. I visited Liz and Graham there once during a camper van trip and immediately knew I had to put the location into a novel. I loved the idea of Janie raising her

---

[2] https://www.dalmallyrailwaystation.co.uk/

family in a working railway station and making a community there. Please note, I have totally fictionalised the building and location in the book.

Acknowledgements

Thanks go as ever to my no-nonsense editor Sara-Jayne Slack, to my loyal draft-reader Sarah Carby, for her suggestions of tweaks and improvements that always make sense and make the story better.

To Deb Urbacz for her beta reads, to J.L. Dixon, Stacey Hammond and Demelda Penkitty for the cover quotes.

To Kelly Lacey of Love Books Tours, who I totally trust to organise the best possible book tours for all my books, and to the dedicated and hardworking book blogging and bookstagram community, especially those who make my novels come alive with their reviews.

Thanks to Phil for the formatting and producing. Thanks to readers who have bought my previous books and have told me how they were affected by them. It makes the hours of writing and editing worthwhile. All I want to do is connect.

About the Author

When she's not writing or editing, Tracey Scott-Townsend spends her time working on her allotment garden where she hopes to have her best-ever harvest of vegetables this year. Tracey also spends several days a week as a volunteer with a local charity that helps refugees.

A mother of four grown children, she is now a first-time granny and looks forward to spending time with her grandson and his mum and dad on their off-grid homestead in central Portugal.

Tracey's novels explore the pressing themes at the heart of human existence – finding personal space in an often-confusing world, environment, choices, family relationships, love and grief. Geographic sense of place is also important, and each new novel reflects the locations she has recently travelled to. Festival in Time is her seventh novel.

Lightning Source UK Ltd.
Milton Keynes UK
UKHW010916280622
405068UK00001B/41